I0748426

GLOBES DISEASE®

Editors: P. A. Cronin/Editor, Marie Antionette/Cauzing Elevation Publishing, LLC, Marie/the Edit Agency

Cover art: Phatpuppy Art Studios
Photography: Teresa Yeh
Cover design: The Bookish Brunette
Book design: MC Writing Services

First Printing, 2016
ISBN: 978-0-9961233-0-3
Library of Congress Control Number: 2016903489

KeebleInk Publishing, Chatsworth, CA, USA
www.keebleink.com

Learn more at www.globesdisease.com

GLOBES DISEASE®

❊

LANCE OLIVER KEEBLE

CONTENTS

I dedicate this book to my Mother. Without her I wouldn't be who I am today. She read to me from the moment I could sit up. She taught me to read, to imagine, to contemplate and to question the world. She encouraged me to put pen to paper.

Though she was a single mother, she was not alone. She surrounded me with a tribe. I learned from them all. My role models came from a variety of professions, nationalities and backgrounds. My mother was a great example, earning her Master's Degree when I was 13. She was diligent, strong and loving, nurturing me and weathering the storms of my rebellions.

Rest in Peace Mom, I'm okay...

PROLOGUE

TERRY

5 years ago…

PAIN! That is what Terry kept saying to himself, "Pain, pain, pain!" He was in the back of an ambulance. Through his pain-filled haze, he could make out the paramedics. One of them kept shaking him awake to ask questions Terry wasn't sure he was answering correctly. He thought he was going to bleed to death. He wanted to give in. He wanted to die so there would be no more pain. How could he be in so much pain and still be alive? The paramedic shook him out of his thoughts. "No!" The only answer he had for them was "No!" "No, I am not a diabetic. No, I am not an alcoholic. No, I am not a drug-popping executive. I have no history of heart problems, no high blood pressure and my cholesterol is fine. The only thing I have a history of, at this very moment, is pain!" Terry wanted it to stop. Terry wasn't too out of it though. He could tell by the way that the paramedics looked at one another that he was in bad shape.

They stuck an IV in each arm. The fluids were very cold. Terry thought, "If ripping out the IVs in my arms would end my misery, I would do it immediately!" There were two paramedics, male and female. The man was on the radio talking, describing his injuries. Terry heard phrases like, "Multiple lacerations and punctures." Some of the words he couldn't make out. He heard them discuss his blood loss. The female paramedic looked down at him and told him he would be okay. He knew that was simply bullshit. "Ugh, make it stop! Too much pain!" Just when Terry thought he couldn't take it anymore, he heard the other paramedic mention morphine. "Sweet

Jesus! Narcotic nirvana, opiate analgesic bliss!" The female promptly grabbed a syringe, a bottle and began drawing from it. He looked at her and asked, with a blood filled smile, "You're about to give me the good stuff right?" The woman responded, "Oh yeah baby, you just relax and we'll get you to *Ange de Vie Hôpital* (Angel of Life Hospital) in no time. You'll be back to pushing pencils very soon." Terry felt new hope. He thought to himself, "I can die in peace now."

The heat of the drug swirled around the clear liquid that had been chilling his bones. He began to have a bitter taste in his mouth. As the morphine entered his body, Terry felt the effects almost immediately. He thought of his life, his twin sister, his job, his insecurities, and his efforts to avoid confrontation, so that he could *make it* in this world. Terry questioned why he moved to a place known as "La Mort Douce" (The Sweet Death). He asked himself, "Why in the world would I go hunting in the first place? I was the *only one* there. I should have known better than to try to impress the higher ups. Haven't I watched enough science fiction and horror movies? The black guy and the new guy always get it first!" Terry was both that day. He would have appreciated it had some of his coworkers or friends warned him that the le Parc du Gévaudan (the Park of Gevaudan) was dangerous and that the wild animals that lived in those parts were actually wild. Terry was expecting "Mutual of Omaha" or "Disney movie" wild, not "I survived" or "I shouldn't be alive" wild.

"Damn!" It would have been helpful if they had told him that the stories about La Mort Douce were true. He probably wouldn't have moved here. Terry started to feel lightheaded and began to float. The pain in his body had become dull throbs as he continued to bleed out. Terry felt the allure of sweet sleep and heard the angelic sound of hospital nurses telling him to hang in there. His last thoughts before facing his drug induced caliginous abyss was, "You mean they were serious about naming this place, La Mort Douce?"

Terry awoke with a start. There was a television in the corner of his hospital room. It was on, but there was no sound coming from it.

Terry briefly worried he had become deaf from his incident. A man he had never seen before was standing amongst a sea of cards and flowers. Instead of wondering, "Why is this strange man in my room?" all Terry could think of was, "Wow, I didn't know this many people liked me." The man was medium height and build with bowl cut black hair. His voice was soft with a low timbre to it. Terry thought it odd that he would notice something like that. He had never noticed details like that before. "Hello Terry, my name is Harold Garcia. I represent The Institute for the Research of Globes Disease. It has come to our attention that you were in a terrible hunting accident." Terry looked up to the ceiling and thought, "Thank God! At least I am not deaf." Terry began to respond, but his voice came out hoarse and low. He looked at the man and attempted to apologize; Harold waved him off. "No need sir. I understand your injuries were severe. Eventually, you will need more than this hospital can provide for your recovery and we are looking for volunteers." Harold calmly produced a business card and put it in Terry's hands. "We help heal people like you. If and when you're ready, contact us; we will be happy to make an appointment for you."

The man exited so quickly that Terry had no time to ask any of the questions popping into his mind. "What is this Institute? How do they know about my accident? What is Globes Disease? How long have I been in the hospital? What the hell is so wrong with me, that this hospital cannot fix it?" Lying there, staring at the door, he saw the hazy form of his sister. He stared at her with deep intent, questioning her with his eyes, "Did you see the guy that was just in here, the one that looked like he was Secret Service or MIB?" Twins usually notice that kind of thing. Maybe Jerry was so distraught that she didn't notice. Tears were streaming down her face as she occupied the doorway like a beautiful mist, an oasis-like hallucination. She glided across the floor and held her hand over his head to comfort him. It felt like one of those water misters people have in their backyards in the summer time. He could feel her breath in his hair when she leaned down, as if to kiss him. He tried to speak, but became flustered when nothing intelligible came out. He had always taken the ability to speak for granted; now it was quite a trying effort. Jerry hovered over him and looked into his eyes. Terry looked back at her and hoarsely forced the words, "How long?"

"Two days," answered the doctor, who had just entered Terry's room. Like a whisper, Jerry was no longer there; just this bearded man with curly hair and a white coat, who looked pale from being indoors too much. The doctor reminded Terry of a rabbi he once knew. "Hello Mr. Andersen, my name is Doctor Needleman. I operated on you. Your injuries were so bad; we didn't think you were going to make it. For those who do survive injuries like yours, it usually takes several months to recover. You are quite the medical miracle, however, and if you keep healing at this rate, you will be out of here in a few days. Some patients suffer infections, deformities, and disabilities. There are no guarantees, but it looks as though you may only need some physical therapy and possibly some trauma counseling. All my suggestions and recommendations will be in my report. I will send it to your employer and provide you with copies.

You are a lucky man, Mr. Andersen. Lucky to have a job that is willing to give you all the time you need to recover, with full medical benefits and pay! Lucky indeed! You must be very important to them." Terry thought cynically, "My Company is being so accommodating to avoid litigation and accusations of negligence. I am sure there will be paperwork to sign releasing them from all liability for injuries sustained on a company hunting excursion; as soon and my arms heal." Terry recognized he had to work on his attitude. He was such a pessimist. His sister was the opposite, a complete optimist. "Maybe they are doing this out of the kindness of their hearts," she would say if she were here. Wasn't she? No, Jerry couldn't be here, that would be impossible. "Yeah right," Terry would have responded to her. "What was this Institute's angle? Why was his employer being so accommodating? Were the two in cahoots?" He looked down at the card Harold had given him. Again, his sister's mist was there, looking down at the card as well. As if to say, "What would it hurt to call?" He palmed it so no one could see. Terry decided to hang on to it for a while, until he had more information and time to think.

WEEKS AFTER THE ATTACK

Terry felt great, better than before the attack. Maybe it was the hope his sister's appearance gave him in his hospital room. Nevertheless, he could not understand why the doctors and The Institute insisted he get help. Deep in his soul, he felt his sister's urging. Terry was so deep in thought; he forgot he was in his car. He barely realized he had arrived at a large concrete and glass building. As he parked and set the brake, he could see Jerry in his rearview mirror nodding her encouragement. He could swear he could hear her voice urging him, "Go and see what they have to say. What could it hurt?" Terry exited the car, he had been sitting there for God knows how long, still plagued with indecision. He walked up the well-manicured walkway and looked back at his twin sister, but she wasn't there. Maybe he was already dead and this was some holy light guiding him to believe he was alive. He thought to himself, "Maybe this optimism stuff does work." Terry closed his eyes and there she was again. She blew him a kiss and mouthed the words, "I love you." Terry opened his eyes, took a deep breath and entered the building.

QUAKE

30 years ago...

Quake woke from a night of partying with his Rugby team. From the moment he enrolled in this college, they had found a way for him to be involved in as many contact sports as they could find for him, because of his size. He didn't even understand the rules of rugby. Like football, wrestling, lacrosse and the occasional times he went in for hockey, he liked to hit people and knock them down. He was good at it. He was a natural athlete and a freak of nature. He was large, extremely fast and agile for his body type. His coach said, "Quake is what you would get if you mixed an elephant with Sea Biscuit." He was size, mass and speed rolled into one massive body. He was a natural, with a personality to boot. Gregarious in nature, he could win over the stodgiest of people, once they got over his substantial dimensions. The other reason players liked him on their teams was because he was a consummate partier. Quake rarely drank to excess and hangovers were virtually nonexistent with his metabolism and stature. Tonight was no different. The other guys had all passed out, except for Ano Warfield, one of the few people equally as strong, if not stronger, than he was. Ano was a giant, 6'5" 275 pounds of solid Austrian muscle, compared to Quake's mere, 6'3" 255 pounds. Sports came easy to Ano, as well, and he knocked people down a lot too. Quake liked that about him. They got along well.

Ano and Quake had a lot in common, except for their taste in women. Quake liked his women shapely and intelligent. Give him a woman he could hold on to, someone who could keep him warm at night. He didn't like the feel of thin women. Even the thought of watching them undress made him shudder, "Yuck." They looked too much like children to him, with their small breasts and flat bottoms. He frowned just thinking about it. For some reason, the little pixie sized girls loved Ano. Ano loved them too and judging from the sounds in the next room, there was plenty of loving going on. That is probably what awakened Quake. He had his suspicions as to why Ano only picked little woman and it caused him to smirk a little. Oh well, that was somebody else's problem as far as Quake was concerned. Quake would happily take a woman with naturally large breasts accompanied by a great ass any day. He rose from the couch he had slept on. His consistently mussed up hair often enhanced Quake's six-foot frame. The reddish blond nest that set atop his skull seemed to have a mind of its own. Quake decided there was no need to try to tame it now. The dorm reeked of alcohol and body odor. Quake needed fresh air.

Quake stepped out onto the patio and looked up at the moon; a waxing gibbous. In mid yawn, he looked across the grass separating the dorms from the walkways and saw Diana. He had been watching her for three semesters. There was no way he could mistake that walk of hers. "She's not a party girl, what is she doing up so late?" He noticed her bags were heavy with books. "Oh yeah, spring terms are coming up; she must have been studying. Who's the creepy guy, headed in her direction?" he asked himself. "He doesn't look like he's from here." Quake vaulted his large frame over the 4-foot patio wall. He stumbled, but remained upright. Judging from her body language, Diana did not seem too happy to see the stranger. The stranger grabbed Diana and Quake's adrenaline overrode whatever alcohol remained in his system. Quake sprinted through the verdant area, leading to the walkway where Diana and the creepy stranger were. In no time, he was behind the stranger ready to deliver some discipline and a lesson in manners.

DIANA

Diana, a studious strawberry blonde had walked the college campus late in the evening before, but never this late. She was so intent on finishing her research that she had failed to notice the time. Diana was in a hurry to return to her dorm. She was exhausted. Diana noticed a young man walking her way. She could have sworn he had just been headed the other way. "Why did that guy change direction?" Diana wondered nervously. Probably a late night partier, the boys at this school tended to take the weekend recreations a little too far. Diana began to feel anxious and she was getting a creepy vibe from this guy. She began to wish she hadn't been so absent-minded about the time. Diana decided to avoid eye contact. She didn't want to give this guy any indication she was interested. As he drew closer, the hairs on the back of her neck began to stand on end. She looked up briefly. All she saw was dark hair, a dark complexion and a deep, dark void where eyes should have been. There was no glint of light to draw from or indicate if he even had eyes. Diana looked away and tried to calm her uneasiness with the thoughts of the Taser she carried in her purse.

Diana couldn't put her finger on what it was, but the boy gave her the heebie-jeebies. She did her best to keep from going into a full panic, telling herself she was just being silly and paranoid, though she unzipped her purse; just in case. She scanned the immediate area for anyone she might know. She was more than a little relieved when she noticed there was someone on a patio not too far away. Diana hoped whoever it was would have the good sense to call 911 if things got out of hand. She prayed they wouldn't be one of those who didn't want to get involved. Distracted by that thought, Diana lost track of the stranger's distance until it was too late and he blocked her path. Diana tried to suppress her fear and resolved that if he touched her she would Taser him. She put her hand in her purse and moved to pass around him without making eye contact. The stranger was having none of that and grabbed Diana.

Her heart raced, yet time seemed to move in slow motion. She looked up into his face. The terror she felt looking into his eyes was something she'd never experienced. Diana finally understood the meaning of the phrase "frozen with fear". Somehow, through the fear, she fired the Taser. The darts flew through the air and made contact. All those hours practicing in the backyard with her father and brothers kicked in. Diana's quick action had taken her by surprise. She stared at the wires in his chest. It was then Diana allowed herself a normal reaction. She screamed.

Time stood still. Nothing seemed to move in real time, except the stranger. Diana watched the stranger brush the darts away as if he were simply brushing off cat hair. She gulped and prepared to give him another shock, even though it appeared to have had no effect on him. It was all she could think to do to save herself. His countenance seemed to darken even more and the creepy stranger grinned. It was an evil, menacing grin and Diana was out of options.

QUAKE

Diana couldn't say for certain when the big guy named Quake showed up. All she knew was she was seconds away from a total breakdown when he arrived. Diana mumbled to herself, "Earthquake." Quake was surprised she knew who he was. The boy in front of her looked perplexed. He was so preoccupied with Diana that he didn't seem to notice Quake's ever-looming presence behind him. When she looked past the creepy stranger's shoulders at her hero, she sighed in relief. That indicator was all this stranger needed. He spun around to face Quake. Quake's voice boomed through the fresh morning air, "Hey little man, I don't think the lady here wants to be bothered." The dark creep looked Quake up and down and scoffed, "Back off kid, I ain't the push over you think I am." He started to turn around and grab Diana's arm again, but Quake grabbed the stranger by the shoulder. The man swiftly turned back around and pushed Quake. Both Diana and Quake were surprised by this action; no regular person had ever been known to move this massive man. Quake's temperament changed from mediator to enforcer, Diana smirked and thought, "Oh Boy, you're gonna get your ass kicked now."

"You're barking up the wrong tree, little fella," Quake warned. The stranger growled and lunged at him. Quake was often assumed to be slow moving, because of his size. The stranger made the same mistake. Quake quickly dispatched him with a right cross that sent him sailing. He and Diana stood over the seemingly unconscious man. Quake looked at Diana and said, "Why don't you go back to your dorm, I will take care of this creep..." Before Quake finished his sentence, the stranger was back on his feet. Quake quickly jumped in front of Diana and squared himself for another attack. The stranger laughed and lunged again. Battle ensued. The men matched one another punch for punch, blow for blow. Diana screamed for help; lights all over the area began to come on. Window shades and doors began to open. The two continued their battle. Quake punched the stranger with a haymaker causing him to tumble backwards, but again the stranger was quickly back on his feet. The stranger lunged at Quake a third time, but this time Quake caught him by the arms. Quake head-butted the stranger and both staggered. Dizzy, his head spinning, Quake quickly realized head-butts only work in the movies. Quake grabbed the stranger by the shoulders and maneuvered him around into a headlock. Since fighting hadn't worked, Quake decided to rely on his wrestling background. The strategy seemed effective. The stranger's breathing became labored and slow. Quake was confident he would soon choke the stranger unconscious. Suddenly, the stranger wriggled loose and bit Quake. "What the…!" Quake yelled. The stranger escaped Quake's massive arms, turned and gave Quake a devilish grin. Wiping Quakes blood from his mouth he said wryly, "I warned you," before running off and disappearing into the morning darkness.

VLAD

The stranger ran for a while, pumped up on adrenaline, and he eventually found himself at a park. He was exhausted. The fight had taken a lot out of him. It had been a long time since he had an adversary of that size and he prided himself on his ability to handle big guys. This Quake fellow was no average human. He had some skill and lethal abilities that could come in handy later. The stranger didn't like running from a fight, but he didn't need the inconvenience of witnesses. He didn't like leaving such a dangerous man behind either, but he had no choice. Besides, "He who fights and runs away..." The girl was his target. He had been stalking and studying her for some time now. He didn't want anyone identifying him, especially if he returned to claim his prize. The stranger took a deep breath; he needed rest and time to heal. Unfortunately, before he could resolve what his next move would be, he heard footsteps behind him. "Damn, twice in one day!" he chastised himself for being too distracted to notice someone sneaking up on him. This one smelled different; there was barely a heartbeat. The voice behind him was odd, deep, young. He turned to see a tall and very pale man in a long, thick fur coat. This pale stranger in the long coat smiled, revealing sharp fangs. He spoke in a very thick Russian accent, "Hello, Sobaka (Dog), my name is Vlad."

TERRY & QUAKE

Present day

Terry had worked his way from the large parking structure and reached the entrance in no time. He was looking down; reading the card Harold had given him. He stared at it, as if some clue as to what the Institute was all about would be revealed in the small print. He nervously confirmed the address again. Terry wasn't paying attention when he passed through the large glass doors into the building, complete with armed security, and he collided with what he first thought was a large pillar. Terry quickly rose from the floor. He adjusted himself and looked up, surprised to find that the pillar he had crashed into had messy red hair and an engaging smile. Terry was embarrassed and offered his apologies, partly for not paying attention and then for staring so intently. Terry always considered himself a big man, but next to Quake, he felt small.

"Excuse me," Quake boomed. "No, excuse me!" Terry countered with a smile. The large man extended his massive hand, offering it to Terry. Terry did the same. It was a long handshake, during which they sized each other up. "Hi, my name is Ragnorock." Quake thundered. "Hello, my name is Andersen," Terry said with a smile. "Sorry, I wasn't paying attention." Quake grinned big and wide, "No problem Andersen. You bounce back pretty well. Most guys would still be sitting on the floor after bumping into me." Quake chuckled, as he punched playfully at Terry's arm. In spite of himself, Terry found himself wincing in anticipation of the blow. Quake never made contact. Quake had learned early on that even in jest, he could cause someone serious pain. Though Quake suspected Andersen could have handled the punch, he still didn't want to chance it. If Quake misjudged and hurt him, he thought, "This guy could very well give me a run for my money." Quake continued talking, "You seem like you're an athletic fella. You work out at the local gym?" "Nope," responded Terry, with a huge smile, "Rehab!"

GLOBES DISEASE

TERRY

5 years ago…

When Terry Andersen was first told of his disease he didn't know what to do. How could this happen to him? How could this type of thing even exist? La Mort Douce had a sordid past for sure, but damn, who names a place "The Sweet Death" anyway? Located between Quebec and the States, hardly anyone knew where it was for a few hundred years, allowing countless atrocities to go unnoticed. However, since the 70s, all manner of people had begun to move here. As long as they could afford to. Some Native Americans and Native Canadians returned, most from "The Seven Nations" tribes, including the Iroquois and the Mohawk. "Don't let that melting pot ideal fool you." Terry had a professor who once said, "We should stop saying melting pot, because melting pot implies we all ceased being who we were and all became the same; a collective." She thought we resembled a salad. Well, if this town was a salad, the lettuce ran the show and the rest of us have to be croutons.

Well, now the dark crouton had something he hadn't even known existed. Something he once thought couldn't be real, and yet it was. He had IT now. Terry looked into his bathroom mirror. Staring back at him was the early morning malaise that normally overcame him before heading off to work. This morning was different. Terry's reflection, a dark man in his 40s with deep dimples, strong cheek bones and what he thought was a friendly face, seemed extremely tense. A woman he dated once told him she thought him to be clean cut and intensely appealing. His eyes however, she said, "Were severely serious." "Interesting description," he thought. He wasn't sure if it was his color or height that caused many at work to call him "Intimidating." The description felt suspect all the same.

Terry's thoughts often wandered in strange directions, generally away from what bothered him most, yet his mind eventually came back to it, without fail. He sighed, a single encounter, one bullshit incident and he now had IT; his destiny had been redirected. Terry figured there would be legitimate literature on this, but dammit-to-hell, no medical book he'd picked up covered the combination of symptoms he had: Unexplained lapses in time, increased hunger and metabolism, irritability, high sex drive, unexplained bruises and wounds that healed more quickly than normal. Terry also struggled with being exhausted during the day from bouts of insomnia.

All of these were symptoms recognized by the doctor he'd called on the card that strange visitor gave to him in the hospital. He realized later on that the same number was in newspaper ads he'd seen as well. What was it called again? Globes Disease? Apparently, it was a fluid borne illness passed from carrier to carrier. Shoot, he had tried looking it up with no success. Maybe it was covered under some other subject. Maybe it was biblical, myth or folklore. What little he did know, didn't make any sense to him.

God willing, maybe he'd finally found help. Maybe there would be a suggestion or something beyond science that provided a cure. Terry was desperate. It was sad really. Now he, like others before him, would have to pave the way for researching a cure. A real life guinea pig! Ain't that a crock? The doctor told him, when he inquired, that there could be no animal test subjects for something like this. That he, like a few others they had found, would have to volunteer for human trials.

It was early morning when Terry walked out of his condo. A brick Victorian structure, gutted and remodeled to modern standards. Terry purchased both floors so he wouldn't feel like he was living in an apartment. The condo concept was a joke. So many people were living in apartments re-purposed as condominiums. The air felt summer-like, even though it was September. Terry hadn't called in sick to his office. That was somewhat of an after thought. He walked the streets slightly dazed. He needed to talk to someone who could help him mull over what to do. Who could he talk to? Who would believe him? Who would understand? He had worked so hard trying to break through the so-called "Ceiling", that in his battle for success and empowerment, most of his friends and associates had become casualties. He longed to hear the voice of his sister Jerry. She had always been sanctuary throughout a childhood of preoccupied parents and siblings too old to relate. Jerry was his mother, his playmate, his nanny, his best friend and his twin. He missed her, deeply. Terry longed for her closeness and the bond they once shared.

Sharing the womb together was an advantage that helped them overcome a cruel world bent on robbing them of happiness later in life. They had long abandoned hanging on to one another so they could conquer their own shares of the American dream. They waged separate battles against a country they weren't even invited to. "Give us your poor and hungry," he scoffed. It never truly applied to those who had arrived through Charleston or New Orleans, dragged here to "till the soil." Soil, stolen from the other orphans of this country. "Come on Terry, those issues are nothing compared to this mystery you carry in your veins." Terry said trying to resolve himself. He sighed, took stock of his surroundings and continued his thoughts. He wondered to himself, "If I could call Jerry, What would I say?"

Terry was deep in thought, yet he still registered the subtle things that occurred often and every day around him. Things that the average person wouldn't notice. Things that, if you hadn't grown up in America looking like Terry, you might never notice. He was sensitive to nuances that others would never know existed. They were subliminal; a momentary blink in the TV screen of his mind's eye. A mother protectively pulls her blonde haired, snowy-skinned offspring closer to her, as they stand on the corner waiting for the light. A woman moves her purse to her other shoulder in an elevator. It's that kind of subconscious behavior that leaves a person doubting himself, especially now. "Is it because of the way I look? Can they see my affliction? Am I hypersensitive or just plain paranoid?"

The looks and reactions that people of color experience happen so often that only the more severe responses usually garner notice. A curious second glance from children that later becomes fascination and then fear. Too often, turning into hatred rather than understanding. This cycle is typically perpetrated and perpetuated by incidents of police brutality that lump much of an entire race as gang-bangers or career criminals, simply because one member fits the description of a suspect in the area. News blurbs of a medieval hanging or the vehicular dragging of an innocent person, trying to provide for his family, are disheartening. A young person struck down because the shooter feared for his life, purely based on the color of his victim. Terry experienced it many times in meetings with his so-called peers. They often stared blankly at him, unable to get past his pigment or his vocal inflection. They couldn't relate to him and often spoke in that nasally condescending tone that grates the spine like the master's whips of years ago. He out worked them; out talked them and eventually they saw past all that. Soon enough, he'd become one of them; one of the good ones. The only vindication is success. Success takes you further from that which you wish to glorify; your lineage, your past, your history and your pride, but a man's gotta eat.

Terry shook himself out of the spiral into an abyss of hate. Recovered from the vertigo, he changed direction and headed for the newsstand, grabbed a paper and continued towards the center of town. Maybe some fresh air and a look on the bright side would help clear his mind of so much chaos. There were others far worse off than he. Others who wished they could be where he is right now. Guided by his new direction he breathed deeply to regain his composure in an attempt to settle the confusion and turmoil in his mind. He reigned in his thoughts amongst the pedestrians, as they amble toward various destinations; the pedestrians unaware of the danger he had become. Terry began to organize his thoughts, fighting the feeling of apathy. Some things that used to be important didn't seem so valid anymore. He wished to rescue himself in a calm atmosphere and with aplomb. He needed to collect himself. As the sun closed in on high noon he forged into Le Parc Central, (Central Park).

Terry sat watching the activity in the park. There were people playing with frisbees, mothers watching over their children in the sand, mid-morning joggers and birds being fed. He enjoyed looking at the small man made pond and wondered how often this place of beauty had been desecrated by crime, moral deprivation and drugs. How many couples had made love in the rose garden? How often had the rose garden witnessed proposals, first kisses, conversations, arguments and resolutions? He stared at the afternoon sky; blurring the moon's Waxing Gibbous with a thinly clouded light blue.

Terry decided to distract himself by reading the paper. On the front page was news of a serial killer tearing apart streetwalkers, pimps, drug dealers and derelicts. Well, that was too depressing. It made him reflect on the selectiveness of the American news media. He thought of how concern about killers and psychopaths never seemed to make the front page until some virginal coed made the list of victims; or if a killer took out a group of victims in some grand fashion, causing mass terror and chaos. He knew his thoughts were becoming disturbed again when he continued to think about how serial killers were often glorified as geniuses; men of complex psychology. Terry tried to shake off the negativity. He knew he had to escape the paranoia and mistrust.

As he sat looking at the park's layout, a frisbee landed near him. A dog approached to retrieve it, but stopped and gave him an inquisitive look. The canine picked up the disk, began to walk away, stopped again and looked back at Terry. In the distance the dogs' owner called out to him, shaking them both from an awkward moment of recognition. The dog took off running, happy to return the frisbee to his owner.

Terry considered heading home, he continued his overwhelming thought process and pondered, "Why get angry over something constant and unchanged in a country built on a shaky foundation? You know the rules", he told himself, "Just play the game. Play to win." It is what Terry had done all these years. Lately he'd been feeling as if the game had been lost, his world pushed off course by the ravages of dumb fate. Damn, how long would he sit still watching the world go by, feeling sorry for himself? This new challenge had nothing to do with the politics of the world. This was personal. He realized he would have to align himself with those whom he routinely mistrusted. For his benefit as well as theirs, he would make this compromise.

Terry stood and wiped the sweat off his face. The noon sun had climbed higher and it was getting hotter. He supposed he should get to a phone, since he had promised to call the office and let them know whether or not he would come in, though it should seem obvious by now. He made the arduous walk back home, went to his car, opened the door, reached in, unplugged his phone from the charger and dialed. He thought to himself dryly, "Maybe, I'll get hit by a bus and won't have to worry about any of this."

As the weekend approached, Terry became increasingly anxious. He waited for Jerry to return, as she had done in the hospital, an ethereal genie to comfort his tortured soul. That's what she did when she was alive, saved people. He reflected on the times she'd saved him in the past. As children, she became strong for him as he did for her. Outside their home, he was her knight, fending off all those who oppressed her; boys, girls, even teachers. To the outside world, he was the hero, the strong one. He continuously came to her aid in every situation imaginable for a young girl becoming a woman. To him, truth be told, she was the true rock; his pillar when things went awry and their world seemed to fall apart, when he was ready to give himself over to despair. Jerry seemed to always be there, reaching out to save him. She would hold him and console him, mending his inner wounds.

His way of thanking her and securing her, his very own selfless savior, was to make sure the world never got to her, like it had gotten to him. Terry was her armor outside, Jerry was his armor at home. Home was his Achilles' heel and she'd often nursed his psyche back to health. When he suffered from too much thinking, he had to remind himself that he couldn't call her. How many times had he broken down in tears when he pulled her number up to dial? Terry couldn't bring himself to erase his sister's number from his phone.

As the weeks pressed on, Terry found himself paying more attention to astronomy. Often studying the calendar, checking the moon cycles and tides. He was stir crazy and needed his sister like never before. He flipped through a myriad of TV channel's, however, the networks were having a dismal season of repeats and recycled sitcoms. So, as he had in his childhood, before abandoning them for CNN, he tuned in to old cheesy black and white Lon Chaney movies. Terry was again drifting into a negative spiral when he faded off to sleep. The phone rang. It was Jerry; she was on her way, tonight! With only a few days left to decide whether to volunteer for experimental treatments that may or may not lead to a cure, Jerry was finally coming to rescue him. Terry felt as if half his weight had dissipated. She would know what to do. His twin sister would give him the strength to decide.

Jerry approached the door and Terry thought how beautiful she was. Her jet-black hair barely touched her shoulders, as she exited the car Terry had provided for her. Company connections had occasional benefits. She had pressed her hair and the wind was making it bounce as she bounded up the steps. Jerry was ecstatic to see him. Her business suit fit her lean body perfectly. "She had strong hips, perfect for children", thought Terry, though he never understood why she'd never even considered having children, ever. "Jesus, I'm starting to think like Mom." He had forgotten in all this, his own self worth. Terry passed the mirror and realized they had always been described as "good looking kids". His skin was a shade darker, his jaw more square. Their intense, expressive eyes and almost purplish-red lips matched. Coarse hair was another thing they shared in childhood, but Jerry had found ways to improve on that. Terry had taken a simpler approach and kept his hair short; it had looked funny for years until his athletic 6 ft. frame finally caught up with his head. Eventually he had become an ominous equation in his world filled with numbers and figures.

Terry was elated that his sister was here. He was also surprised by another emotion. He felt fear. He'd never allowed himself that, often replacing it with anger and bravado. Anger was his armor, it made things easier to handle. Jerry's presence allowed him to let his guard down.

They embraced as Terry welcomed his sister into his home. Jerry stayed strong while he told her he had been struck with a disease that presently had no cure. He wept as he expressed his fears to her. How no one could ever truly have his trust like she did. She held him, she listened and as the night drew to a close she advised him, and in some instances chastised him. How dare he put his pain and hatred above his safety and the safety of others? She felt he was being selfish and Jerry read Terry the riot act. He had to quit brooding about not having it easy, no one did. Having a hard life did not make him special. If Terry really wanted to set himself apart from others, he needed to face his fears and overcome them. He needed to think and act in the here and now, not the past. Jerry told him how much she loved him, needed him in this world and that she would stand by him, no matter how horrible this thing was. That night they cried. That night Terry smiled again, his savior had returned. The phone continued to ring; Terry awoke to an old film he vaguely thought might have inspired Michael Jackson's Thriller video. Jerry was not there. Tears filled Terry's eyes as he answered the phone. It was the Institute, interrupting the dream of his long dead sister.

A day passed and the decision made. After talking to his sister, Terry committed to the research. Jerry truly was with him in spirit. She was there as he awakened. She was next to him in the mirror as he combed his hair and shaved. She was there in the car traveling to the Institute.

Once at the Institute, forms were filled out, waivers signed and he soon found himself in an observation room. Technicians and assistants strapped Terry into a chair that bore an eerie similarity to an electric chair. Terry shuddered at the thought. The staff affixed electrical pads to his head, face and arms. They stuck him with IVs and plugged them into monitors. As the sun set, they seemed to hurry their pace. Terry looked at his surroundings. He could see Jerry behind a massive glass, thick and foreboding, in a room full of people in white coats. Jerry noticed there was a variety of people working there. It was obvious there was no lack of skill or empathy. As for issues like race or sex, the staff did not appear to notice or care about those things. They were all there for the same cause; to find a cure for him. Jerry had long ago, gotten past such concerns and the influence of Terry's negative view of the world. She was the optimistic voice in his ears. She was here with Terry, even if no one else could see her.

"They called it Globes Disease" Terry thought. Once a month, sometimes twice during a blue moon, victims of this disease are transformed into something more primal than anything we were meant to be." Soon the earth's silver satellite began to rise in plain view through windows. Terry began to feel a hot sweat burn as it seeped from his pores. His brain was ablaze and his chest felt as if his heart were a rock tearing through rice paper. His skin itched like a plague of fire ants had been set upon him. The tips of his fingers and toes felt like bamboo was being pulled through them. Jerry looked on in horror and her form began to waver. New shadows were cast from the approaching moon, distorting Terry's vision. Terry struggled through the searing agony and torment to keep his sister's face in sight. Jerry was Terry's kindred spirit, womb mate and twin; his whole life. He loved her more than any human being could comprehend; his connection was one only a twin could relate to. She left the window and Terry almost panicked, until he felt her next to him; her hand hovered over his by millimeters. Her touch felt like a cool mist.

Terry told himself that he was doing this for his sister and for any human faced with this circumstance. Terry convinced himself that it was the right thing to do. For the sake of all those victims in the paper, all those facing an early visit to the morgue. For the sake of all those who survived an attack as he had. For the sake of a cure, for the sake of science; he would be a pioneer. Despite being engulfed in pain, Terry was glad he had volunteered. His face felt like lava, as if hot iron was burning its way through him from the inside out.

Terry thought through all the pain and horror. He was positive that this affliction, had not distinguished him by race, creed, color or sex. This was a disease against humanity. Terry struggled through spine warping anguish to look at his sister, floating and glimmering by his side, one more time. Her tears were his comfort; a reminder that what he was doing was right. In the darkness, the pain that he had sacrificed himself to, took hold. Terry lost all but an iota of who he was before he blacked out. In that moment, as if outside himself, he heard something. A deep sound, muffled yet loud, , faint yet clear. Terry heard a howl as he lost himself to the depths of a caliginous abyss…

ARTY

Aristotle Kanin, his friends called him Arty. His family had varying ideas when it came to their loving nicknames for him. His little sister Annie had loved him from the day she laid eyes on him. She'd followed him everywhere as soon as she could walk. She had never been able to pronounce his name. Even now, as an adult, she continued the running gag and called him Artsy. She called him that out of love and teasing admiration. The looks she gives him are still rewarding to him. It had been that way from the time he helped her steal her first cookie. Through all their failures and successes, they'd loved each other unconditionally.

Other members of his family used names like fag, faggy Arty, and gay boy to mention a few. It hurt more than he would ever let on. After all, he thought, he was the perfect son; despite whom he chose to love. He was a decent student and a great athlete through high school and into college. He finally ended the quest to please his father when he grew weary of having to hide who he was from his teammates and family members. Only Annie had attempted to understand. College was different and he met others with similar lifestyles. He'd served his country and was a decorated officer with an honorable discharge from the Marine Corp. After college and the service, he'd become a businessman. "I'm an American Success Story", he said to himself. "But all the world cares about is whom I choose to love. Doesn't make sense does it?"

Arty had cut himself off from the world he'd grown up in, yet it didn't surprise him that Annie still sought him out. She drove five hours from her perfect suburban nightmare, into the city, just to tell him that she loved her big brother and chastised him for thinking he could leave her out of his life. As tears flowed down her cheeks and glistened in the light; a strange reflection off her perfect dimples, Arty understood and opened up to her. He shared his pain, his fears and he promised her he would never cut her off again. Despite what the rest of their perfect family had to say, his sister had never cared that Arty was gay.

"The perfect family. What an oxymoron!" he thought to himself. Arty was 30. He stood 5 feet, 10 inches tall with dirty blond hair and a muscular build. He had a smooth handsome Greek face that both men and women seemed to love. What a joke; his mother was a drunk and his father was a womanizer. Of his brothers, the oldest was a career criminal and the second born was a child molester. Of his three sisters the oldest was a run away and the middle one could do no wrong, despite never having really done anything with her life. Her accomplishments included kissing up to their parents. She had married and divorced countless times. She was constantly in and out of relationships, as well as dead-end jobs, but somehow she carried the grand distinction of being the favorite. No matter how much he and Annie excelled, it was never enough. Whoever said the youngest children are always the spoiled ones, didn't know squat. Annie and Arty couldn't wait to get out of their family home. "Tell me who is truly normal in this family?", Arty thought.

Arty's true family consisted of his current lover, his friends and Annie, with whom he'd recently reunited. In spite of the hours they spent together in reunion, and the various lengthy phone calls, he was holding back. How could he tell Annie something he still had not told Jeremy, the love of his life? Jeremy was his backbone. A complement to Arty's flighty behavior, Jeremy was level headed and always on track. Arty was occasionally promiscuous; Jeremy was faithful, forgiving and absurdly loyal. He protected Arty, looked after him and loved him unconditionally. Arty couldn't reveal his affliction without revealing his indiscretions. "I don't want to hurt the only man who has accepted me totally and completely." Arty contemplated these issues as he muddled through the workday routines of a career he had studied so hard to acquire. His job was another one of many successes he had used in an attempt to try and please his father.

Obvious motivations that were only recently revealed to him by his therapist. "I have to think this through." Arty struggled with himself internally only to be pulled from his thoughts by his ever-ringing phone. "Pavlov, you asshole!" he thought. You're responsible for all those dinner bells, phones, pagers, PDAs, smartphones, trains and clock alarms. "Your theories have enslaved men, not Rover or Lassie." "Nobody uses a bell to fucking feed his or her dogs. But if you want a human to come running? Ring a fucking bell!"

It was the Institute. An appointment had been made. This was all new to Arty. What was the name of that place again? What an interesting name, The Institute for the Research of Globes Disease, that's it! He had to tell Jeremy now. Forms needed to be filled out. Only one person could accompany a patient. That would be a tough decision. Should it be Annie, who had just come back into his life or Jeremy? Who should be there? What kind of patients did they have? How many were gay? God knows who this rare disease has afflicted. Women? Children? Heterosexuals as well as us so-called accursed sinners? Hmm, I wonder if that means I'm doubly cursed. I wonder if the "Religious Right" will find a way to blame this on my, "lifestyle"?

Arty sat alone in the bar, staring at a television perched in the upper corner. All the chatter floated by him like the smoke collecting on the ceiling. He was so deep in thought that conversations around him didn't register. He didn't notice the occasional man checking him out or trying to get his attention. He couldn't relate to the news of war and the threats to his country on the television screen in front of him. His mortality didn't rest on world events or safe sexual encounters. He was lost in the horror of his situation. The fear of the unknown. Having to tell someone he loved that he was sick. Someone had to come with him, because according to the nurse on the phone, he would be in no shape to do much for himself when all was said and done. He also knew he needed emotional support. A familiar face, a loved one to help him through this. He finished his drink and thanked the bartender who had served him hundreds of times. He paid and he tipped. Arty was both nervous and excited with anticipation. He was ready to move forward.

Arty was surprised to see his sister and Jeremy waiting for him when he walked through the door. Due to his distractions, he couldn't remember if they were there when he left or if he'd called them to meet him at home. He kissed them both and poured on the hospitality. Somber as the air was, he tried to give them his usual sparkle. He sat down and began telling his story. He remembered what his mother taught him and he didn't want to be like her. When she broke something in the house or wrecked the car, she would promptly replace it or have it fixed before Dad came home. It often worked because father was almost always late. "Son", she would slur, "Some things are better left unsaid". Tonight would not be one of those times. Arty told his story with tact and frankness. The undertones were there, but Jeremy ignored them. All Annie wanted to know was what was wrong and how could she help?

Neither of them believed him, they thought it was one of his pranks. They started to come around when he showed them the card and brochures. Arty was not sure what was more surprising. Both his lover Jeremy and Annie insisted on going with him, and that they believed in him and had faith in him despite all their misgivings, were facts that shocked him. To Arty's own surprise he relented. He called the Institute and pleaded special circumstances, allowing both to accompany him. To his surprise, the Institute had no problem with it.

Time to celebrate. They agreed to dinner and a movie. To Arty's elation, the night became an exceedingly rewarding experience. Somehow they managed to take the most horrendous situation and use it to merge his family and his personal life. It was worth more than any cure; any research, anything ever to occur at this point in his life. Arty thought to himself "I could die now, but at least I got my wish. Forgiveness, and unconditional love from the two most important people in my life."

Full from an incredible meal and a mutually enjoyed film, they exited the theatre together, laughing and talking. All the crying and questions from hours ago were over with. The city's negative setting had been replaced with a "Stop and smell the roses", feel of ambient lights and city sounds. The sounds from the car horns, bus engines, helicopters and sirens reverberated in Arty's ears like a rock symphony. They walked their usual route to the loft that Arty and Jeremy shared. A two block jaunt and an alleyway would eventually lead to a rear stairwell depositing them into their brightly painted kitchen.

They turned down an alleyway identical to the one they always used to get home. They laughed and teased one another for getting turned around. Before they could correct their mistake, their rosy feelings were interrupted with "Cat calls" falling out of the city sky. They tried to ignore the ignorant men who idiotically called his lovely sister a transvestite and he and Jeremy fags, but the hate mongers continued. The insipid verbal assault put a damper on the night's reconciliation and it brought Arty back to reality. Where did they come from? The question needed no answer, because the assailants were in hot pursuit. The trio did what all street-smart urbanites would do. They ran.

"Damn, this city, so many alleys" Arty exclaimed to himself. Terror made all the alleys look the same. The city passageways of La Mort Douce betrayed them. Arty fell when they reached an alleyway with a dead-end and the haranguers were closing in. Jeremy and Annie attempted to turn around and help Arty. Arty insisted Jeremy and Annie continue to the end of the alley and climb the chain link fence ahead of them. Annie was crying, but made it to the fence. She somehow managed to squeeze through the chained double gates. Once through she began to run. Jeremy began his climb just as Arty reached him and eventually made it over as Arty urged him on. Arty began his ascent, but stopped suddenly. Arty looked at Jeremy and Annie and changed his mind. He jumped back down to the dangerous side. Jeremy began screaming at him to resume his climb. Annie turned around when she heard Jeremy's screams and realized things were about to get worse.

The darkened night revealed a moon reflecting off puddles of water and urine throughout the alley. Arty waited as long as he could, until he was certain Annie and Jeremy were safe. He was wrong, Annie and Jeremy were fervently screaming at him through the fence they had just traversed. They begged him to climb over. Arty didn't have much time. The alley, his disease, The Fates; it seemed they all had other ideas. His heart began to race and his chest felt afire. He felt a lust stronger than any he'd ever experienced during a sex binge. He was thrilled more than any parachute jump or business deal could ever have provided. Arty gave a last human look at his family, before closing his eyes.

His back was to his attackers when the first blow landed. He felt the initial strike. Despite the violence, Arty's pain from the blows soon disappeared. The pain from the violence was replaced with what increasingly felt like burning skin and frostbite all at once. His very pores felt as if someone were threading needles through them. His head pounded, with his heartbeat, Annie's voice, Jeremy's screams and the heavy breathing and heartbeats of the fools who had chased him and were beating him down. The blood borne affliction that he had thought would be his ruin had come to his rescue.

He raised his hand and for some inexplicable reason the attackers stopped. He turned to them, blood oozing from wounds that were already starting to heal. There was a fury in his eyes they could see in his blood soaked face, even in the darkness of the alley. He knew they were getting a true introduction to his affliction by their looks of shock. Their dismay was an indication that the feral disease was taking over his body. He knew the last of his humanity was disappearing as their eyes widened. These purveyors of hate, who had closed in on him from behind, wielding chains and bats, got to see it all. Up close and personal.

Arty fed off the pleasure he felt from the attacker's surprise. Before he disappeared into the disease, he had the feeling of a turning tide. He relished in that moment. To these fools, now frozen in fear, Jeremy, Annie and Arty were victims, but not anymore, not tonight. Just this once he needed to see someone get exactly what they deserved. Arty craved that satisfaction. His humanity hung by a thread when he growled at them.

The last thing Arty saw was the look of terror on their faces. They were frozen in place, weapons raised and ready to relaunch their attack. The last thing Arty heard was the screams, horrendous growls and the rending of these potential victimizers flesh. Once again before the full moonlit night, Aristotle Kanin was no more. Globes Disease had taken over. The curse he wished to excise had once again come to life. The animal within him had awakened and passed a final judgment.

JODI

Jodi Sakarui considered herself a bit of a rebel. Her family were conformists, at least that's how Jodi saw it. Compared to her family and their traditions, she was a black sheep. Even though there were better, more positive words in Japanese for rebel, she often heard the word "Gaijin" (foreigner). It was a terrible name to call a Japanese person. That, among other words she preferred not to think of, only inspired her to rebel that much more. Her family lived in a two story Victorian in La Mort Douce. The exterior looked like a traditional home from those stupid black and white movies she had seen on TNT. The moment you walk in, the looks and smells were that of any from the Homeland. Which homeland? Japan? As far as Jodi was concerned, Japan was not her home.

"Why should I follow tradition?" Jodi mulled, "For fuck sakes we have been in America for four generations. Grand-Dad was put in the American camps, what? Like a million years ago? Back in 1942 or some shit like that, right? For all intents and purposes, I am an American now. Shit! Who am I kidding, who looks at my round face, yellow tinged skin and almond shaped eyes and thinks American? I am no more a Japanese than I am American. How many Asian women have been crowned Ms. America? Two?" Jodi thought sarcastically.

At 16, Jodi looked 13 and often dressed a lot younger. Imagine a Gothic Catholic schoolgirl. She often wore pigtails captured in red bows, black pleated skirts, patent leather boots, leggings, her arms covered in torn lace and uniform shirts in whatever color fit her mood. Jodi smoked cigarettes and marijuana, drank beer, cut up in school, and fought regularly. All in rebellion against her buttoned down upbringing. Her mother refused to give her a car like the rest of her friend's parents, so she rode her skateboard wherever she was inclined to go. She found it funny to show up at family functions, dressed like a punk rocker or a Goth-Girl. In fact, she had even considered being a Suicide Girl, but even that seemed conformist at present, beside, it wasn't as if she would make the Showtime special.

She scoured the web site and became elated by what she read. She saw every color, every hue and every size girl you could imagine. When the two TV specials came out, she freaked. She was beyond excited, she TiVo'd both of them, waited until her mother was asleep and watched them back-to-back. What a fucking surprise; they were all white and skinny on the show! 'Oh God! Jodi's thinking was excessively negative, and her thoughts were making her want to throw up.

"Fuck this!" she thought, "It's time to get out". Night skating wasn't new to Jodi. She did it all the time. In fact, the night she got attacked was a night she had climbed out the window and headed to the skate park. That didn't stop her though. The weather was just beginning to warm up, spring was approaching and the moon lit up everything like the overhead lights at the basketball court opposite where she skated. It certainly was easier than trying to skate during the day and having to fight with the other kids who asked her questions like, why she was there or if she was waiting for her boyfriend. When they found out she was a Bowl Rider, she was cool until, they realized she could out skate them. Then they wanted to kick her ass or told her to, Fuck Off! Mostly they just assumed she played for the "other team" and shunned her completely and called her a dyke.

Jodi didn't like being discriminated against. Especially by people who had no more claim to the sport of skating and surfing than she did. Jodi remembered once being told that California skaters were inspired by surfing and surfing is Hawaiian. Jodi didn't even know if that was true, but it fueled her indignation. She told herself to, "Snap out of it! Concentrate, open the window and bail quietly." All this thinking was a distraction, it caused her to feel worse. Jodi resolved to revel in being an outsider. Jodi collected herself, grabbed her board and her backpack and climbed out of her window into a night lit by a perfectly round moon.

All the dogs in the neighborhood were howling as she made her escape. She closed the window quickly so the sounds wouldn't carry through the house. Jodi never considered that the howling could have been a warning of danger or anything else; she was intent on her mission tonight. She had been on her computer all day waiting to see if any sexual deviants would hit her up. Finally, some old pervert did. She was going to exact justice like that TV show, but she would do it better than Chris Hansen and with no budget or studio backing.

Jodi recalled the night of her accident. She remembered skating through the tunnel, on her way home from the park, when she'd seen this rad looking guy smoking a joint. The hairs on the back of her neck had tingled a bit, but Jodi ignored the feeling because the guy seemed so cool. He'd worn a long, dark coat, like those guys in old black and white movies or those vampires in movies where the super-hero guy with a sword hunts them. He was sexy, dangerous looking and strangely inviting with the aura of a man who could sweep a girl off her feet. She had wanted to see more of this man's face. So she thought, "What the hell". Jodi slowed down, picked up her board, and walked over to him; swaying her hips in an oft practiced sexy walk. She quietly cleared her throat and in her most seductive voice, asked him if he had any matches.

Instead of reaching in his pocket for a light, the mystery man had grabbed her with a smooth swiftness that completely startled her. Initially Jodi had frozen, but then her survival instincts kicked in. She'd hit him with her board, elbowed his throat, and given him every move that had saved her before with guys who'd gotten out of line. "Shit!" He was the strongest person she had ever encountered.

When she finally saw his face, all she could focus on was his eyes. They were dark, cold and deadly staring back at her. The veins in the whites of his eyes had appeared to grow with every pulse of her heart. With no effort at all, he'd lifted her, embraced her like a child and moved to lay her down. Jodi had thought then that it was all over. She'd be raped then killed and her body left in that tunnel. Fear consumed her. She thought about all the stupid things she had done; defying her parents, skating through that tunnel, talking to the gorgeous killer. She'd wiggled and squirmed, but nothing had freed her from his grasp.

Her heart had raced, adrenaline had made her temples ache and she'd squeezed her eyes shut; tight enough to add to the throbbing pain in her skull. She had known her life was over but she could neither face her killer nor certain demise. She had realized pretty quickly that she was his prey and he would never let her go. Jodi's heart had beat double-time as his cold, stale breath moved closer. Directly over her, she had heard the most guttural, unholy growl she'd ever heard in her short life. Her attacker had looked up, snarled and hissed in response. She'd dared to open her eyes when his grip loosened. In an instant, things had changed. Suddenly, Jodi's attacker had become the prey.

The impact of what hit them had tossed her into a wall. Jodi had lain there with cuts and bruises from head to toe; bleeding through her clothes onto the cold concrete. Her pain had somehow overcome her delirium and kept her awake long enough to smell the oddest scent she had ever inhaled. Not simply animal yet not simply man,but a raw, metallic mixture of both. The tunnels fluorescent lighting had been poor, so she had only seen shadowy forms dancing in a deadly whirl of snarls and violence. The battling figures had resembled a scene from Godzilla vs. King Ghidorah. "Stupid movie, why in the hell would that come to mind?" Jodi wondered just before she blacked out.

The rest of that experience remained foggy. When had the ambulance come? Who'd called them? Why wasn't she dead? While the rape kit hadn't shown signs of sexual assault, Jodi had still felt violated. She never understood why the doctors and nurses repeatedly said she only had bumps and bruises, "How the hell did I heal so fast?" she wondered. "I was shredded." She remembered looking up inside the ambulance when she'd heard the sirens; she had been bleeding from cuts, bites and scratches over her entire body. Jodi still felt the scars, even after the physical evidence had disappeared.

Jodi was already harboring anger and the attack served only to fuel her fire. She continued to channel her anger by combing the Internet looking for him and predators like him. Jodi overwhelmingly felt the need to get even.

The cold night air shook her from her memories and puckered her skin. Parts of her that weren't covered with clothing seemed more sensitive to the frosty air. The click clack of the wheels from her board bounced off the concrete. Night was so much more still than day to her. Jodi could tell Indian Summer was almost over; the air felt crisper, cooler. Jodi felt alive at night, even more so after the attack. She seemed more sensitive to everything. She found herself picking up a cacophony of sounds from traffic, sirens, street voices, wind, rustling leaves and so much more. All of them seemed to assault her hearing.

All those sounds together resembled the hushed murmur often heard during a school play. It had been a little less than a year since that frightful night. While Jodi had survived the experience, she was worse off for it, as she had become even angrier. She thrived in the night and enjoyed the potential danger. In fact, Jodi welcomed it.

Jodi turned in at the park, headed over towards the swings, and carelessly kicked the dew dampened sand around, keeping her eyes out for needles and doggie bombs left by the local addicts and yuppy puppies. She settled onto a damp plastic swing in her punk skirt and kicked herself back and forth for a while. Eventually she stopped her momentum with her feet, reached in her jacket pocket and pulled out some envelopes wrapped in old rubber bands. Out fell a carefully torn advertisement she'd found in the back of the free newspaper. It read, "Globes Disease, do you have it? Do you black out? Do you wake up in strange places? Do you have unexplained fits of rage? Do you heal faster than normal? If you answered yes to these questions, you may have Globes Disease. Call us, direct or collect, at 1-518-555-9653 or visit our website at www.GlobesDisease.com."

Jodi picked up the crumpled ad and put it back in her pocket. She unbound and examined the letters. All had return addresses from Japan. Most of the letters were in Kanji, except the envelopes themselves. Some pages were in English and those were for her. They were all from Jon Ichiban Sakarui. Jodi was annoyed. Her mother neither said anything positive about her father nor let on that he even cared enough to make contact. She realized he wasn't perfect or as buttoned down as her mother's family. He was like her, Next-Gen Japanese. For the first time in her life, Jodi didn't feel as different after reading the letters. She was not in search of validation through older men. She had a father; she did not need a perv to be her daddy figure. Jodi felt anger and resentment for her mother gaining ground inside her.

When Jodi found the letters earlier that day and confronted her mother about them, it did not go well. Her mother threw out words like Haji, which means shame, claiming she was trying to save her from the influence by the new ways of western culture. "That is such bullshit! Isn't pinning all your unrealized hopes and dreams on your children some kind of child abuse?" Jodi was furious and didn't want anything to do with her family. She hated them almost as much as she hated the crusty old fucks that derived pleasure from feeling up young girls. "HAH! My mother wants to protect me from the new ways, but the old ways are fucking me up more than western culture ever could." Jodi's thoughts drifted again. She told herself, "They will all pay." She was gonna take out this one last pervert, then her family and when she was done she would call and find out about this Globes Disease thing.

With luck, being a minor would keep her from the electric chair. Telling the authorities about her affliction might get her labeled crazy and earn her a stay in the loony bin for a while. Nevertheless, at 18, she could claim she'd been cured of her psychoses and be released with her records sealed. When all this was over, she would go to Japan, seek out her father, start a new life and finally be happy. She understood many Japanese left Japan for smaller towns and rural areas, because the big cities in Japan had caught up with the western world and their modern ways. Many of those cities had become so modern, there was no way the residents could live life in the old way. Cities like Osaka, which is where she would go.

A sedan pulled up and ended her daydreaming. A businessman exited the vehicle, approached her quietly and sat on the swing adjacent to her. Jodi's rage began to build, bubbling like an ancient volcano. She would use her entire teenage lifetime and focus it on this moment. She held herself in check for this purpose. She needed to maintain control. Jodi felt his excitement grow as she acknowledged him with a nod. The night air was thick with tension. Jodi's skin heated, causing steam to rise from her skin. She held back just a bit longer, like a child who desperately had to pee, but had to finish the next level of a video game before going. She needed that ache, that urging pain before she could issue her brand of judgment. The man leaned closer; a buttoned-up wolf in sheep's clothing. He would soon discover who the real wolf was. She reminded herself to lock into her mind that while she was in her mindless rage to be sure to visit her mother. The time had arrived and this creep was the catalyst Jodi required. Jodi was ready to rid herself of all the adults who would do her harm. As she readied her mind and stoked her rage, Jodi could hear the thump of her own heartbeat. The last thing Jodi remembered feeling was the stranger touching her leg; the last thing Jodi heard was this perverted stranger's scream.

SAL

Salvatore Dario, Sal to his friends, had worked at The Institute for the Research of Globes Disease for a few years. He wasn't much of an intellectual but he worked hard and was fortunate to have a good job, especially in La Mort Douce. A high school friend had gotten him in and he'd done the rest. Sal had always been a charmer, tall, with dark curly hair and the gift of gab. His buddies used to say he could charm the panties off a nun. The funniest part about that was they also joked that nuns were closet lesbians. Sal chuckled to himself; he knew if his mother had ever heard him and his friends say something like that she'd have popped him upside his head for blasphemy.

That's how he'd grown up. His family always pushing or slugging one another. It was kind of the Sicilian way of showing affection. Sal was well into his twenties. At 6' 1", he weighed in at 220 pounds, with a boxers build, though he was the runt of the family. He was an impressive fighter. In fact, he was the only one who'd never had his nose broken or his jaw dislocated in a family of boys reared on boxing. Their father had worked two jobs. The only time Sal and his brothers got to spend time with him was when they'd gone to the gym with him for amateur boxing matches or sparring sessions. He'd seen his dad spar with pros who would come to town to stay fresh during long stretches between bouts. He'd felt privileged on those occasions when he'd gotten to enjoy a meal with his dad. Breakfast or dinner, but rarely both in the same day. Often his dad lectured them about education and making it in a world fast being taken over by minorities and immigrants, like they had once been. He told them the world was theirs for the taking and it was their responsibility to claim it. As descendants of Italian-American immigrants, who'd persevered through years of suspicion and oppression to succeed in this country, the discipline of both his parents; hard working boxer Dad and Catholic Mom running the family home, had shaped Sal's habits. He rose every morning at 6 o'clock, without fail. No matter how late he stayed up. Sal cleaned up, made meals and worked out in the early morning before making his way to school. Sal continued that process in his adult life and work habits.

Sal's father had been adamant, "No fucking hand outs; make your own way", so that was how he lived his life. He couldn't abide whiners. "Hey, more than likely, you dug yourself into the hole you're in. Fight your own way out". "Unless you're born fucked up, like no leg, a bum arm or some shit like that, stop begging and fucking do something about it!", was what Sal would say to anyone who challenged his views. For the first time in his young life, he now realized how circumstances beyond a person's control could jump up and take a bite, because it had happened to him at work.

Sal replayed the incident over and over in his mind and could only come up with two things. He had either gotten complacent or suffered poetic justice, because he had to admit; for the poor bastards that had come through the Institute the last few years, he'd had no compassion. They were often pitiful and eventually violent, which was why he was there. Sal and a few other ex-ball players from the community college were the facility's muscle. They held down, smacked down and strapped down anyone and everyone who got out of hand. Some of those desperate saps had proved unbelievably strong. During the peak of the month's research cycle, some of the patients panicked. At those times things could get ugly, but Sal had believed that was all under their control.

Sal and his counterparts had their bouncer routine down pat. When patients got out of line, they held them down or strapped them in, for medical staff to administer injections. By gurney or wheel chair the men rolled them into a vaulted room with a skylight. Many patients broke free of the chairs, but none of them had ever gotten out of the room after being subdued by Sal and the bouncers, with one big exception.

The day Sal was infected was not typical and neither was the patient. She was a 5' 6", blonde with long legs, straight hips and a smooth sloping ass that Sal thought was out of this world. She also had a rack to die for and Sal couldn't take his eyes off of her. Sal had thought that, if he broke his usual coolness and showed some compassion, maybe when this beautiful woman was cured, he would ask her out. So, he'd let his guard down for the first time; he'd gone soft and briefly forgot his training. The Institute constantly reiterated that, during the throes of Globes Disease, even the meekest person could be more dangerous than imaginable. In this instance he'd taken the warning for granted, "What could a little girl like her do? Besides she's strapped in." Sal nearly salivated at the mere memory of accidentally brushing against her unbelievable cans, while she was strapped in. They had made it worth taking the minuscule risk. Moreover, it absolutely was a perk of the job.

This woman, stunning as she was, had fooled Sal. She had lulled him into a false sense of control and then she'd bitten him on the arm with her perfect white teeth, drawing blood and changing his life forever. The pain was intense, like nothing he had ever felt before and certainly not from a woman. Girls he had dated, mistreated and dumped in the past had attacked Sal for his transgressions. He had been bitten, scratched, kicked and punched. Hell, he fancied himself a modern day Tony Manero, straight out of Saturday Night Fever. Irate women were an expected hazard. There would always be some scorned, fiery, raven-haired woman he would have to hold at bay. He liked them feisty, but he knew where to draw the line. "Hmph, I may be a little bit of a perv, but I'm no rapist or abuser."

The woman had been extraordinarily strong and extremely difficult to control. Sal couldn't free his arm when she'd clamped down on it and, for the first time in his life, he actually thought he might have to hit a woman. Then again, was she even a woman when she bit him? With the disease raging through her veins, the Institute's doctors theorized about the timing of her metamorphosis and Sal's attack. Usually patients were in the vault by the time they changed. The psyche issues Sal had witnessed in patients normally occurred just before or after the change, but the timing of his bite from that beautiful woman was all wrong, or so he had thought. No one had ever gotten the best of him and Sal had needed help for the first time. It took two brawny orderlies to get her off of him, strap her down and swiftly roll her into the vault.

Sal had somehow eluded the Institute's scrutiny. He wasn't about to allow them to quarantine him. Besides, whatever the negative effects of this thing might be, the positives were awesome. It was like being on steroids and Viagra at the same time. In less than 14 days, he must have bagged at least 20 barflies and techno club hotties. At the gym he felt godlike. He was quicker and stronger in just weeks. Those other guys? "Naturals" they were called at the gym; he owned them during sparring sessions. Sal felt like he did, back when he was on 'roids. His temperament had changed and his thoughts had become violent, even murderous. He was increasingly feeling anti-social. All of which is probably why he was enraged, not scared when his doorbell rang and he saw two orderlies from work, whose names he never bothered to learn. "What the hell are they doing here?" Sal thought, "Well, damn! As he opened the chained door, to confront them, he didn't see the other ten, until it was too late. He tried to close the door, but he was too slow. They shoved the door open, breaking the chain. He had held his own for a while, until he felt a needle pierce his skin.

When he came to, he was strapped in the same fucking chair he had strapped so many others into. The vault door slammed and Sal found himself hating life. He was infected. He had become one of them! He'd be poked with countless needles and would be probed and experimented on because of it. Men he had worked with for several years were doing to him what they had long done to so many others. He thought of the waiver he'd signed when he was hired. They were going to get their money's worth. If he thought the bite was excruciating, the pain he felt now was inconceivable. Sal could feel his skin itching, crawling, burning and a numbness that felt as if he were being electrocuted. It was absurd that he couldn't sit still. He squirmed and fought without success. "So this is what those people deal with," he thought. "The Institute for the Research of Globes Disease" Salvatore scoffed, was just a generic way to say, "The Study of Lycanthropy."

Study? More like experiment. It didn't feel like they were gonna study anything. Sal felt like a guinea pig. That afflicted bitch had infected him and now he was losing hope. He sat there feeling sorry for himself, writhing in pain and looking up at the skylight; all while strapped down. He had once tortured and observed patients without compassion in the same manner. The ever brightening full moon had risen and now peeked into his view. His skull throbbed and he felt like lava was being poured into his brain and was spilling out of every orifice in his head. He closed his searing eyes and screamed at the top of his lungs. All Salvatore Dario could think of, before losing himself to this disease was, "I fucking hate werewolves!"

THE ACHE

QUAKE & DIANA RAGNOROCK

Present day

Quake woke up sweaty. His pajama bottoms were drenched and stuck to his skin. The fire in his lungs felt like the first drag on a cigarette. He had awakened in a panic, gasping for air. He inhaled slowly and deeply, in an effort to cool the inferno in his chest. The desire was overwhelming, and his whole body ached with the need for satisfaction. He could feel the pull of the moon and his humanity fighting against it. His brain throbbed from the rush of testosterone and adrenaline. There was a burning in his chest and the heat raced through the chambers of his heart. He was exhausted, fatigued and jittery all at the same time. He felt excruciating pain and uncontrollable lust from lungs to loins. Quake's nerves sparked and he hungered for flesh. His skin was pyretic to the touch. The cravings, which resembled what an addict might feel after days of sobriety, were primal, sexual and untamed. Quake concentrated on his breathing and held on to himself through the fervor, trying to control it. Quake looked at his beautiful wife as she slept. Usually she was up when he had these moments. "She must be as exhausted as I am," thought Quake. Obviously, she had watched over him the whole night. He thought, as she lay there with bedcovers haphazardly exposing all his favorite parts, "For a woman just over 50 she rivals any of the Pixie's tempting me at the electronics stores". To Quake, Diana was sexier and far more gorgeous. His body could not resist her and watching her sleep increased his desire for her. Quake knew that sex would delay his impending transformation. The Institute told him it had something to do with hormones or something like that. Hell, all that mumbo jumbo was too complicated. Quake did not want to think, He wanted to bury himself in Diana, flesh-to-flesh.

Diana felt Quake's eyes on her and rolled over to look at him. She could see the turmoil raging in him; she anticipated and cherished these moments. Diana loved it rough every now and again. She smiled and thought, "Well, it is for the sake of science". The big lummox was the love of her life. Through thick and thin, good and bad, she believed they would survive it all. They had so far. His blondish red hair was always a mess. He was a broad, solid man and handsome in a Nordic God kind of way. She loved every inch of him and most of the time he was romantic and sweet. However, during the gibbous moons, she welcomed the galvanizing variation from his usual tenderness. It took her days to heal, but it was oh so worth it. She leaned in and kissed him. "You have a rough night, Quake? It's early and breakfast needs to be made, but we could work up a big hunger", Diana purred. Diana climbed on top of him, letting her gown fall off her shoulder. She gave him a half smile, leaned in and kissed him again.

Quake always tried to be delicate, but Diana's lace strap was no match for his passionate caress and it ripped despite his efforts. Diana was glad she hadn't worn her panties to bed; they would not have survived. The tenderness of the moment disappeared as Diana switched gears. She climbed off him and crawled across the bed on all fours. She grabbed the post with both hands, leaned into it and looked over her shoulder. Quake jumped up and moved toward her. She nuzzled her bottom into his groin as he approached and nibbled her neck. Usually Quake took his time during lovemaking, but there was no patience this time, it was rough and satisfying.

The lovers exchanged knowing glances from across the breakfast table, blushing, flirting and playing footsies. Jeez! They were over

50 but they still behaved as if they were in their twenties. Breakfast was full of silent conversations through eye contact and giggles. Quake was calm and Diana was sublimely satisfied. After breakfast, they went down to the basement where Diana gave Quake a shot of Valium and locked him into the silver-lined cage in the far corner. His man cave consisted of a bar, big screen TV, pool table and exercise area. Diana kissed Quake and told him how much she loved him, and they waited.

As the Valium kicked in, both their minds wandered, his drug induced, hers littered with worries. They had been through this numerous times. Diana sat in her chair listening to music and thumbing through magazines, her heart racing. Quake would soon be gone and the creature would be in the cage. The beast was a killer and nothing like the man whose body it would eventually appropriate.

Quake was the consummate gentle giant, always had been, except when he played sports in high school and college. Back then; he was a bruiser, the kind of kid that would tear off your head when the game was on. Off the field, everyone knew that Quake would give someone in need the last of his food, his money or the shirt off his back, though he was no push over. If someone pulled one over on him once, it never happened again. His friends joked that if he did allow it to happen again, it was because he needed a good reason to tear them up for some other indiscretion. Otherwise, he was loyal, faithful and loving to a fault. Quake's love for Diana fueled all his work to control or cure his disease.

Diana and Quake met in college. He once confessed to her that college was easier for him than high school, because for once he wasn't the biggest guy there. College was a breeze with his reputation on and off the field. He was one of the loudest, most popular jocks and a force of reckoning. He had gone to numerous parties and consumed countless beers, bought for him by admirers and peers. His presence provided order, a little intimidation and a lot of magnificent entertainment. Occasionally, he had to prove his mettle, but generally, people loved and welcomed him.

Quake would rumble a room whenever he entered. His loud voice and laughter was a definite key to his unforgettable presence. That is how it happened. Diana was a freshman, he a sophomore. Some jerk at a party got out of line and Quake gave him a thunderous and painful lesson in manners. She had been his damsel and he had been her hero ever since. Protecting her caused what he had become, but he would do it again in a heartbeat.

Quake's infection with Globes Disease happened years ago, but neither of them cared to remember that moment. He wasn't the first of his kind. He wasn't special; at least that's how he felt. What made him unique was being one of the first to control it without complete medical intervention. Control doesn't come easy; in fact, it is downright painful and hard as hell. The ache is incredible and surges from the core, then crawls over and through his skin. That pain alone had caused many a man to give in to it. Quake had given in a few times, but somewhere along the way, for Diana's sake, he had vowed to do everything he could to prevent the change, or at least not kill when he did. Quake hadn't killed a human in almost 15 years and never wanted to let Diana down like that again.

Quake took to Yoga, Tai Chi and meditated regularly. Eventually, he had gained a reasonable amount of control. Today was one of those days he felt he couldn't go it alone. Diana understood communication was the most difficult thing for couples to achieve. Quake had been a professional ball player, briefly and then a cop. Communication didn't come easy to him. Still, Diana believed in and stuck by him. It was tough, but their years together helped, especially before he learned to control the change. Once he told her what he remembered after a change had passed, she had felt more secure. With that insight, she was able to help Quake whenever and wherever she could. Five years ago, he contacted a newly established medical facility in the area after they had placed ads in the paper. Both he and

Diana were hopeful that they could cure him of his affliction. Quake also wanted to find others that understood the pain, the fire that had burned and tortured him. For all these years Diana had known of his affliction and that Quake felt alone, save for her unwavering support. He often told her that she was his one and only true love. Diana believed him she felt the same way.

Diana had decided a long time ago that she would be there for him, no matter what happened. She knew the potential for danger but she also knew the potential rewards as well. Diana believed that, as long as Quake was honest and willing to try anything to cure or control the disease, then she was willing to hang in there for him. She paused in her recollections and looked up from her reading material. Somehow she sensed that Quake, was not going to win today's battle with the beast. It had been a long time since he had lost complete control. Sometimes the werewolf in him seemed more dangerous. Diana often left the room when Quake changed because she was afraid. "It" had already tried to kill her from within the cage a few times. This time, for some odd reason, she stayed. She could feel that he needed her. Diana's love for Quake was her greatest strength and it gave her courage.

This time was no different. Quake's beast thrashed against the cage. It howled and yelped from the pain of transformation. The silver-lined cage came courtesy of The Institute. They often tried new and improved equipment on their volunteers and this was the latest. The beast lunged repeatedly. Diana trembled and shuddered when it looked at her through the bars. The eyes were not her husband's; nothing about this thing resembled Quake. She had seen movies and read books. Some believed that the person engulfed with this terrible affliction was still inside and trying to get out. She believed that theory was utter bull crap. Quake was gone. The thing that now focused its attention on her from inside the cage wanted to kill her. It watched her and attacked the cage furiously. It stopped and peered at her. It seemed to assess the cage. The idea that this thing was trying to figure out how to get out of the cage was unsettling and she definitely did not want to credit this animal with anything resembling intelligence.

Diana decided it was time to leave. She pushed her chair back and grabbed her book. She moved slowly towards the stairs and worked her way up to the door, making every effort not to provoke the beast. She could hear it crashing in the cage; then there was silence. She didn't want to look she was too frightened. Diana heard a clanking sound and thought he was probably trying to touch the bars again, but her instincts told her to get out. The moment Diana grabbed the doorknob; she felt hot angry breath on the top of her head. The smell of the animal made her heart nearly pound out of her chest. Diana realized at that moment the same thing the beast must have, the cage was made of silver but the lock was not.

GOLDY

Goldeen Johnson gazed into her bathroom mirror. She couldn't see what others saw in her, only tired eyes and countless imperfections. What stood out to her was the mole on her neck, her not so perfect breasts, her thighs; a little thick and jiggly in her opinion, and her ass; better to not even think about it. Goldy lamented to herself, "Seems like these days having a firm round behind is only acceptable for a Puerto Rican pop star". Goldy turned away from the mirror, the self-loathing and the mental torture. The evening was at hand and she had an appointment with a very old Lycanthrope. She had meditated all day to fight off the effects of the full moon taunting her from the daylight sky. It was a provocative moon, giving rise to her feral beast.

Goldy sighed, looking in the mirror once more. She was facing the task of unleashing her hair from the confines of her scarf and her daily beauty ritual. Many men hate short hair and don't much care for weaves or braids. Most of the men she dated complained about how long it took her to get ready, of course they'd complained about how long most women spent getting ready. Men like the results, but not the process. Men want beauty to be automatic, like movies or magic. Beauty is truly like both, an illusion. Press and comb is an art and rollers are a chore. Mom always said, "There is pain in beauty." The stigmas black women suffer when it comes to their hair often forced Goldy to defend herself. She relished the chance to point out that black women aren't the only ones who get perms, weaves and extensions.

Goldy was a natural beauty. This was a painful fact for her. Did men love her for who she is or what she looked like on their arm?

Did they love her or the chance to conquer the elusive prize? As far as she knew, most people she knew didn't see beauty as she did. They saw it as an asset and compared her to some of Hollywood's most timeless beauties, like Beverly Johnson, Rachael Welch and Sophia Loren all wrapped up in a humble physical therapist. Goldy's skin was caramel colored and even toned so she rarely needed foundation. She had a quiet, stunning quality about her with a captivating essence. She could have been a model. When she had considered it, back in the day, she hadn't been tall enough, thin enough, or fair enough. She sighed as she applied her lip-gloss and eyeliner. She hated having fallen captive to her thoughts.

Goldy had always made the effort to be one of the good girls. She tried to refocus, but her mind wandered to her boomerang child and her job. She thought about how her experiences and philosophies had evolved. Goldy was not overly religious, but she did pray and believe there was a higher power, somewhere. She had ethics, though time and experience had shaped her definition of them. It took plenty of trial and error to practice the "Do-unto others…" mantra. Goldy believed in being a lady, a woman with class. No matter the situation or affliction, no one should ever see more than what you want to show. She allowed no one, especially no man, to venture inside her mind, body or soul, without invitation. She had created a wall of protection against betrayal, hurt and judgment made even more painful and lonely by having Globes Disease.

Goldy's youth was interesting to say the least, growing up in California. Los Angeles was nothing like the movies and TV portrayed it to be. There was no shortage of ghettos and violence. Plenty of the people who lived there had never seen their very own sandy polluted beaches. It took forever to get anywhere and the skies were polluted enough to impede enjoying the sun. There was plenty to do, if you had money. Skiing was only hours away, even if they did manufacture the snow, numerous sports to watch, countless clubs, movie theaters, restaurants and the like. The poor might find their way to some of this entertainment, but the rich could do it all in one day. It wouldn't be wrong to think that places, such as Los Angeles, California, had so much to do that one could get bored having done it all. It is a city with fickle loyalties; a tough audience to sell out tickets and seating for sports teams and entertainers. Despite distractions and self-absorbed people, Goldy's parents had found time to have fun and educate their children by taking them to museums, plays and other cultural events. There was no shortage of education in their household. Discrimination existed and Goldy's parents invested a lot to ensure their children received the same education their wealthier white counterparts received. Goldy's parents had shielded them from such counterproductive activities as drugs and gangs, taught them self-respect to avoid teen pregnancy and so many other things that infected and plagued kids across America. Goldy and her siblings were not completely sheltered, though. They all found some piece of counter-culture to dabble in. For the most part, they were great kids that got into minimal mischief. They learned, grew and moved on from their youth, largely unscathed.

Goldy's Mom was a strong, assertive, outspoken and caring woman who loved to talk. Her Dad was a passive, laid-back, dependable man. He was no pushover, but he believed the happiness of his wife and daughters came first. He was stern with their two boys for a reason. Their combination made for a long and interesting marriage. There were challenges, of course. Her father's efforts made it easy for the entire family, especially the women. Their parental involvement paid off. They all came together in her father's later years, when he became ill. There was an abundance of levity in the family dynamic, even in those trying times. Her Mom and Dad needled one another frequently. With age and illness, it had taken her Dad a little bit longer to utter his digs and quips, but they all patiently waited for them. They laughed and joked in return when their father finally delivered his punchlines, as if his impairments did not exist. The loving atmosphere, where everyone lightheartedly teased one another constantly, was a memorable experience. There were fights and hurt feelings on occasion, but overall everyone knew no one was going anywhere. Maybe that is what confused her about what her life had become and despite all she had accomplished, why she saw herself the way she did. She did not consider herself attractive, smart or successful the way others perceived her to be. She considered herself a 'recovering failure'.

Words couldn't describe how painful it was for Goldy as a woman with three failed marriages. As if that wasn't bad enough, people judged her for having had more than her share of men. Goldy actually hadn't had many lovers at all she was old fashioned that way. She was an eternal optimist, but like many women, she bought into the idea of the 'All-American male'. Goldy had tried to be the ideal woman, often to her own detriment.

Goldy's first husband was a striking, charming, engaging and unbelievably sexy man. The kind of man any woman would want to have children with and she did. After the birth of their son, she got back in shape and did everything she could to please her husband and make theirs a successful marriage. She was educated, good looking, a good wife and a great Mom. That wasn't enough for him, and apparently, Goldy wasn't either. He just had to have more women. For a while, she had tolerated his actions. She figured they had just gotten married too young, but she had believed he would eventually grow out of his wandering ways. She tolerated it, because she loved him. Her Mom and Dad were together for years. Couples have challenges, so, stand by your man" through thick and thin, for better or worse is what she did. That is what her family taught.

Goldy contracted a sexually transmitted disease from her husband and lost their second child because of it. She had taken everything he did to her, but when it hurt the children, that was the final straw. No matter how strong a woman is, how much in love she is or how deep the pain she endures is; no woman will completely get over nor will she ever forget the death of her child; unborn or not. The separation and divorce were painful, but that pain had not lasted long. He found another woman to support him. It had been difficult raising a child under those circumstances, but she did her best. Once Goldy's son went away to Howard University, she finally allowed another man into her life.

Her second husband was a drug addict. Goldy didn't know it until their honeymoon when he overdosed in the hotel bathroom and she had resuscitated him. Unfortunately, his overdose had set a precedent for their month long marriage and it didn't end as well as she would have liked. She had wanted to save him, but as the saying goes, "No good deed goes unpunished" and it ended as dramatically as it had begun.

One evening he came to as she was reviving him and stabbed her with the needle he had used in his arm. It was a purely drug induced accident but the effect was the same. Some heroin remained in the syringe, though not enough to do her any real harm. There was, however, enough infected blood to change her life forever. When they were dating, she hadn't given much thought to the fact that he was gone at night on odd but consistent occasions. Goldy had assumed his disappearing acts related to his drug habit, until she experienced her first full moon. She came to realize his heroin use was an attempt to keep from changing. It was his way of quieting the beast within. Goldy decided she would learn to quiet the beast without the use of illegal drugs. That decision lead down a long arduous road.

Eventually Goldy had married a third time. That marriage was a turning point for her and taught her a lot about herself. She learned that even the beast could not push her past her limits like that abusive man could. He devolved from giving compliments to making minor complaints about her and her looks to giving reminders to keep it together to outright insults and put-downs. His erotic lovemaking had begun gently enough but ultimately turned into pushing, grabbing and slapping her around. It had affected her self-esteem, but the last straw came after her son had tried to defend her. For his intervention, he had been badly beaten, and had to be taken to the emergency room for his injuries. Goldy and her son promptly fled to her mother's home and protection.

Goldy determined she would put an end to her tumultuous life. After watching TV reports about a girl named Jodi Sakarui, who claimed to be a werewolf using her powers to exact justice on child molesters, Goldy decided Jodi would not be the only Were to pass judgment on someone using their animal as an instrument. One night, Goldy left her son with her mother. She sat naked in a park, hidden and meditating about her husband and his demise. She awoke the next morning in her mother's garden, crept into the house, showered and watched the news to see if there was a report about an animal attack in her husband's neighborhood. The knock on her mother's front door was the local police, confirming that she had succeeded. It also confirmed her suspicions that maybe her disease could at least be, channeled if not, controlled. After the dust settled, she vowed she would never harm anyone in that manner again. Instead, Goldy began helping others. That too, proved to be a complex challenge.

Goldy shook off the negativity, finished applying her eyeliner then frowned. She knew the past still affected her and felt she had wasted too much of herself on the wrong men. Deep down, Goldy believed she was past her prime with no chance for true and meaningful love. The reality that she wasn't past her prime eluded her. How she saw herself was not how others viewed her. For a woman at the back end of 40, she still attracted many men. She didn't want others to define her by whether or not she had a man in her life, so she vowed not to think that way anymore. There were no knights in shining armor. Three marriages and a life changing disease had caused her to redirect her focus. Initially she practiced for herself, but eventually she developed a desire to help others like her, with what she called, "Zen-lycan-therapy". She devoted herself to helping others gain some semblance of control over an uncontrollable disease.

Extensive travel, the study of Yoga, Zen and many African philosophies had helped her create a method to control her own inner-beast. In doing so, she had assisted others and had made a substantial amount of money in the process. Helping others provided her with the ability to raise and educate her son properly. He was a well-traveled, self-sufficient, modest young man who was gorgeous and charismatic like his father. She was proud of how well her son had turned out, despite her misfortunes. Now, her goal was to help others cope with and control their disease, and help cure them of Lycanthropy. That is why she was in this town on the blurry border of Canada and the United States. Goldy had redirected her maternal instinct to help save the odd, dangerous town of La Mort Douce.

The morning air felt good, when she exited her home. Goldy looked up at the moon, it was bright even in the morning sky. The moon in a daytime sky was still a dangerous influence. Before she had learned how to control the thing inside her, any waxing, waning or full moon, day or night, could cause her to change. She chuckled to herself as she hit the remote car alarm, opened the back door and tossed all the things she was carrying onto the back seat. How had she kept this thing a secret from her family, especially her son and the few men she did allow into her life? Goldy programmed her GPS and continued to think about men. She wasn't willing to open herself up for that type of trade-off, pain for pleasure, just yet.

There was one gentleman, classically tall, dark and handsome with a strong jaw line and sad, sensitive eyes that she found herself thinking about. His name was Terry. They had noticed one another but they both seemed too afraid to make the first move. Goldy laughed, "What a shame at this age, we're both waiting for that movie moment when we look into each other's eyes and sparks fly." Maybe if she examined the shredded mess of her heart, she could enjoy those sparks for once and finally let someone in, again.

Matters of the heart would have to wait. Being deep in thought got Goldy to her destination in no time. She had arrived at the home of her morning appointment. She parked, shut off the car, turned off the GPS and got out of the car. Goldy straightened her clothing and grabbed her things. She said to herself aloud, "First impressions are so important and this is a rare find, a Lycanthrope older than me, and seeking my help". She was hopeful that they could learn from one another. Maybe he knew some thing's the Institute couldn't or wouldn't reveal. She looked to confirm that she was indeed at the correct address. The name on the mailbox, Ragnorock, just oozed masculinity. She pictured a man in a Viking helmet answering the door. She giggled to herself as she made her way to the front door. Goldy rang the doorbell, but her thoughts interrupted by a feeling, part female and part beastly instinct. Something was terribly wrong.

VLADIMIR ROMANOV

Vladimir Romanov had been watching the news. They were extolling the merits of some research Institute volunteering to help a child serial killer who claimed to be a werewolf. The story indicated she was a child when she allegedly committed her crimes but tried as an adult. It was difficult to fathom the adorable golden-skinned angel, Jodi Sakarui, would receive the death penalty. Vlad did not feel she deserved a death ordered by inept lawmakers. Life and death are simply the natural order of things.

Vlad found himself outside a large windowed building, staring at a huge television in the biggest electronics franchise in the country. Curiosity caused him to enter the store. "This small town is slowly ceasing to be small," he thought to himself. La Mort Douce was once a mining town many years ago; taking in all immigrants, even the Russian ones, but this place had changed considerably from when Russians were the minority. The bulk of the Russian migration happened just after the assassination of Alexander the II in 1881. It had been a town for Hunters, then miners, and eventually yuppie tourists. Now, werewolves were here. This place had changed more in the last 10 to 15 years than it had in the last 105 and Vlad wondered if he should stay here much longer. Where should he go? Maybe back to the motherland or somewhere in the States. Vampires are loners, like sharks. Being immortal requires a singular mindset.

A companion was out of the question as far as Vlad was concerned. "I like to be alone," he thought to himself. Imagine a roommate or spouse forever, by year 200 or 300 a person would probably want to jump off a cliff. Vampires would go crazy and kill one another, sacrifice themselves to the sun or even rip their own throats out. "May I help you?" sang a woman's voice, yanking Vlad out of his thoughts. A gorgeous, dirty blonde pixie of a woman stood in front of him, introduced herself as Heather, smiled, winked and asked Vlad again if he needed assistance. Heather saw what many women saw in Vlad, a handsome dark stranger with an air of danger about him. Vlad had barely shown his face, his long-coat collar hid most of his features and his long wavy hair did the rest. Vlad was like a Venus flytrap; he rarely ever had to hunt. He didn't need to use Glamouring as often as other vampires did. After all these years, he didn't question his 'Mojo'. His vampirism was both blessing and curse. Heather was an attractive woman, but too small for his hundred-year-old body. Vlad required more blood than what this little morsel had pumping through her veins. Vlad wondered, "How did she keep her anorexic little body alive?"

"American women try so hard to be thin." Vlad continued his internal conversation. That concept alone was baffling to Vlad, if not for the Midwestern states and a good portion of the East Coast; this country could leave an old vampire starving. Facing dire straits, a vampire could feed on livestock or wild game, but Vlad was not fond of that survival trick. Nothing was as sweet as the succulent blood of a human. There just wasn't enough for a complete meal in this one. Heather would merely be a snack. She had been talking so much that Vlad did not think she had taken a breath while speaking.

Heather was nothing compared to Oksana, full and sexy, she was the love he'd left so many years ago, in the northern part of Moscow when his family immigrated here in the early 1900s. Once in America, Vlad had planned to send for her, but that had never happened. He walked away before Heather could launch another pitch. Vlad had two loose ends to tie up.

Vlad exited the store, leaving behind the perplexed Heather. The cold air was a comfort to him. It reminded him of home; though in some ways he regretted returning to the place he'd immigrated. Vlad became a vampire here. He hunted for a few decades, and then returned home to Mother Russia, but like they say, "One can never truly go back home". He had changed and so had his hometown, 30 miles from the Kremlin. Oksana had changed as well. Vlad had remained as he was once he was a vampire; Oksana had moved on and aged. Vlad stayed in Russia as long as he could stand the unfamiliarity of his home. In fact, he became Moscow's self-appointed werewolf exterminator.

There were fewer werewolves in Russia, after Vlad's return, for two reasons. First, Vlad hated them so much he killed as many of them he could track; second, the cold weather. Often, during or after, they'd freeze to death when they changed back to human. Naked, lost and disoriented, they would lose their way and die, vulnerable and exposed trying to get back home. This was the epitome of their idiocy to him. Stupid creatures, lacking tact and class, they were definitely not part of the natural order, thus Vlad felt it was his right to rid the world of their mangy existence.

Vlad headed to Le Parc Moyen. It had taken a few years, but he finally tracked his objective. Normally he wasn't the vengeful type, but the meal that flea-ridden hellhound had cost him, was also a witness to his presence in La Mort Douce. Vlad hated having human witnesses to his identity even more than losing prey. Humans that knew of vampires made easy conduits to vampire Hunters. 60 years had passed since the last time he was on their radar. He liked it that way and had no desire to be again. Killing Hunters was quite an inconvenience. Hunters knew all the strengths and weaknesses of vampires and were generally quite tenacious. Vlad had tracked his filthy adversary back to the very same spot of their first encounter. He stood at the tunnel and waited, as he had for Jodi. Vlad produced a joint, lit it and took a deep hit. Hmm, why did this herb appeal to him so much more than cigarettes or cigars? Maybe because, at its most basic, it was still pure, no machine had a hand in its making. For him, the taste was more consistent, clean, pure, and sweet. Vlad would enjoy his joint for only a moment. His elevated sense of smell had picked up the stench of that wet, hairy mess as it drew near. "Stupid creatures, all fangs and claws, no sense," he grumbled aloud.

Vlad took one last drag off his ace and stepped away from the wall. Smoking was an interesting indulgence and quite a lure for young victims. He stood facing the tunnel's end. The werewolf's howl echoed down the tunnel like a trumpet. He thought to himself, "I am glad I am not human, I might have vomited from this creature's stench by now." The beast's next howl seemed like a curious warning. Vlad could sense confusion in the beast as it realized it did not smell fear from him. "Stupid shabby thing, can't it tell we met almost five years ago?"

As the wolf reached the end of the tunnel, its growl indicated familiarity. The silhouette would have made most humans soil themselves and run. Standing on its hind legs, this werewolf was sinuous, tall with a long snout and long claws. Vlad could feel it getting angry and decided to pause a moment before he entered the tunnel. The wolf charged. "Good" he thought, "This one's completely primal." Vlad hoped the distance would tire it out, giving him an advantage. The werewolf, as it made its dash, was already half way to him when it started tearing at the ceiling-lights. Eventually the strategy worked and the tunnel went dark. Seconds before it reached Vlad, he realized the wolf was not as stupid as he had assumed. Vlad flung open his coat and readied himself. His face exposed the only scar, he'd ever received since becoming a vampire was visible, a jagged claw mark on the left side of his face from his ear to his chin, trailing his jaw line. It was a gift from this very werewolf and Vlad wanted to return the favor. As Vlad's eyes adjusted to the lack of light, his fangs and nails grew longer and his eyes changed from a soft brown hue to a dark metallic projecting a cold, deadly stare. His evil grin exposed his long, white, perfectly intimidating fangs. The veins in the whites of his eyes pulsed with his thirst for the kill as he braced for the impact.

The beast was yards away, invisible to human eyesight, but Vlad could see it. To an unenhanced eye, the beast would have seemed to lunge out of the darkness. The beast was snarling, saliva spilling from rows of fangs layered in its gaping snout, ready to rip Vlad's throat. Seconds seemed to take minutes as it leapt. The sheer force of power, speed and fury seemed about to overtake Vlad, like a linebacker dealing the business to a vulnerable quarterback. Vlad reached up, caught the beast by the neck, crushing it with one hand. Air gurgled through the constricted opening and still it fought. Barely able to breathe, it still had fight in it. With his other hand, Vlad grabbed a fist full of long tangled fur and yanked on the top of its head until there was a sickening pop. It ended almost as quickly as it began.

Air bubbled through the blood of its exposed neck. By the time Vlad dropped the flaccid body of the gnarly beast to the pavement, it had begun to revert to its human form. A large breasted woman, about 5' 6", with long legs was sprawled dead, naked and headless before him. Despite the carnage, in death she was quite beautiful, Vlad thought as he examined her blonde head, a prized kill.

Vlad had often wondered how well it would go over to stuff and mount these creatures like humans so often do with what they hunt. Vlad stood over her, looked at her beautiful frame and thought, "What a complete waste of a human, she would have made a lovely and fulfilling meal." If not for the whole werewolf thing, she would have been a perfect candidate to be a turned vampire. "Oh well." Vlad thought. On her wrist, Vlad eyed a band, broken during her transformation. Likely caught in her mangy fur, it lay free after she reverted to human form. He dropped the head and bent down to pick up the wristband, blood dripping from his hands. The unmistakable insignia on it indicated she was a patient at the Institute for the Research of Globes Disease. Vlad pocketed it then straightened himself and casually closed his coat, flipping his collar to cover his face. As if no violence had ever occurred, he simply walked away.

His agenda partially satisfied, Vlad had one more place to go. As he headed west through the town he'd known for a hundred years, he noted all the changes. The businesses that had come and gone the ones that had stayed the same, some handed down, generation to generation. Politicians had come and gone, industry had evolved and Vlad wondered if he would even fit in here anymore or if he had outgrown the old ways and the town.

Vlad looked at the brilliant moon, barely at the beginning of its full moon cycle. "That probably explains why the female Lycanthrope was weaker than anticipated," he theorized. Nevertheless, the moon lit the night better than any streetlight; not that it mattered given Vlad's supernatural vision. He wondered if La Mort Douce had an epidemic on its hands. He considered whether he should stay to help eradicate the problem or move on as planned. Vlad didn't mind performing pest control. These wild animals; were just clumsy vermin.

Vlad swiftly arrived outside the Institute. He'd passed a cabin on the way and figured the place had a basement he could use as temporary shelter from the sun. He planned to stay around until Jodi arrived. He hoped it would be soon, because he sensed something horrible on the horizon. Vlad had yet to decide if he would remain in La Mort Douce or give his motherland one more chance. He didn't want to outstay his welcome in the States, but he had unfinished business. Vlad wanted closure; he wanted the girl.

ANDERSEN

Terry Andersen stared at the flat screen on the wall in his office. The local news carried one story, "The girl who claimed to be a werewolf." Apparently, she had used the Internet to lure men seeking to diddle with underage girls and murdered them. La Mort Douce's first known serial killer, was a minority to boot, just not the right minority to his way of thinking. Terry had to laugh at himself, even he was losing the fine line between militant and racially positive thinking. He whispered to himself, "Terry, just let it go."

According to the news, authorities remanded her to the Institute after a massive investigation, the discovery of a diary, her arrest and trial. Terry, and others like him, knew the child was likely telling the truth, despite the public laughing off her claim. Terry believed she was genuine, though he suspected there was more to the story. He wondered if Lycanthropy would make her truly culpable. He marveled that the news never questioned or brought up the Institute's true purpose for existence. Obviously, the Institute was not forthcoming with everyone about working with Lycanthropes. How could an organization of such magnitude manage to keep so low a profile in the press? Did they claim to be treating psychotics, specializing in those who believed themselves to be Lycanthropes? He wondered what story within the story regarding the existence of this private agency was. Terry did not believe the Institute helped anyone out of simple kindness, so where did they get the money?

Terry shut off the television and turned his chair around to look at the wall of glass behind his desk. Some would call it a window, but he felt trapped by its deceptive clarity. Terry was perplexed as to why he'd retained his position with The Douce Water Company, after such a long absence. He was further puzzled at his inexplicable promotion upon his return. That had come as a huge surprise to Terry, as he'd assumed he would be fired.

Something felt wrong concerning the Institute's intentions. A nagging feeling crept up on Terry. He thought, "I hope the Institute isn't just another version of the Tuskegee Experiment for Lycanthropes. Is the Institute lying about treating participants for Lycanthropy or something even worse? What are they hiding?" Terry couldn't put his finger on anything specific, but something about the whole thing definitely vexed him. He didn't have time to solve that question just then, occupied with other issues as he was, primarily, learning to control his disease until there was a cure. Terry decided to play it through his mind a few times, work through his reservations about the Institute and address it all later, when he could view things with more perspective.

Terry's thoughts drifted to his twin sister. Jerry's apparition had been with him through this ordeal. In his dreams, she had helped him make his decision to seek help with the Institute. After many months, she no longer appeared as often, but he could feel her there with him. Terry imagined that, had she still lived, she would have eventually gone stir crazy here. Most people couldn't take this town and its extreme seasons. The majority of outside traffic and tourism came to this area during spring.

La Mort Douce had the most beautiful spring one could ever experience. In a town overrun by deaths, spring was its reward to the surviving residents, repaying them for their many sacrifices. "Maybe this town was using their dead as fertilizer," Terry morbidly joked to himself. Maybe that explained La Mort Douce's brilliant springtime colors. No computer graphics, movie imagery or special effects could ever recreate those colors. Visitors from throughout the nation came to see the wonder of it. Movie companies, photographers, naturalists and the like, but somehow the town's biggest secret had never been revealed. It was like a family secret that most dared not discuss, for fear of bringing additional negative karma to a place already teetering between hell's angels and heaven's guardians. A town of death and burgeoning evil wrapped in lush plants, trees, gorgeous scenery and spectacular flowers of every genus.

The town was busy. Winter had already left the frightful park that he now viewed through his office window. In the woods, just past Le Parc Moyen, spring was in full force. The hunting grounds to the east, the mountains directly ahead to his north and the suburban tract homes to the west, just past the Ange de Vie Hôpital. How ironic; the only hospital in a town of death calls itself "Angel of Life Hospital."

The Institute stood on an island outside the edge of town, just past the hospital. How they managed that was a mystery. It was prime real estate, supposedly government owned, positioned between the Canadian and American borders; it was on the only strip of land within the bordering lake. A medium sized lake that often proved treacherous.

Escape of any patients could present a litany of problems and would surely put the citizens of La Mort Douce in jeopardy. Imagine feral werewolves escaping the Institute. The location was choice, because even if they could swim off that tiny island, they risked freezing to death and drowning because the water was so cold all year round. Their bodies would change back to human and wash up on either bordering shores.

Some escapees attempted to stay human and swim or ferry themselves across in the most creative of ways, but the same morbid result inevitably occurred. The treacherous weather and landscape claimed many lives, human and super-natural alike; she had no favorites.

The ecosystem in La Mort Douce provided life-sustaining water, including Montagne du Loup and Le Petit Lac de Vostok and one could speculate that the residents were fertilizer. Many people drowned and/or froze to death in the Lake. Russian immigrants chose the name Vostok after one of the coldest and deadliest lakes in Antarctica. Eventually French immigrants altered the name to Le Petit Lac de Vostok. There was a cruel irony throughout the town, concerning its origins and the many names given to its landscape.

Terry shook off his meandering thoughts, once again, and resolved to research all his questions as soon as he was done with his project. Terry chastised himself, "I know you're a genius and all, but at least look at the thing before your meeting this week." Terry sighed, picked up the paperwork and started reading. Life was different now; he was different. Terry felt as if all of his strengths had magnified. He read faster, thought quicker and concentrated better. The downside of these attributes, being that the closer the full moon got, the more the pendulum swung the other way. He found it harder to concentrate, was hungrier, more desirous, and far less patient. He had roughly a three-week window to take advantage of the positive side of being infected. He chuckled to himself, realizing his mind had begun to wander, once again.

The phone rang none too soon; the moon's influence was pulling at Terry's Werewolf fervently. Terry was delighted to find it was Goldy. "Cool!" he thought; she was a welcome distraction. They chatted for a while, catching up. Jerry appeared, as she often did where Goldy was concerned. Her spirit didn't always show itself, but she often whispered in his ear. Jerry's spirit favored this woman and in his dreams, Jerry nagged him about connecting with her.

While on the phone, Terry felt almost schizophrenic and had a hard time discerning whom he was answering, as if Goldy was channeling Jerry. "Yes, I am going to the Institute for my weekly visits. Yes, I am working out. No I haven't built a containment unit in the house like they advised." Goldy was very motherly in her approach as she confirmed their appointment for yoga and meditation. Goldy was his instructor; referred by someone because she specialized in Terry's unique needs. Goldy was so extremely gorgeous, making her slightly intimidating, but her spirit was a comfort. There was definitely an attraction, on Terry's part.

Goldy was surprisingly youthful for a forty something. Her spectacular figure, phenomenal face and personality could make even the most confident of men swoon. Terry needed to get off the phone; he didn't want Goldy to know he was attracted to her, at least not yet. He was waiting for the perfect occasion, so he forced himself to concentrate past the ache in his loins, as Goldy continued their phone consultation. He used every trick he could think of to block the part of him that wanted so desperately to ask this seemingly unobtainable woman out. Whispers of settling down to marriage, and kids with Goldy drifted in and out of his thoughts. Eventually Terry extracted himself from the conversation, using work as his reason. Goldy finally relented, once Terry promised to continue working with her. He hung up the phone covered in sweat.

Terry thought to himself, with a nod to the persistent whisper of his sister, "Settle down? Who would marry someone like me, especially given this infection?" Being a successful black man in a town of limited diversity was tough enough. A great number of places catered to folks in his tax bracket, but many of those same places didn't always have black women inside. Terry remembered a conversation with a doorman who'd casually shared with him the requirements as to who could enter. Most of the women described were not women of color. Even Jerry, when she was alive, had complained of having a hard time getting past the velvet rope. He found that both strange and curious, in this day and age. Terry sighed, looked at his paperwork, put it down, and sighed again. Nice girls and professional women were difficult enough to meet without so much other interference. Terry felt helpless against his conflicted mind, gone astray from his work. He thought of how meeting Goldy had been a very pleasant surprise. He knew she understood him, but that didn't mean she felt the same as he did. He turned, looked out the window again and sighed once more. He needed to fill the void his sister left, years ago. He was lonely and longed for a soul mate.

Terry attempted again to reign in his focus, as he stared out his glass enclosure towards the hunting grounds. One moment, forever implanted in his mind and in his blood stream. "Dumb ass me, trying to fit in." He reflected on his first and last time hunting; out there with men he didn't know, dressed like Elmer J. Fudd to boot. The guys had all gotten a good laugh and Terry had taken it all in stride. He'd even begun to have fun, until he found himself separated from the group while tracking a buck. As he'd lain low in brush, the buck spooked by something from his right and suddenly, something slammed into Terry. The impact was so hard, Terry thought some asshole lost control of an ATV and had run him over. When he looked up, he faced a wolf, the likes of which he had never seen. Fortunately, all that gear he'd purchased protected him from the initial strike, but it didn't hold long. The mega-wolf had torn through all barriers of clothing in short order and Terry had believed he was dead-meat. The mega-wolf had been unable to kill Terry right away and that seemed to annoy and infuriate the beast. Frustrated, it picked up Terry and shook him like a chew toy; possibly to dislodge him from his armor.

Terry had landed with a thud, like a discarded rag doll. The wolf, on top of him stared at Terry, its growl unworldly, eyes filled with a rage and anger he had never seen in any animal. Its thick breath was visible in the cold, like smoke from a mythical dragon. Hot, steam poured from its mouth and his hairy assailant bared its teeth even broader. The beast had ripped away at his down coat and flung him all about. Terry had screamed in terror as his body slammed into the ground repeatedly, with incredible force. Terry had begun to welcome death as delirium set in. The air knocked out of his lungs, he hadn't been able to catch his breath. Lightheaded, his injuries had pulsed along to the cadence of his rapid heartbeat. Terry had felt teeth make contact with his skin and in that moment, as the creatures large mouth was about to split him open; Terry knew he was about to die.

Terry didn't know why the animal did what it did, but he faced it and looked deep into its eyes and said, "P-p-please no, don't kill me." Somehow, through all the rage and hunger, it had stopped and stared down at him. For a second, the eyes looked almost human and appeared to understand what Terry said. Gunfire had interrupted the pause in violence; a pause that felt like hours. The wolf growled in the direction of Terry's fellow Hunters and refocused its attention back to the preservation of its meal. An enormous paw had pressed down on Terry's chest, as if to lay claim to his prize. "That thing had no intention of sharing me," Terry thought with morose humor. The wolf had reared his head back, maybe to bite him again or possibly to drag him off to his lair. The gunfire had continued until one of many bullets hit the beast in his eye. It had let out a heart dropping, unholy howl and took off. Terry had looked up to see his hunting party standing over him and then he did what anyone would do under those circumstances, he passed out.

Terry regained his composure and resumed looking out the window. Suddenly Terry felt something vaguely similar to the connection with his sister, except this feeling was primal not spiritual. This feeling was urgent and often came upon him just before and just after the full moon. Terry somehow felt, via a new and strange vibe, that there were others like him out there. There were certain Lycanthropes he felt a connection with, almost as if they were communicating with him. "Maybe they share the same maker." Terry thought. "Something out there is more dangerous than I am. I hope whoever or whatever it is, seeks help, because the bloodshed in this town has got to stop." Terry had an inkling something was waiting, lurking, for a chance to get out. It wasn't he and it wasn't what was inside him. The phone rang, shaking him back to reality, leaving him no more time to dwell on thoughts and feelings. He mumbled, "Must be time to get back to business." Terry answered the phone with longing, loneliness and a little hope in his heart, "Douce Water Company, this is Terry Andersen speaking, how may I help you?"

JOHNSON & THE RAGNOROCKS

Goldy rang the Ragnorock's doorbell. As the sound from the chime subsided, she sensed danger. Something was wrong. She smelled a familiar scent. Goldy didn't expect that her introduction to the Ragnorocks would be like this. She dropped everything at the front door and ran to the side of the house. Goldy was up and over the fence in no time, following the smells and sounds as they became stronger. She held on to her human self long enough to gain the privacy of the Ragnorocks yard. Once out of sight of the neighbors, she allowed herself to transform. She was good at it. Many had slow torturous transformations, but Goldy completed her metamorphosis in less than 60 seconds. In this case, it was good for what was needed but bad for her attire. She always worked hard to look professional, "What the hell," Goldy resolved, "This is an emergency."

Goldy's transformation was still very painful and the itching lingered as her paws hit the cool grass of the well-manicured backyard. The animal rage was welling up, though the vestiges of her humanity kept repeating to the beast within her, "Save the human, stop the animal." She was mere yards from the rear door of the house and the overwhelming smell of human had permeated her nostrils, nearly distracting her from the mental mantra. The human was fresh and ripe for the taking. She smelled the fear and heard the heartbeat of a human female and Goldy's beast wanted to claim it as her own. First, she needed to stop the male from taking her prize; that was the last thought Goldy had as her werewolf completely overtook her. Goldy had become a large, wiry werewolf with a singular purpose, "Save the human, stop the animal."

Goldy's werewolf bounded through the rear door of the Ragnorocks home, instantly rending it into splinters. This freshly transformed animal was on a mission. She turned sharply, skidding on the kitchen floor, knocking over the table and smashing into the lower cabinet doors. Righting herself, she leapt, demolishing the basement door. She was in a completely feral state as she barreled down the stairs. The woman's screams from the other side of the last door sent her crashing through it. Goldy, in a complete rage, collided with one of the biggest, reddest werewolves she had ever come across. Her momentum and the surprise of her entrance was enough to knock him off the woman, but the battle had just begun. By all appearances the red beast was going to kill two females in that basement. Goldy's wolf struck quickly and knocked the red wolf against the cage. The silver burned his back and he stood up straight from the pain. His head hit the ceiling of the basement and he grunted, howled and growled. From the corner of her eye, Goldy saw Diana get up and run away. Goldy's mission was partially complete.

The male was preparing to strike back and Goldy braced herself, her hind claws digging into the floor. At the very moment when Quake's werewolf would have pounced, two shots boomed, followed by two audible thuds. Diana may have forgotten the cage lock made of silver, but she had remembered the tranquilizer rifle. Diana stood tall as she cocked the rifle and quickly reloaded, ready to fire again, her heart beating faster than it ever had before. Quake looked down at the two syringes that had caused him such pain, followed by lethargy. He growled.

Moments before, when Diana realized Quake had escaped the custom cage, she couldn't speak or yell. Diana had fallen to the ground and crawled through its legs in attempt to escape. For something so large and hairy, it had pivoted effortlessly and all she could do was scurry on her butt; until her head smacked into a wall. She lost her bearings and she couldn't remember where the door was. All she knew, was she was going to die, as the beast lunged and snapped his teeth at her; saliva dripping on her clothes and exposed skin. The heat from the drool felt like burns to Diana's flesh and its hot breath was foul. It seemed to take pleasure in her fear, almost savoring it. It even appeared to lick it lips!

Diana had looked over at the wall where the rifle and tranquilizers were and saw no possible chance of getting to them. "Shit! I'm dead," Diana realized. Then suddenly, she'd heard loud noises upstairs, like a car had just smashed into the kitchen. She tracked the sounds with her eyes as it powered through the door leading to the basement stairs. Quake's beast, who was towering over her, had leaned back as if to prepare for an initial bite. Diana couldn't contain her fear any longer. It welled up in her, much like the passion that she and Quake shared earlier that morning, as she reached a new level of emotion and terror, she opened her mouth and released a blood curdling scream.

Suddenly, Quake's beast had tumbled away from her in a flurry of violence. That he was no longer standing over her jolted Diana out of her frozen state of terror. The She-Were hadn't finished bringing down Quake. Diana had come back to her senses during Goldy's entrance and self-preservation was tantamount. This new werewolf bought her the opportunity to get to the tranquilizer gun. The Valium shots Diana had administered earlier began to do their work; there just hadn't been enough. The tranquilizers added to the Valium in Quake's blood stream, gave Diana hope that maybe they all had a chance to survive this ordeal.

Diana had stood firm, rifle in hand, ready to silence both creatures if need be. She wouldn't take any chances. Tears streamed down her face, blurring her vision, but she didn't waiver and took aim. Quake's wolf had leaned back, stumbled and eventually sat down. Diana wasted no time as she aimed the gun at the female werewolf. Judging by the demolished doors Diana knew this new Were was just as capable of killing her as Quake. She'd wiped her tears on her shoulder even as she kept the rifle steady. Her vision clearing, she had the new animal in her sites. The beast's silhouette seemed to shimmer. Diana's vision hadn't yet cleared completely, but she followed its movements. She applied slow, steady tension to the trigger. Just as she heard Quake fall to the floor, a woman's voice said, "Don't shoot!"

Diana found herself face to face with the most striking, mocha-skinned woman she had ever seen. Goldy stood before Diana; shaking and nude; looking as if she couldn't harm a fly. All Diana could think to ask is, "How were you able to do that? Protect me as werewolf and not try to kill me?" Glancing around the room, Diana noted Quake in his cage, snoring away in his naked human form

Goldy, while exhausted, had still maintained her sense of self-preservation, which negated any fatigue. She walked over to Diana, who was still pointing the gun at her, and politely asked her to point the gun elsewhere. Diana, still beset with shock, was simply too tired and frightened. Goldy gently pushed the rifle away and enfolded Diana in a hug. Speaking calmly and clearly, she said, "My name is Goldeen Johnson. You must be Mrs. Ragnorock?" After a long pause, she stepped back from the reassuring hug, and asked, "Mrs. Ragnorock, would you have any spare clothes I could borrow?" Goldy looked down at Quake, snoring away and said, "I wouldn't want anyone else to see me like this." The women shared an awkward laugh and in that moment of relief, they bonded. Diana had visibly relaxed. She motioned towards Quake; "I might be able to spare some clothing, if you'll help me heave that man of mine out to the car so I can get him over to the Institute." The tension from the danger was broken over and the pair shared a moment of humor. Goldy responded with a wink, "Sure, let me just make a call to a friend who can help us, while you fetch those clothes." They hugged again, chuckling.

Diana handed over her cell phone and ran up the stairs. Goldy dialed the one man in La Mort Douce she trusted. She just hoped he would come, because after something like this, she longed to see him. Actually, she needed him. She wanted their friendship, to progress into a romantic relationship; she just wasn't sure how to approach the situation. "If this isn't the perfect excuse to break the ice, what is?" she mused. Goldy took a deep breath as the phone began to ring on the other end, "Life is way too short Goldy, take a chance," she told herself. The phone clicked and a deep male voice answered, "Douce Water Company, this is Terry Andersen speaking, how may I help you?"

SAKARUI

Tears silently trailed down her cheeks as a police radio droned on with the steady cadence of road noise. Jodi, a Hitogoroshi (murderer), sat handcuffed in the back seat of a patrol car headed for the Institute. She couldn't figure out why she was crying. Worse, she couldn't seem to stop. Jodi thought she had broken that habit a long time ago. Maybe she felt embarrassment, shame or regret for being caught and publicly humiliated. Jodi wanted and needed to go to the Institute for help.

Wanting help had nothing to do with regret. Her family got theirs for hiding the truth about her father. Her father did exist. He did try to keep contact. Countless filthy old bastards that had tried to lure her into their sex schemes got what they deserved. Yuck! Perverts deserved to die for taking advantage of children. Seriously, what kind of person would want to mess around with a child's body when plenty of adult women looked young like Jodi? There were countless childlike pixies with more womanly parts. Jodi was not ready to have sex yet.

Erotic thoughts had never entered her youthful mind, until the stranger. There was something different about him. As she rode in the back of the police cruiser, she found herself thinking of him, imagining things she had never wanted to. He was on her mind so much that she could have sworn she'd seen him several times on the way to the Institute. In reality, it was just her loins talking. Ugh, Jodi attempted to reign in her thoughts. What was real, were those feelings of desire mixed with a sense of foreboding and danger yet she couldn't quite shake the unwanted desire. How could one person or creature do that to a girl? Jodi had dedicated her short life to shutting those emotions down, using rage and contempt as motivation. It annoyed Jodi that she was having sexual fantasies about someone who'd tried to kill her.

Jodi shivered and turned her thoughts back to the events leading up to her current predicament. How did they find, let alone decipher, her diary? What clued them in, the detectives, federal agents and the like? Jodi had foolishly thought that if there were no bodies or weapons, they couldn't convict anyone. She was wrong. Jodi considered that, maybe; she should have watched more reality crime shows and not so many of the predator catching ones. Jodi knew it was too late to worry about it now.

Jodi and her escorts had arrived at the Institute; she couldn't recall the route they'd taken to get there. This was northwest of the park, where she'd met the stranger. The very park she'd used to exact her brand of justice. She had never been this far, but wherever she was; it was freaking cold for this time of year.

Police Officers gently pulled Jodi, still in handcuffs, from the cruiser. "How low key bondage is this?" Jodi thought with a chuckle. She closed her eyes, not from the light, but habit. The last few years, camera flashes of curious news people constantly accosted her. They had shouted questions at her, the serial killer child and self-proclaimed werewolf; after all, she was big news for the media circus. Bitten at 13, her childlike look remained, though Jodi wasn't entirely sure if it was because of the disease or genetics. That disease sucked ass and Jodi wanted to get rid of it for good to look, feel and live a normal life. Realizing there was no media, Jodi opened her eyes.

The building was HUGE! She couldn't believe she had never noticed it from town. The structure was metal, concrete and a whole lot of glass. "Shit, I bet they got killer air conditioning in there." Jodi thought looking up in awe. Werewolves' body temperatures ran significantly higher than humans did.

Once Jodi got inside, she found the Institute a completely different place than the jails and psychiatric wards she had resided in. It was clean, decorated in neutral colors with thick glass everywhere.

An Asian woman greeted them. "Nice touch…" Jodi thought sarcastically. "This broad looks like that Asian newscaster, what's her name? Lisa Ling." The woman instructed them that the handcuffs be removed, though the cops were obviously not entirely sure. The woman eventually quelled their fears, with a little help from the two dark skinned brutes in white standing behind her. "Fuck," Jodi thought, "I don't want trouble. I just want a shower." She was itching all over and it was driving her mad and body grooming had reached the point of necessity. "Being a Lycanthrope blows!" thought Jodi. Lost in thought, Jodi didn't hear half the crap that perky bitch was saying, until they arrived at her room and the woman said, "All your needs will be completely taken care of. The restrictions you've been subjected to the past few years will not be nearly as stringent." The Newscaster look-alike went on to say that, Jodi's 'special needs' would also be taken care of. "What the hell does that mean?" Jodi wondered, as she stepped into her room and the door closed, ever so gently behind her. Her sharp ears picked up the whirr and the click of the automatic locks. The greetings and the polite people suggested she was a guest, the door confirmed what Jodi already knew; she was not a guest, she was a prisoner.

Jodi explored her new room, it was the largest room she ever had in her short little life, though it needed some color. Jodi didn't know how long she would be here, but she knew she would have to leave her mark somehow. She longed for a sharpie and made a mental note to ask for one, as well as what kind of magazines she could read. She sat on the bed, "Boy, this bed is comfortable", Jodi exclaimed in amazement. She spied a television mounted in the corner, but what she really wanted was a radio or an iPod. "Reality Check, Ms. Sakarui, you're incarcerated. This is not a freakin' resort." Before she could continue the conversation with herself, she noticed a document on the large white desk. She walked over and read an itinerary filled with a never-ending schedule of doctor and psychiatrist visits.

Jodi checked the dresser drawers and found clothing in her size, but definitely not her style. Still, they were better than the bright orange prison jumpsuit she was currently wearing. She smirked; obviously, she would have to give these new clothes a touch of her personality as well. First things first, she needed a shower. Under the water flow, Jodi lost herself in the sounds, the feel of the soap; luxuries she had gone without the last few years. A person never realizes how much freedom they have, until that freedom has been lost. Jodi was enjoying this freedom, even with conditions. She exited the bathroom wearing a towel and dried her hair. Suddenly she got a chill, followed by a feeling that someone was watching her. Looking around, she realized the room had tiny cameras everywhere. She doubled back and found them in the bathroom as well. "What the hell!" she screamed. Rage began to well inside, she was beginning to get that old feeling, like with the perverts and she knew she needed to control the rage.

She got a flash of that old newspaper ad she'd had in her pocket at the park not so long ago and recalled that this was the place she was going to use to help her before she was arrested. The Globes Disease ads, these guys weren't perverts; they were here to help. Finally, Jodi had hope for a cure and maybe she could be free again. Jodi's heart raced with optimism. She sat on the bed; her feelings abruptly overshadowed by something else. Jodi felt overrun with a deep dark sense of dread, a jarring apprehension, and fear that she might not make it out of this place alive.

KANIN

Aristotle Kanin woke up in the cold wet grass of morning, weak, thirsty and his skin itched. As he vigorously scratched, he realized he was nude. He could hear water and his need to quench his thirst was overwhelming. He strained his eyes to look around, but the sun felt like hot pokers burning into his skull. He rolled over onto his stomach, the damp earth beneath him was cold against his bare chest. This moment was ungraceful, but his need to hydrate superseded his sens de modèle, sense of style. He stayed low because he wasn't sure where he was or whether anyone could see him. He crawled through the brush and grass, his pride scraping on the rocks and dirt along with his chest and loins. When he reached the water, he stuck his hands in and cupped the clear liquid. The water was nirvana, the true meaning of spring fresh. His eyes rolled up into his head and he lapped at it consuming as much as possible. He drank until his belly was numb.

Arty took in a deep breath and rolled on his back. He was so completely gratified he didn't mind the discomfort of nature at his back like a lumpy, wet, mushy pillow. Normally the thought of dirt or bugs anywhere on his person would send him into a conniption fit, but at this point in time, he couldn't care less. All that mattered was that he had slaked his thirst. The heat of the sun was balancing out the oddly cool spring La Mort Douce was experiencing. Maybe there was something to this Globes Disease. Arty wondered if there truly was a cure, would he even want it? He smiled to himself; he did like the extra testosterone surge, just one of the many side effects of Globes Disease. He enjoyed being a glutton every full moon and the extra attention he got from his changed demeanor. He was so butch! Despite betraying his lover, he enjoyed getting laid and the extra energy his disease gave him to handle all the strange that came his way was a bonus. The boost to Arty's ego was splendid and honestly, he loved the killing as much as he loved the sex with strangers.

The killing was invigorating for Arty. He didn't always remember what happened but the movie-like flashbacks, were addictive. Arty lay there listening to the water amble past him, the rustle of animals, birds overhead, felt the ants on his skin and savored the memory of what he'd done to those gay-bashing assholes when they'd attacked him. In his head, he could hear their screams, begging for mercy. He chuckled. He liked how someone wielding a bat and chain, intent on beating another person to death, had the nerve to ask for mercy. "Why would they want to hurt us? Arty thought, "Because of who I choose to love? Shouldn't love between consenting adults be applauded? Would the news be willing to report about what happened in that alley if I had been a religious martyr?" The press was eager to give details about the three or four shredded bodies of the very men who tried to ruin his life. He simply wanted the right to love whomever he chose.

"Arty, you are so full of crap. Choose to love, with all the cheating you do? You change into a massive wolf, have sex and commit murder; both for the thrill and because you can't help yourself. Admit it, you're a sick fuck, but you don't want to be cured," Arty chastised himself, with a laugh. He loved the hunt and conquering men bigger and stronger. The type of men who had bullied him his whole life. "When you change", he told himself, "You're killing your father, all the people who turned their back on you and kids from your youth that ostracized you for not being like them. You're killing all who stare, assassinating those who take people's personal lives and put them up for political and religious debate. You are ridding the world of bullies and you do it because you find pleasure in it, regardless of consequence."

Arty thought of his lover Jeremy. "Why can't you be more like him?" He's articulate, proud and caring. He doesn't live a lie, is proud of who he is, loves life and people. Jeremy is willing to help others and he never hides. Arty hid everything; his gay lifestyle and lust for blood and killing. Arty began to miss Jeremy and his sister Annie; he knew they would be worried and he needed to get to them. Finally, he sat up and looked around. Man, was he far from home. He recognized the area, he had been here before, years ago, as a kid. At some point, the authorities started chasing teenagers away from the area. He remembered some stories on the news a few years back, featuring countless debates about the government and some agency taking possession of an island. They wanted to build a facility on the island. The city council wanted to know what the agency needed the land for. Obviously they lost that battle and governmental secrecy won out over the public's right to know.

Arty realized he needed clothes to get back home. He just wasn't sure if he could muster up the nerve to walk over to someone, while completely nude, and say, "Excuse me, I changed into a giant dog earlier and now that I have changed back to human, I could use some clothes. Do you have any I can borrow? I'm good for it." Arty chuckled nervously and decided he had no choice but to swallow his pride, endure the embarrassment, and head over to the large concrete and glass complex to ask for help and clothing.

Just as Arty started to lift himself off the ground, a police car approached. He lowered himself to the ground again. He was scared. "Are they looking for me? Could they have tracked me here?" He was wondering if more police were on the way and whether they would bring K-9s, when he noticed they were helping a young girl from the back of the squad car. "What the hell is that all about? What could she have done?" He wondered aloud. She appeared to wipe tears away as she emerged. He sat up a little when he saw she was in ankle chains and handcuffs. "Damn, she is trussed up like a hardened criminal."

As the girl was being escorted into the glass-laden building, she stopped cold, turned her head in Arty's direction and squinted. Immediately he recognized her from the news, "Jodi something. She's just a misguided Were-child." Arty could swear she was staring right at him. He flattened himself down as low as possible. The girl paused, for what seemed like minutes, staring at him or was it past him? Arty couldn't tell. In that moment he had confirmed both what this place was and what she was. The pair of police officers, each holding an arm, continued escorting Jodi in, but the child didn't stop looking his way until she was through the door. "That was spooky," thought Arty. As he watched, a woman flanked by two terrifying guards approached Jodi.

Once the girl was inside, Arty felt free to survey the area a little more. He raised his head and looked around, hoping to get a clearer view. He really needed to get home to his lover Jeremy and his sister Annie. Arty shook off his discomfort and convinced himself the girl had been looking past him. He turned around and adjusted his vision so he could decipher things at a distance. Being a Lycanthrope had many advantages; keen sight, acute hearing, and an incredible sense of smell; even when in human form. Arty spotted a cabin off in the distance, barely noticeable through the trees and brush. He was relieved. Walking several miles, barefoot and nude was not ideal, but going over to the Institute would raise way too many questions. None of which he wanted to answer. Seeing the cabin helped him gain some resolve, as he remained hidden and worked his way in that direction.

Before Arty could make good progress he was forced to duck down again as two more vehicles approached the complex. Two women exited the first car, a middle-aged white woman and a younger black woman, neither of whom he recognized. A tall, black man in his 40s, wearing a business suit exited the second car. He had a menacing look about him. They seemed to be in a rush, jumping out of their cars, to open the back doors of the man's sedan. Arty's view was partially blocked, but it looked like something huge was in the back seat. This flurry of activity could not be a good sign and Arty decided he was not going to hang around to find out what else was coming; he had his own problems to deal with. He also had a nagging feeling in the pit of his stomach that something more dangerous was lurking in La Mort Douce and he had no desire to encounter anything or anyone, especially if they were more dangerous than himself. He set off for the cabin in hopes of finding some clothes, a phone, and possibly some help. Arty wanted to be as far away from danger as possible and was hopeful that the cabin would be a safe haven.

THE INSTITUTE

The moon was in its waxing gibbous and had been visible through the afternoon sky. The Institute's windows seemed filled with it. Looking up, it was there, a daunting figure, like a warning beacon, ominously giving premonition of dangers to come. All day security had been active, breaking up scuffles, handling patients and using all available personnel for tests and treatments. The guests of the Institute had been restless most of the day. The closer the moon got to being full, the more palpable the tension within the Institute. The howling, yelling and talking worsened. It was building up like the wail of a siren. A person new to the Institute would swear they'd entered an insane asylum. The main lobby was off limits during full moons to most patients. Of the patients who normally had control, only about half were able to control their changes during this time; the patients who had little or no control at all, were difficult to corral together and eventually had to be sequestered in their rooms, cages or specially equipped labs until the full moon phase was complete. Those who maintained control, when brought out, had to wear silver chains on their wrists and ankles.

The 10 x 15 foot long oval security desk was in the center of the main lobby, just in front of the entrance, plenty of room for three to five guards. Only three guards occupied the main guard desk, due to the uptick in activity. Randy DèShaun was one of them. His hands were full with two admissions. A young girl who was being escorted to her room by the police and Sue, an administrator; The second was a very large, red haired man he'd only seen a few times before, accompanied by an older white woman and a black couple. Randy couldn't recall that behemoth admitted as a patient while he was on duty, though. The man appeared heavily sedated and the group seemed to have difficulty keeping him upright. Randy knew things were tense and slowly headed towards chaotic, but he really had no place to put the big lug. All he could do was offer them a seat on one of the many lobby couches until Sue returned. He laughed to himself. He had called Sue, Lisa for years until she finally corrected him. He liked Sue; she was strong, intelligent and efficient. She made working here easy, even on the worst of days.

Randy began to feel uneasy when he noticed Sue had not returned. As time pressed on Randy's humor left him. Even with "Big Red" out of it, he couldn't seem to focus with all the noise and howling. He was uneasy and hoped Sue would return soon. Randy knew the crew he had with him was not going to be able to handle, "Big Red" over there, whether human or werewolf. That thought was the cause of his discomfort. The older woman who appeared to be "Big Red's" wife, tried to give Randy a comforting smile, as if to say, "Don't worry," but Randy wasn't buying it. A sudden chill interrupted his thoughts and a sense of fear overcame him as the last of the sun slowly gave way to a night sky that carried a nearly full moon that had increased tensions in the building substantially. Randy looked at the console to ease his mind, 10 screens all periodically toggled images of all areas of the building from security cameras. "Funny," Randy thought, as he cleaned his glasses, he could have sworn he saw the screens flicker. "Why didn't the other guards notice this?" "Maybe" he rationalized, "Maybe it's just me. Maybe you're just hypersensitive, Randy."

VLAD

Vlad awoke, still full from his pre-nap meal, and walked up the basement stairs. The moment he opened the door, he knew something was different. He could smell one of the dogs he loved to hunt had been in the cabin, probably seeking refuge from a night of mindless mayhem and killing. He could tell the dog had long since gone, but now he had its scent in his nostrils. "What a coincidence," he thought. "They continue to provide me opportunities to kill them, stupid dogs." The apparent infestation of these creatures made it difficult to leave La Mort Douce. "What was going on in this God forsaken town? Was there a plague?" Vlad wondered aloud. He hoped the female mutt he'd been searching for was at the Institute. That would make hunting her much simpler. If not, Vlad resolved he would hunt her later after killing whatever was in that building tonight. The scent of the other werewolf that had been in the cabin was still in his nostrils, tracking the moronic thing would be easy. The cabin reeked of its stench, left over human flesh and blood obviously caught in its fur or on its skin. "Sloppy bottom feeders, they are uncivilized at killing and eating. Ugh. Very well it is settled, as soon as I am done here, this new one dies as well." Vlad decided. "Eventually," he thought with a sigh, "I will have to leave this place, this town, no matter how good the hunting is." Why leave? Because Vlad grew weary of this place, the changes, the difference in the air and the loss of what it once was. Change is inevitable, but it's not an easy thing to deal with, particularly for vampires. Living for centuries was no picnic.

Vlad gathered his coat, and set off for the Institute. Vast as it was, the structure lacked the grandeur of buildings in Russia. Americans loved building squared off structures with no character. His contempt for this culture continued to grow, making it easy for him to embark on these bold and dangerous hunts. Vlad did not care. He had watched the building long enough to know that the inhabitants would want to keep secret anything that occurred there. That secrecy fed his selfish motivations to kill the girl. If Vlad also destroyed a few of her furry comrades in the process, he would count that as a bonus. Vlad arrived swiftly and stood outside the structure. There was an overabundance of cameras. Normally he wouldn't concern himself with human technology, but in this case, he felt it necessary to use Obfuscation. The viewer wouldn't detect him or the telltale blurring that would show up on technology, such as cameras, DVRs, and phones. Vlad wanted the element of surprise. He usually didn't have to focus on things like Glamouring, Obfuscation, subliminal suggestion, mind control or light magic, but there were so many mutts in the building and he needed to locate all of them. Vlad planned to be thorough, so he stood just outside the view of humans and cameras to concentrate. Vlad closed his eyes, for a few well-spent minutes and then he was ready to make his move. They wouldn't be able to call for help, alert anyone or record him. Vlad was pleased with himself. The time to retrieve the child named Jodi had come.

SAKARUI

Jodi was bored and began to get antsy. Normally this time of the month she would be hunting; stuck in her new room she was beginning to feel stir crazy. The place was abuzz with activity and chaos. Jodi didn't care about all that, she just wanted to get started with the cure. She needed to be normal. She had noticed after her infection that she didn't seem to age as fast, but she could heal quickly. Jodi didn't appreciate the fact that she still looked like a child though. The defect of the disease worked in her favor when it came to killing, but she didn't like feeding into the stereotype that she looked so young because she was Asian American. Inside she felt like an adult, many years older than her age, especially with all that had occurred. What she had endured would have aged anyone's soul. She sighed and thought about another problem. Jodi sat down, rolled her eyes and said aloud, "Shit, I hope they have razors in this room."

After opening every drawer and cabinet in her room, Jodi found all the things she needed. When she'd finished her grooming, Jodi remained restless. The howling and wailing of the other guests did nothing to calm that restlessness. Jodi wanted to make a phone call. She needed to talk to someone. Normally she considered herself a loner and with her family gone; albeit by her own hands, she still craved family support. All Jodi had now, was her father. She called him whenever she moved to a new place or facility. He'd answered only twice, but he did tell her he loved her and that was enough to give her hope and make her believe that they were developing a father-daughter relationship. She needed the solace and reassurance he provided and anything else that would placate her hatred and thirst for revenge against the world.

Jodi had to focus and shake off her dread to keep from becoming a monster again. That took control and practice. Jodi held those who couldn't control themselves in contempt. "How was it possible that the imbeciles here had not yet learned to control their gift? Shit, I had control within a year of being bitten." "Gift, huh?" That was the first time Jodi acknowledged the disease was a gift. Was her subconscious telling her she really did not want a cure? Jodi knew she was going adrift and in an attempt to ignore her own thoughts and self-analysis, she walked over to the intercom, pressed the button and simply stated, "I want my phone call." Minutes later, she heard the ever so subtle whirr and click of the electronic rotary locks. The door opened to reveal the happy lady and a huge guy in a hospital uniform.

The pair escorted Jodi to a phone bank down the long hallway leading to the lobby. Just as she was about to make her call, two Weres attempted to transform. The silver restraints kept that from happening, but enraged them enough that the two began fighting with one another. Staff swarmed them immediately to contain and sedate them. For some reason, call it impulse, fear, or whatever, Jodi put the phone down and slowly headed for the lobby. Maybe it was the change of heart she felt in her room or simply the opportunity to regain her freedom. Regardless, it was just too tempting not to try to slip away. In hindsight, it was likely her sense that something bad was coming that prompted the urge for self-preservation to take over. Jodi wasn't certain she just acted. Her instincts had told her to leave, and the only way out of the Institute Jodi knew of was through the lobby and that's where she headed.

DARIO

Salvatore Dario stood in line with chains on his wrist and ankles, but to him, the restraints didn't matter. He had a handcuff-key on him at all times. He just never felt the inclination to use it. "Funny huh?" he thought. "I hate being here, but I haven't tried to escape yet either." He wasn't happy about being a patient at the Institute but he had ulterior motives. First, Sal wanted a cure. Second, Sal wanted revenge. Maybe satisfaction was a better word. Sal wanted to see the blonde woman who had bitten him, once they captured her. She had changed his whole life and then escaped. Sal was seriously unhappy that he was stuck in this hellhole with all these jerks, while she was free. He wasn't like them and felt he didn't deserve to be in this predicament. He was an upstanding person who wanted to help others and got Globes Disease for his troubles. The guy behind him bumped into him and mumbled an apology between pained growls. He gathered the poor sap was attempting to keep himself from changing. Sal and his group were transferring to the testing area, but something felt off to him as they approached the lobby area.

Having worked here, Sal had the advantage of having walked this place a thousand times. Being a patient gave Sal a completely new perspective on the Institute. To think he'd once considered it a mundane place of employment! The windows teased him with glimpses of the outside world. The new moon was coming and he thanked God he had learned to control the change, though he still had trouble during the blue moon. A full moon that occurred twice in a month would challenge any werewolf. Sal told himself, "Hey, you can't have it all, but at least a cure is in the works."

Tonight, everything felt different, the mood, the activity just weren't right. Two men in line attempted to change, and a shoving match ensued, once again bringing Sal from his meandering thoughts. "Here comes the needle squad." Sal chuckled, remembering the old days; he'd loved beating up the freaks. Beyond the chaos, Sal saw the little girl who had been on TV. "Shit, she was telling the truth!" He whispered gleefully to himself, "Now the Institute has her!" As Sal looked past the skirmish in Jodi's direction, he saw her look around and set the phone down. She quickly made for the lobby. Sal was no squealer, but he felt compelled to follow her. Finally, he had a good reason to use that key.

THE LOBBY

Time seemed to stand still when Vlad entered the lobby. The noises from the patients throughout the Institute echoed and the tension in the building immediately thickened. The three guards at the security booth were tinkering with their monitors. Terry, Goldy and Diana all looked up simultaneously, immediately sensing that something was not right about the ominous figure that had just walked into the building. Vlad was dangerous and dark, his hair and clothes, adding to his portentous aura. Before Vlad could speak to the guards, Jodi and Vlad locked eyes. Jodi mouthed the words, "Oh, Shit!" Behind her, Sal saw her body stiffen. The whole room focused on Vlad as he bared his face, they all simultaneously fixated on his scar and fangs.

The human's reaction time was quite impressive. Randy De Shaun, lead security officer, signaled his two men. They were up and over the counter faster than Vlad expected, not that it made any difference. The men were ill prepared to battle a vampire, who grabbed one in each hand. The first was in his right hand. Vlad's fingers tore through muscle, bone and flesh. Blood sprayed out in tempo with the man's heartbeat. He pulled him in close and finished the job, tearing the front half of his throat, larynx and both carotids out with his fangs. The second didn't fare any better. Vlad had him by the throat, and brought him in close as he tossed the other body to the tile floor where it made a sickening splat-like thud. It took less than 30 seconds for warm red liquid to pool around it. Vlad choked the second guard with his grip; the man flopped around like a fish on a hook. Vlad bit into his head like an apple, tearing half of his skull and skin away.

Bullets riddled Vlad's body and he dropped his second victim before he was finished with him. The bullets burned and were slightly painful, more annoying, than uncomfortable. Vlad turned to face the gunfire as Randy De Shaun finished off a whole clip. Vlad set his sights on Randy, grabbing him and tossing him over his shoulder before Randy could even think, much less reload. He didn't bother to see where the body had landed. Jodi fell to the floor, crawled backwards and then cowered in the corner against the wall, scared out of her mind. Vlad quickly and purposefully approached her. The Russian juggernaut dispatched all those that tried to intercede. By the time he was within 10 feet of her, he'd killed five more guards and two Weres; snapping their necks, tearing out their throats, crushing them and tossing them aside as if they were merely toys. Sal witnessed it all and was amazed at how quickly the carnage had piled up. Inexplicably, Sal could only think that he would normally hear the squeak of shoes on the hospital floor as people traversed the halls. This night, the sounds were splashes from the blood-covered floor. Interesting the things one thinks about in times of stress and chaos.

Sal was close enough to catch the scent of this monster of a man, this undead human. He noticed Vlad carried the odor of the blonde. He'd recognized hers amid all Vlad's victims just prior to the blood bath in the lobby. Sal ran over to Jodi and yelled, "He's after you, stupid! Run!" Sal set himself to the task of transforming, not checking to see if the girl heeded his command. The change was painful, but he was in the right clothing; patient smocks and slippers. All he had to deal with was the burning and tearing feelings of his werewolf's flesh and hair emerging. He postured and howled, having changed into what he hated most. Jodi shared a common bond with him; they were werewolves and he would protect a young girl he didn't even know.

Diana, Terry and Goldy stood stunned by what had transpired before them. It all happened in a flash; the guards, the gunfire, and the vampire tearing through people to get to the girl they all recognized from the news. They witnessed an Italian looking guy change into a Were and plant himself in front of Jodi to protect her. Simultaneously they exchanged a look and collectively decided to act without ever exchanging words. Diana ran over to see if Randy was alive. Goldy and Terry kicked off their shoes. Terry took off his coat. Unfortunately, Quake wouldn't be helpful anytime soon. Goldy and Terry ran towards the action, while stripping away their clothing. Randy wasn't bleeding anywhere Diana could see and he looked bad, but he was still conscious. She hollered, "Where is the first aid kit?" Randy pointed to the guard station and muttered, "Top drawer." Diana yelled again over the noise and chaos, "Does it have an Epi-pen?"

Sal, in full werewolf mode, was tall and muscular, with short hair and long ears. He was about to charge when Vlad appeared in front of him before he got a chance. Sal slashed twice, Vlad ducked, which caused him to miss on his initial attack. Vlad reached in to grab Sal but Sal sliced his arm. The cut was deep and blood flowed; but the wound began to disappear almost instantly. The pain of healing angered Vlad and he dug the fingers of his other hand deep into the beast's shoulder and began tearing at the limb. Bone and muscle began cracking, popping and tearing. Sal's agonized howling and growling resonated through the lobby. "Revenge! An arm for an arm," muttered Vlad. Sal went berserk from the pain, hitting, tearing, biting, and pulling at his adversary. Sal dug his hind legs into Vlad's torso, his claws tearing and scratching at Vlad's chest. Some onlookers froze in horror as they witnessed the strange and bloody tug of war between Vlad and Sal.

Terry and Goldy remained focused as they ran across the blood-slicked floor, changing as they traversed. Goldy completed her transformation first and she took the lead. She was sinewy and lethal. Terry, seconds behind her, was long and black, with massive shoulders. Their enemy was a common one and all the Weres focused singularly on stopping the most dangerous thing in the building. It was as if they shared a singular thought to destroy the vampire. The two didn't make it in time to help Sal. His screams, the sickening noises and a horrific pop echoed into the room. Blood gushed out of Sal's shoulder socket and he went limp from pain and exhaustion. Sal was beaten. Vlad's torso was shredded and bleeding, but healing was a lot slower than his arm. He hadn't expected such a valiant fight from a mutt and he was seriously pissed that his clothing was ruined. Vlad's chest was on fire; his own blood had spilled and he was not pleased. He knew he wouldn't survive many more injuries like this. Werewolves and vampires could eventually do one another in. Just their differing bodily fluids and chemistry mixing at too high a percentage might mean the end for Vlad if he wasn't careful.

Terry slammed into Vlad, before he could focus on healing himself and catching Jodi. The impact caused Sal to fly out of his grasp and across the room. Sal had passed out from the pain and massive blood loss. He transformed back to his human self where he lay on the bloody tile floor. He was a grim addition to the carnage. Vlad hit the floor as Terry landed on top of him. All his muscle gave Terry a huge advantage. Goldy was faster, but Terry could jump farther. Vlad was on his back, holding Terry at bay. Terry was tearing, biting at Vlad and tried to dig his hind legs in but Vlad was not going to allow new injuries without a fight. He used his own legs and dug his feet into the beast's abdomen. Vlad was growing weary of this violent dance, so with both hands, he began to squeeze the werewolf's neck.

Terry's fur was thick, particularly around his neck; almost like a lions mane. He was no easy adversary to choke. Vlad succeeded just in time though, because Goldy was nearly on him. Vlad pushed Terry aside quickly and scowled at Goldy, sizing her up as she postured and howled. As far as Vlad was concerned, she wasn't much of a threat. He knew he could not sustain any further injuries. Goldy was quick and the fight would be tough if he tried to trade blows with her. Vlad swiftly gained his feet and charged her just as Goldy was about to reach him. Vlad caught Goldy off guard, as she'd underestimated his speed. He grabbed her by the neck with one hand and bludgeoned her on the top of the head with the other. She fell to the floor and the skirmish was over. Werewolves had no experience in battle, but their raw potential was dangerous nonetheless and Vlad didn't want any accidental wins for the dogs. His thoughts were short-lived, interrupted by all the people running around, screaming, and weeping. The noise was deafening. Vlad concentrated until he was able to ignore all of it. Straightening himself, he adjusted his tattered clothing, took off his blood-soaked coat and surveyed his surroundings. It was time to get Jodi and finish what he had come to the Institute to do. Kill the child.

THE SHOWDOWN

Jodi Sakarui hadn't felt this kind of fear since the horrendous night she was infected; the very same night she met Vlad. That terror was gripping her again, but when she heard Sal tell her to run Jodi overcame her fear enough to do it. As her senses came around again, she heard the carnage behind her. Jodi felt Vlad's presence and feared she would die that night. As she passed the men still confined by silver, she realized that maybe her curse would help her get away. After a terror fueled mad dash by her, she reached the end of the corridor and turned the corner, searching for a place to hide. If there was any chance of surviving this nightmare, getting outside was her best hope. If not, at least get in an area of the building that when the sun came up she might have a fighting chance. She knew she was too small and too young to fight him, but if she could change and maybe she could hold him off until a miracle happened. As she ran, she prayed for the very first time in her life. She stopped when she came to a building map on the wall. Locating the "You are here" indicator, she picked a destination. Concentrating hard, she repeated to herself, "observation center, observation center, observation center..."

She held on to that thought as her heart rate sped up and a fiery burn spread over her skin. Her head burned as if filled with hot coals and her face felt as if it was splitting. She didn't intend to scream, but she was terrified. With all the other distractions, the pain was more excruciating than usual. Her screams echoed in her ears and undoubtedly down the hallways. Screams soon turned into gut-wrenching howls and Jodi's transformation was complete. Her werewolf bound down the hall heading towards the observation center.

Terry Andersen awoke next to Goldy Johnson. Even lying there, changing back to human, she was gorgeous. Terry realized two things right then. First, he was falling for Goldy. Second, he needed to improve his fighting skills, big time. He'd gotten his ass kicked by a werewolf, while holding a shotgun and then while in werewolf form he got his ass kicked by a got-damned vampire. "What the hell is next, Frankenstein?" Terry had just sat up when Goldy opened her eyes. She sat up and they stared at one another. They were human again; bruised but not severely injured; battered but not bleeding, their clothes in shambles, surrounded by chaos. They both spoke at the same time, "Are you all right?" "Yes, are you?" which caused them both to smile, briefly. Terry stood and helped Goldy to her feet. They continued to look into one another's eyes. A loud, ear-piercing howl broke their connection. It was the sound of a very young werewolf. They both looked where Jodi had been and realized she was gone. They had just turned back to one another when a delirious Sal said, "We gotta save the little girl!" Running over to him, Goldy called over the in-house rescue crew for help. One rescuer grabbed Sal under his intact arm and the other rescuer put an arm around Sal's waist on his severed side. Once they were certain Sal was going to be safe, Terry and Goldy looked at one another again and at the same time they said, "Let's save the girl!"

Salvatore Dario labored to breathe. He felt hot blood pour out of his shoulder, where his arm had been, soaking his clothes and watching it pool on the floor. His consciousness was slipping in and out, and yet he felt himself healing ever so slowly. Sal hoped he wasn't going to die this way. He hoped that he would get a chance to die as a human, preferably cured. The scene in the lobby made his spirit falter. All that he'd concerned himself with before suddenly seemed less important. It occurred to him that, maybe, he had this infection for a reason and if he survived this ordeal, he should start helping others. Sal was beginning to feel faint and was getting ready to make a pact with God when he felt someone grab him. Gloved hands checked his pulse, he heard a voice through the chaos say, "This one is alive and we might be able to save him." Sal muttered softly, "Thank God!"

Vladimir Romanov could hear the girl as he stalked the hallways. He noticed a group of 10 or so of the vermin he hated so deeply, all bound in silver and unable to change. Vlad was beginning to like this place. He initially thought they were here to create more werewolves, but quickly realized that wasn't the case. They had made it easy for him though. "Hmm, lure them here, bind them in silver, how considerate of them," he thought. Vlad dispatched every one of them; he bit them, slashed their throats, some of the smaller ones he dismembered for his amusement. He held them up as they squirmed and kicked, popped off their limbs and dropped them on the hall floor where they bled to death. How they died or whether they died in pain or not was no concern of his. Vlad simply did not care. It was mild entertainment for him. The distraction of this mini massacre allowed his body the time required to heal before he finished off the child. They'd screamed, fought and begged for mercy; and Vlad had enjoyed every second. He didn't often get to kill these furry wastes of skin when they were weak humans. Vlad crushed the last one's throat, listening to it snap under his foot. He chuckled, straightened his clothing and proceeded to sniff Jodi out. Curious, she didn't smell human anymore, "She must have changed." He thought to himself. Vlad found this interesting, because she was too small, weak and inexperienced to handle him. Jodi's transformation allowed Vlad to hunt her with more ease. "Ugh", he interrupted his own thoughts with disgust, "These mangy things reek."

Diana Ragnorock was exhausted. She chastised herself aloud, "A woman my age shouldn't be running around like this. Though, most women my age would have passed out or had a heart attack under these circumstances." She couldn't figure out how she'd gotten to the observation center before anyone else, because this was the last open room to check in. She was so hopped up she hadn't realized she still had that darn Epi-pen in her hand. She threw the empty applicator down, as she was going to need both hands to pull the trigger on the tranquilizer gun she had tucked in her waistband. It was still there. She took a long, slow, deep breath to collect herself. Diana wasn't sure what state Jodi would be in, so when she heard a noise by the computers, adjacent to the observation area, she whispered, "Hey, little girl, are you here?" Jodi's werewolf peeked out, her long ears perked up at attention and her sinewy body was tense. She was surprisingly small, at least compared to what Diana was used to seeing when it came to werewolves. Her heartbeat rocketed up and she thought, "Oh Shit." Before she could decide what to do, Jodi began to change back to human and immediately began crying, which took Diana by surprise. The half-naked child ran over. Her body, wracked with sobs and fear, was shaking violently. Instinctively, Diana knew there was no threat from her and enveloped Jodi in an embrace and Jodi held her tight. Diana comforted her. "Don't worry child, help is on the way." Before Diana could say more, Jodi tensed up. Diana held her at arm's length, looked her in the eyes and asked, "What's wrong, child?" Jodi's eyes told Diana everything she needed to know even as her own instincts suddenly screamed DANGER!

A deep voice with a thick Russian accent echoed through the room. "I must apologize for intruding on your moment human, but the child and I, well, we've had unfinished business for some time now." Diana spun around, out of fear or reflex, she didn't know, but she had the gun out and was pumping dart after dart into Vlad even as he grabbed and lifted her with one hand. He did it with such ease that she briefly felt weightless. Meanwhile, Jodi was already changing into a werewolf again. Transformation didn't help her though, as Vlad grabbed Jodi by a hind leg with his other hand. He held her out at arm's length, not wanting to risk further injuries so close to daybreak. He had spent all night cleansing the world of countless Lycanthropes, not to mention numerous humans. He was sated from so much human blood, but not satisfied with his hunt. He pulled Diana in close and considered ripping out her throat, "Make it quick," he thought. As for the child, the sport of chasing was over and now he could swing her by the ankles and slam her into walls until she was unconscious. Then he'd finally get to tear the limbs from Jodi's frail, weak, limp body. That was the plan… until pain, such as he had never experienced during his entire existence, interceded. It assailed his powerful vampire senses and permeated his undead nervous system in ways he didn't think possible. The pain originated at the back of his neck, traveling down his spine, paralyzing his intentions and forcing him to drop both of his conquests.

Quake's werewolf bit down hard on the back of Vlad's neck, singularly intent on killing the vampire. Quake had not tangled with a vampire in many years and he had not feasted on any human or undead flesh in over 15, so he was not going to deny himself this meal with no cages, no drugs, no restraints; just mayhem. The taste of Vlad's blood ignited Quake's fury. Vlad began to groan and yell as Quake tore away at him. He thrashed around in an attempt to extricate himself from the jaws of one of the largest werewolves he had ever encountered. Quake could feel the Vampire's wound beginning to heal, so he continued to tear and rip away at it. Vlad's struggling propelled them into a wall, slamming Quake with the momentum. The impact shook the room. Vlad tried desperately to get out of Quake's grasp, without success. The flesh Quake had been working feverishly on exposed Vlad's spine and Quake dug his claws into Vlad's back. He reared his snout back, intent on ripping Vlad's spine out of his body, Vlad managed to reach over his head and flip Quake over his shoulders. Stumbling from the momentum, Vlad tried to right himself. He could feel blood flowing over his back, neck and shoulders. Quake landed like a large cat on the blood-slicked floor and charged Vlad. Vlad had no time to battle this behemoth; he was losing too much of his newly acquired and much needed blood. He looked for an exit, but Terry and Goldy's werewolves blocked the double doors, snarling and posturing. He turned to the only other door and saw Jodi's Were alongside the one-armed-Were, Sal, warning him off. Vlad had to decide quickly, but unfortunately, that tiny hesitation was just long enough to end his chance of escape. Quake overwhelmed Vlad, knocking him to the floor. They tore at one another ripping, biting, and snapping. Every time Vlad dislodged Quake and attempt to stand up, Quake pounced again.

Vlad's last attempt to shake off Quake was successful. He quickly cleared his mind to distract himself from the weakness and massive pain. Blood was pouring out of him like water. Reviewing his options, he saw Terry and Goldy, still poised at the entrance and Jodi and Sal still guarding the other exit. The sun was coming up and Vlad was ready to cut his losses. He determined that a child and a one armed werewolf would be the easier challenge. Vlad took off in that direction, desperate to escape the Big Red Beast that had been giving him grief. While he was a worthy adversary it was, alas, a battle for another time, odin na odin, one on one. Vlad's next victims had the look of fear in their eyes. As Vlad closed in on them, their expressions changed and he knew he had to hurry. Vlad had a dark foreboding feeling. His sense of self-preservation superseded any other thought. At this point, he knew it was suicide to continue this battle; he was more than willing to save this fight for another night. He needed time to think and strategize. Vlad's last-ditch effort to stay alive was futile, his slow healing neck and exposed spine made him too vulnerable and, reminiscent of a lion, Quake pounced on him again.

Feeling his life force dwindling finally overshadowed Vlad's pain as Quake ripped his spine out of his body. It hung from Quakes mouth like a limp snake. Vlad's thoughts obscured in the last milliseconds of his life, by the growls, grunts and deafening howls of Quake's victory. As Quake severed his head from his 200-year-old body, Vlad's mind had one last mental gasp, "*Я трахающий оборотней ненависти,* I fucking hate werewolves."

THE CABIN

Fear gripped Harold Garcia as he ran away from the decimation at the Institute. He clutched the thick manila envelope containing hard copies and blue-ray files to his chest, his knuckles white from his tight grip and frozen by the unseasonably icy air. His breath puffed like smoke as he stumbled through the trees. Eventually he spotted a cabin and sighed with relief. He knew he was lost. The cabin would give him time to locate a map on his phone. He would have to send a text soon. "Oh shit!" He thought when he heard something behind him, pounding through the snow. Harold knew he would have to cover more ground and then send his text. He really needed to hide the envelope, just in case he didn't make it. He muttered aloud, "Lord, help me. Someone has to know! God, I hate human-beings."

TERRY'S JOURNAL

September 29th 2009

Lycanthropes are passion-filled fireballs, full of life, emotions, animalistic desires and urges. We feel hunger, anger, passion and pain amped to the nth degree. Our feral nature is deep and dark; like a sexual urge that can never be completely satisfied. The fear, terror and shame we experience after transforming is laden with agonizing guilt. There is one small moment of peace before succumbing to the beast within and that is our only solace. It is true torment and hell that werewolves experience.

It is akin to sexual addiction, which is a natural part of the human psyche; only this urge is 100 times that. The supernatural ability to change into a wanton beast is forever in our souls. Rare is the werewolf that has any control over the raw, pure and undaunted emotions as the moon grows to full.

Terry Andersen

HAROLD GARCIA

Harold was astonished that he actually made it to the cabin. He entered quickly, slammed the door and leaned against it, as if his weight had any chance of deterring whatever was after him. His breathing was heavy, his bones ached from the cold, but his body was afire with fear. He fumbled with the envelope in his hands, trying to keep all the files, papers, discs and USBs contained while he tried desperately to get his phone out of his pocket. He finally extracted it and was relieved to see he had enough signal bars. Immediately, he started to text. His hands trembled and he misspelled many words. Each time he had to delete something, he muttered a curse. Spell check is more an irritant than an aid. Harold just needed to make his message coherent. All the while, he could hear the tempo of a large, four footed creature pounding the ground and approaching quickly.

The sickly sweet smell of death permeated the cabin, which only added to Harold's fear. Before he could consider what might have happened in that cabin, Harold's pursuer landed on the porch, shaking the entire cabin. Harold looked around for a place to hide and headed for the door to the basement. Suddenly the front door exploded, knocking him to the floor. Papers, files and phone flew everywhere as he hit the floor. His head throbbed and blood poured down his face. A beast was snapping and snarling at him through the door that landed on top of him, which was, currently, the only thing keeping Harold alive. The weight of the door and the beast was crushing him and Harold couldn't catch his breath. He prayed as the beast attacked the door. Harold began to feel lightheaded under the weight.

Harold was in this predicament because he strongly believed he had no choice but to expose the Institute and the widespread conspiracy that surrounded it. Anyone not on board with the Institute's plans inevitably disappeared and was sure some of the patients knew that. He'd discovered that the Institute had allowed the blonde to bite Sal and eventually escape. Somehow, they had manipulated the system so that Jodi was transferred there, in hopes that Vlad would follow her. They'd succeeded, but in a far more terrible way than intended. Dr. von Shelley wanted Vlad's DNA, though Harold did not know why or how the Institute would benefit from having it. The werewolf antidote was completed and all that remained were trials and research, which required recently bitten victims. The antidote, thus far, only worked in the first 24 to 48 hours. Who was going to volunteer for that? "Why, why, why?" is all Harold could think. When he'd accidentally discovered "Operation Pack Mentality", he knew he had to get proof and then tell someone. Harold's quest to acquire proof is likely the cause of his exposure.

Harold had read about a group referred to as The Hunters. His role had been to recruit those infected with Globes Disease, but he'd believed it was to cure them. Apparently, that was not the case. The Institute's goal was actually to control the beasts. "Lord, help me," Harold whispered. It seemed logical that if werewolves were real then vampires were too. It was art, imitating life, so to speak. Dr. von Shelley seemed very determined to reach some specific goal Harold had not discovered yet. He just knew that the implications could be Global. Would the public come to believe century's worth of folklore, some invented to desensitize them and hide reality? Obviously, the Institute intended to use these beings for personal and/or military gain. The Institute was playing a dangerous game. People had died and that would continue, unless someone stopped them. Harold thought, "I have to get this information about Dr. von Shelley and the Institute to the press."

Bam! The door slammed Harold's body again, breaking through his reverie and crushing his ribs and sternum from the pressure. The pressure on his pelvis and spine was agonizing and he struggled to breathe. The werewolf penetrated the door, the only thing separating him from this furry angel of death. Harold closed his eyes and prayed harder, mentally crossing himself and reciting the Hail Mary. It was a struggle, but eventually he managed to send the frantic text message. Harold felt the hot breath of the creature on his face and neck as he prepared himself for death.

There was a pause, seconds felt like hours, and then Harold heard something that sounded like feedback from an old transistor radio. He opened his eyes to find he was face to face with a menacing werewolf, slobbering and blowing huffs of rancid breath that assailed his senses. It was the worst case of dog breath he had ever experienced. The beast was staring into his eyes as Harold lay there, quaking with fear. Warm liquid permeated Harold's pants as he lost control of his bladder. The wolf's eyes shifted slightly, smelling the urine. The high-pitched feedback sounded again and the wolf's eyes fluttered and rolled up into its head. Harold wasn't sure what he was observing, but for a split second, the eyes seemed almost human, just as quickly they registered anguish. The beast stood up on his hind legs, his head mere inches from the ceiling, towering over Harold in the cabin's doorway. A pain-filled howl suddenly rent the air.

The beast reached behind its ears, and scratched away at them with his claws. It seemed as if something was causing him to behave this way. Flesh, fur, blood and computer parts or mechanical pieces rained down on Harold, landing all over the room. The beast began to change back and forth between human and beast. Harold shuddered and dry heaved.

Harold realized quickly that this had to be one of the Institute's experiments gone awry. Apparently the creature had chips and cameras implanted in him while human. Once the command module was in place, they could feed him instructions, before allowing him to transform into a werewolf, which fit with the Institute's plan to control the Lycanthropes. This beast was obviously rejecting the commands. Backing off the door, and Harold, it howled some more. He was certain he had a few cracked ribs, but Harold was relieved to find he could breathe better, but was too afraid to move.

The animal howled, screamed and stumbled. Harold heard more feedback and was certain the Institute was trying to force the animal to kill him. Harold thought, "This is no dog. He has purpose and freewill and isn't about to let a voice in his head deter him." Apparently, the experiment wasn't working which meant Harold still had a chance! As the beast stumbled around in torment, Harold slid out from under the shattered door. The pain and inability to take deep breaths was distracting, but he knew he had to push past it if there was any chance he could escape. Harold used his arms to slide himself across the cabin floor, quickly and painfully distancing himself from the beast; who seemed not to notice. The werewolf continued to howl, bark and grunt as Harold covered the distance to the kitchen. He even dared to feel himself fortunate, an odd feeling given he was not usually lucky. The beast continued howling and barking in anguish. Suddenly, it stopped, jerking violently, arms dropping to it sides. Harold could hear flesh ripping and bones cracking. If he had any urine left, he would have pissed himself all over again. Through the beast's chest emerged a well-manicured, white hand, with blood red fingernails to match the bloody; dripping heart it held in its grip. The heartbeat continued for a few seconds, spraying blood everywhere, as the beast transformed back to human. A clean hand appeared and pushed the dead human to the floor. Harold raised his eyes to face the most beautiful alabaster woman he had ever seen. She was tall and large breasted, with broad shoulders to support them. Long, flowing, dark hair hung down to her straight hips drawing his eyes to her statuesque legs. The beautiful woman had such an intense look about her that chills ran up Harold's spine. "Holy Shit!" was the only thing Harold could muster up to say. When she spoke, her accent was thick and Russian. "Ugh, Sobaka! (Dog)"

The beautiful specter tossed aside the heart and gracefully walked over to Harold. She towered over him, staring into his fear filled eyes. Harold felt the room go cold, as the sauna of terror became the threat of death. She leaned down, maintaining their eye contact, used two fingers on her clean hand to wipe the blood from his forehead. She licked her fingers and stood upright, savoring the flavor of his blood as though it were liqueur. Harold's fear-meter amplified to a completely new level. "Hello human, my name is Oksana Tameira Gavrilovich." She said, then stopped herself and thought for a moment. "Why am I introducing myself to you," she scoffed in her strong Russian accent, "You're not an opponent; you are a meal." Harold's last scream echoed throughout the cabin.

THE INSTITUTE

After Vlad

Dr. von Shelley stopped what she was doing when she heard a technician exclaim, "What the heck is that?" She turned and walked over to him, looking over his shoulder at what he was staring at on the screen. Acknowledging her presence, he continued to talk. Dr. von Shelley was an intimidating woman. She had expressive brown eyes that could pierce a person's countenance, especially when she wore her wire-rimmed glasses. She had thin lips and a tight jaw, and always wore her blonde hair pulled back. She was very tall, which was either impressive or intimidating, depending on who was describing her. She constantly wore a white lab coat, so very few knew what shape she was beneath it. One could see she had strong, broad shoulders, a hint of smallish breasts and athletic calves above low-heeled, sensible black shoes. Dr. von Shelley's forearms and calves were about all the skin anyone who worked with her had ever seen.

The tech pointed to the screen. "We had him, but he started resisting, just like the others." Dr. von Shelley interrupted the technician, "The test subjects are still rejecting the implant. They are too unstable. Maybe we should lobotomize them before we chip them." She theorized aloud, her was English solid, though her German accent was evident. Another voice, deep and gruff with an English-Canadian air, spoke from behind them. "Should we send in a team to retrieve all the files Garcia stole?" Dr. von Shelley turned to face Chuck, leader of one of the elite "Hunter" teams on loan from both the Canadian and US Governments. Chuck was a rugged, scarred and very athletic man with a commanding air about him. He had shaggy, sandy blond hair that hung just slightly across his forehead. Dr. von Shelley thought to herself, "I bet if he didn't cut his hair, it would hang over those intense killer's eyes."

Dr. von Shelley thought a moment, then said, "Let's wait until daylight, it's safer." Taken aback, Chuck said "Safer? We can handle these puppies, day or night. Besides, I thought they could change any time they wanted to?" Dr. von Shelley nodded her head. "Yes, they get stronger the more full the moon is." She explained to Chuck, "With practice, many of them can transform at will, regardless of what phase the moon is in. The moon reflects light on the earth, which is a globe. Legends say the effects of Lycanthropy occur during the full moon, also a globe. The disease itself occurs all over the world, making it a global affliction. The moon is out there whether we can see it in the sky or not. The moon's influence as it gets closer to being full, causes changes in ocean tides, human and animal moods and even lunacy, hence the name Globes Disease. We need to act quickly. Be methodical and cautious. So we will wait." Abruptly, Dr. von Shelley exited the room without looking back.

"Ma'am," Chuck called after Dr. von Shelley, catching up with her in the corridor. "What's going on? Why are we being so cautious?" Dr. von Shelley asked, "Did you see the videos? Did you read the eyewitness accounts? Logic dictates that the same rule of thumb you have for normal animals should also apply to our situation. Where there is one werewolf there are more. Where there is one vampire, there are more. You get the picture; we have to be careful, okay?

How many people did you lose in Massey? Do you remember?" Chuck hung his head. He didn't like it when those who had never been in the trenches brought up things like that. Massey was a sore point for him. He had almost died there. Back then; the Hunters had never experienced that before. No amount of training could have prepared them for what occurred in Massey. Dr. von Shelley continued walking, not bothering to look over her shoulder. She expected

Chuck would follow and listen, and he did, reluctantly. "You know why it happened? Because you fucking jarhead, hard-ass, full metal-jacket jerks do not listen and that is what gets people killed. Well, here in La Mort Douce, you are going to have to listen, because if you don't we will ALL be screwed. You see, it isn't about just you and your team; it's all of us; the whole program. The Chiefs are on my ass and I don't want to lose any more people or time. If those jerks send an audit team here, we are done. They won't just shut us down, they will eliminate the whole lot of us; personnel, the building, all the data and if they are so inclined, this whole werewolf infested town. So, there will be NO going off the reservation from here on out!"

Dr. von Shelley stopped outside her office door, turned and looked into Chuck's eyes. "We have to give them the impression that we have all but gotten rid of most of the werewolf vermin AND that we have control over the remaining few. I can't let them wipe out this whole town, because I may need the remaining beasts for future trials." "We," von Shelley corrected herself. "I need YOU to save this program with your killer instinct, but I need your brains as well. Sacrifice anyone you have to, but not the team or the Institute." Chuck acknowledged her instructions, "Yes ma'am." "Don't you see what I am trying to do here?" Dr. von Shelley continued, "I am trying to create something that's one of a kind, something that is exclusively ours, in Northern America. So please Chuck, not until morning." Dr. von Shelley smiled the best, friendliest smile she could muster, but for Chuck the effort was off-putting.

Dr. von Shelley opened the door to her office. She turned around quickly after a thought popped in her mind. "Chuck, we are not getting enough volunteers. I realize we can't use them the way we use the ones we capture. Obviously if volunteers go missing, their families will begin asking questions we won't want to answers. Things would get precarious in that case. Have your team round up a group of strays for more intense experimentation. We may have to activate, Operation Pack Mentality, so prep your team. Remember, just because La

Mort Douce is infested with werewolves, doesn't mean they are the only things out there. I need you all to be careful. So my orders are, retrieve the Harold contraband in the morning, please." She tried again to smile with the same result. "I will brief you on Operation Pack Mentality as soon as your team is ready, okay?" Chuck relented with a nod and Dr. von Shelley disappeared into her office, closing the door behind her. Chuck stood there with unanswered questions, but he was willing to follow her orders… for now.

DR. VON SHELLEY

Dr. von Shelley threw her keys on her desk and sat down, sighing deeply. She didn't want to think of her history, she simply wanted the past to stay in the past. She just wanted to relax but instead she looked at her computer. Curiosity got the best of her, which irritated her. She grabbed the mouse, clicked a few times and replayed the video the techs had given her from the Vlad attack. "How in the heck did that creature make himself invisible to the cameras?" Eyewitnesses had seen him, but video didn't pick up his image until Quake Ragnorock injured and eventually killed him. She stared at the screen and played it repeatedly, until her phone rang. "Sheesh, can I catch a break?" she said, exasperated. With a sigh, she picked up the phone and said, "Hello."

The Chiefs from both North American agencies had been calling her regularly, General Austin most often. She hated having to explain things repeatedly. Why couldn't he get it? She rolled her eyes and went over it again. In between his excessive chatter, Dr. von Shelley responded the best she could. "Yes General, we have made a breakthrough. No General, not all the test subjects survived. There is one, maybe even two, that are viable, but they are volunteers. General, the problem is we cannot justify the disappearance of volunteers without risking public scrutiny. The best solution is to wait and let the Hunters retrieve them. The Hunters? Well, they are annoying but effective. The DNA issue is resolved, but we may have a new DNA discovery, which could prove advantageous to the military. It is something physiologically similar to cloaking, but in this case, it's not mechanical. More like obfuscation, which is akin to magic or a

Jedi mind trick." Of course, von Shelley had to explain that to General Austin as well. "Jeez, what did this guy do growing up? Did he not ever watch Dracula, or read Anne Rice?" she wondered. "Cure? Yes General, we have a basic cure, but it is limited in its application. General, I thought you had abandoned the cure angle in favor of controlling the subjects?" Dr. von Shelley gritted her teeth; she was feeling irritated, "No, we do not have full control, yet. Cloning would not be good, but genetic blending may help to heal soldiers, cure diseases or even make a better, more aggressive and cunning fighter.

"Controlling them now, that is the main issue, General. The plan is to activate Operation Pack Mentality. We will gather all the strays we can and eradicate any that resist. We have a plethora here in La Mort Douce and certainly could stand to reduce their number. We will make the most of the ones we capture; you just need to trust me. All we need is executive approval, from BOTH agencies." General Austin responded, "You will get your approval, but remember, Dr. von Shelley we will be watching." Dr. von Shelley hung up the phone. She leaned back in her chair and thanked the stars he hadn't wanted to talk to her through videoconference. His constant scowl on his tough African American face was disconcerting. In her opinion, General Austin was far more intimidating than she was and Dr. von Shelley didn't like being intimidated. It occurred to her that she could dish it out, but she couldn't take it. "Oh well back to trying to relax." She sat there in silence for a few minutes, before clicking the mouse and studying the video once again.

THE HUNTERS

Chuck wasn't happy. He didn't like being schmoozed, placated or cajoled. He really didn't like having that woman calling the shots with his team. He felt she was unqualified to understand what men and women in the trenches had to suffer. Still, he relented; she had the authority, as if she were the General himself. Chuck had to respect that, as a man of honor. Chuck didn't like it one iota though. He arrived at the luxury dorms provided by the Institute for him and his team. When he entered, the team was watching a computer screen and laughing together. It was a hard sight to see, given how many they had lost in the Massey Massacre.

Chuck didn't care for the accommodations. He believed such luxury would make his team soft, dulling their edge and their sense of danger. "Shit!" Chuck thought to himself, "If we had been here when that vampire showed up, we could have taken him down." The Hunters had been in La Mort Douce, preoccupied with hunting Weres for a while; long enough to miss his family and be homesick. The military's schedule determines a soldier's schedule, not the soldier. Chuck took a mental head count of his team. He was filled with self-doubt over his own leadership abilities and wasn't sure if they were even ready yet. Chuck didn't want another Massey Massacre.

Seeing Chuck enter the room, Mack approached him. McKenzie Ochoa was tall, lean and an excellent close-in fighter; a real grappler, but more importantly she was their weapons girl. Her dark hair always hung flat to her head, probably her Aztec heritage. She was happy and bright, but always down for a scrap. "Hey Sarge, check this out." Low-Key and Adonis were laughing uncontrollably, a rare occurrence for those two. The two men were huge body building types, though Adonis had packed on a few pounds in the midsection over the years. Adonis liked to say he was Greek and Hawaiian to explain why his skin was lighter than his 10 brothers who were 100% Hawaiian. He nearly always wore a happy face, which hid how dangerous he truly was. It was a frightening thing to experience, because when he was mad, you didn't know until he was practically breaking you in half.

Low-Key was a light-skinned African American who had a California streetwise air about him. He sounded very much like Snoop Dogg. Low-Key was a serious person; to see him laughing was as off-putting as seeing Adonis frown. The two were best of friends, both not as dark as their ethnic backgrounds but both giants, they had found a common bond and were the best of friends, often making jokes to deter commentary about being lighter than their family members. At times, they would claim they were brothers, in jest. They were the muscle. They were dangerous. They were survivors.

Casanova was off to one side smirking. He was a Texan of Japanese heritage. He had the southern accent and Texas ego to boot. Unbelievably handsome, he had a way with women. He always had perfectly combed and gelled hair and the team ribbed him about it often. They liked to joke that his disdain for wearing a helmet would be his ultimate demise. Casanova was their communications expert.

Ray-Anne, known as Ray-Rae, was a dark-skinned New Yorker of multiple ethnic backgrounds. She was from West Harlem and she didn't let anyone forget that fact. She was tough. The only time Ray-Rae showed her softer side was around the oblivious Casanova. He either didn't notice or chose to ignore her. Ray-Rae was their entry specialist. She had a knack for stealth and ballistics.

Lying on the bed near the end of the room was a Hindu called Prabal. He didn't care to be referred to as an Indian. He was quiet, efficient, and a crack sharpshooter. Weapon type didn't matter, so long as it was from the proper distance, he was guaranteed not to miss. His job was to protect the flank on all their missions. Ray-Rae would get them in. Adonis and Low-Key were the front line, with Chuck in the commanding position from the middle. Ray-Rae and Mack would bring up the rear and Casanova would protect them all from afar.

Chuck cracked a smile. He cared for every member of his team. Originally, there were 27 Hunters; this group of 8 is all that remained. That was a sore point for Chuck. He shook off that train of thought; he constantly practiced detachment. It didn't always work, but it was necessary. Chuck walked over to the desk to look at the video, obviously shot with a night-vision camera, though Chuck wasn't sure whose helmet-cam it was. Chuck watched intently as the wearer of the cam, weaved through a dark building. Chuck startled slightly when a werewolf jumped out of the darkness, growling, snarling and slobbering. Before he could even blink, its head exploded in a spray of blood, bone and metal.

Almost immediately, the team fell over in riotous laughter, again. "Damn, Mack, how much silver buck shot did you put in that shot gun?" Ray-Rae queried. Mack was trying to answer through her laughter, "Obviously too much! I guess I'll have to work on that." The crew's uncontrollable laughter swelled up once again. Prabal, grumbled, "How many times are you guys gonna watch that damn thing?" They stopped and looked at one another. Adonis said, in as straight a face as he could muster, "Until it ain't funny no more." The room filled up with cackles, again.

Chuck tried to remain serious. He had to rein them in, yet as commander, he didn't want to be a complete killjoy. All work and no play, right? "Okay team, listen up. We have training exercises today. We are finally gonna get to do what we were brought here for. Prep for Operation Pack Mentality begins at 0930 hours; we'll break at 1130 hours for showers and lunch. Now listen." He cautioned, "Take this seriously; we are just waiting for approval from the Chiefs; which is expected any time. That means we will get to do some exterminating here in La Mort Douce after all." The team got up, in unison, to prepare their gear. "Oh, one more thing, soldiers..." They all paused as Chuck said, "Play that shit one more time, that's fuckin' hilarious." The room acknowledged Chuck's command with a chorus of, "Yes Sir."

ARTY

Arty's life did not improve after sharing his secret. In fact, he and Jeremy were constantly fighting. Arty had accidently injured him during a lover's quarrel. Naturally, he regretted it. At the time, the moon was nearly full and Arty simply lost control. Jeremy's arm and leg had been broken and his face scarred forever. Despite that, Jeremy had stayed with him, remaining loyal and supportive. Annie was an entirely different matter. She had left, giving him an ultimatum, "Get cured, because I will not support a killer, no matter who you are to me." That was truly heartbreaking. Though they'd been born a few years apart, he felt connected to her as if they were twins. He thought of all they had been through and the plans they had made, but nothing mattered when the moon called to him. His blood boiled and the high he experienced was like nothing any drug ever gave him. His passion and lust were constantly in overdrive, but the full moon exacerbated those urges and it was addictive. The killing was fun, what he could remember of it, but the edge of danger before changing into his wolf was what he most loved. The rush he felt, as if standing on a cliff about to jump, thrilled Arty to no end.

Arty had a magnetic personality and with his charisma, he easily drew men to him. The thrill of luring prey drove him to hunt. Flesh wasn't primarily for consumption, as it was for most werewolves, for Arty it was about pleasure. The old cliché about the thrill of the hunt fit to a tee. Under the influence of the moon, sex was incredible, amazing and mind blowing. Nothing else came close to it. Arty cruised the bars, bathhouses and parks during his feral times. There weren't many, but the gay men in La Mort Douce always found a way to hook up with one another. They all knew the secrets spots and private locations where men who preferred to be in the closet could stay there. The men who preferred to hide thrilled Arty. Those who had a dark secret were the corruptible ones and hunting them made his heart race. "Yeah, your women are clueless, your employers don't know, your families have no idea, but I do.", Arty said to himself, gleefully, during each conquest. Finding the macho men that were rough, tough and gruff on the outside was most exhilarating, because they totally submitted to him. Arty couldn't articulate why that thrilled him so much, but it did. At 5 foot 10 inches with dirty blond hair and a muscular build, and a Greek face that men and women seemed to love, he made full use of his looks to take advantage of people. "If they only knew what was hiding inside me," Arty chuckled to himself.

It was late evening and Arty had already been to the local gay bar and wasn't happy with the selection there. He walked through Le Parc Moyens. It was kite weather. Most of the residents of La Mort Douce bundled up against the frigid air. Even though spring was coming, the chill was enough to keep people from going out, which explained why the choice of men was so sparse. There was little justification for being out at night in this cold. Arty didn't feel the coldness of the air in his feral state. In his lunar influenced mindset, his body temperature was well into the 100s. A side effect of Lycanthropy in the harsh cold of La Mort Douce, it was just another thing he liked about having Globes Disease. Arty's rationalization was, "Why give this up? So what if one of the side effects is being a murderer. I can live with that, if the sex stays this incredible, then c'est la vie."

Arty headed south, past the sheriff's station. Funny, Sheriff Bray and all his cronies keep trying to stop the homosexual problem, as if being gay was a disease. The irony of it was the very thing they were so keen to stop was but a stone's throw from the sheriff's station in an old bar/bathhouse. The old style corner shopping area had limited parking shared by a convenience store, a barbershop, a massage parlor and lastly a men's gym and sauna, by day. At night, it housed the bathhouse, accessed through the rear entrance. Arty considered the double entendre and chuckled aloud.

Arty arrived and didn't see many vehicles on the side streets. Normally there were plenty, but he attributed this to the cold. He sighed heavily. He was really hoping to get some strange tonight. He seriously needed release. Arty didn't mind making-love with Jeremy while in the feral state, but after a while Jeremy couldn't keep up and started complaining. He was a scoundrel but he truly loved and cared for Jeremy's well being. Arty took a deep breath, trying to clear his mind, and said to himself, "What the heck, you never know." Approaching the darkened door, he turned and looked at the moon. "Tomorrow it will be full," he thought. "Tonight would be perfect for getting laid." Tomorrow would take all Arty's energy to maintain control over transforming into his werewolf and he wasn't very good at it yet. He had been able to do it a few times, but it was easier when he was sexually satisfied or exhausted. Tequila, morphine and Valium worked wonders, though Arty hated the after effects when he awoke days later.

Reining his erratic thoughts, again, he realized his mind was all over the place; it was merely another manageable side effect. It was difficult to hold back his excitement. His breathing was heavy and his erection was throbbing. All that and he hadn't even met anyone yet. Arty stood by the door wrestling with his thoughts when he smelled cologne heavy with pheromones. The scent was exciting and made it even more difficult to focus. There was an unfamiliar scent in the air as well. "What is that smell?" he wondered, "Paint? It had a hint of metal and oil. Did they buy a new door?" The pheromones overtook his sense of danger. Arty knocked and showed his health club card with the pink smiley face sticker on it. The men's club went to great lengths to avoid detection, using all manner of

"I Spy" measures. Arty smiled, he liked all the secrecy, especially the anonymity. It made what he did easier and more thrilling.

Once inside, the music and darkness overwhelmed any second thoughts he might have had. As the lack of cars parked nearby had indicated, attendance was sparse. Arty went to the bar, bought a drink and eyed an Indian fellow. He was lean, olive skinned and their eye contact was immediate. Arty's breathing became shallow. The guy was hot and looked to be new to the place. Arty walked over to a vending machine that dispensed keys rather than junk food. He put in money, pushed a number and two keys dropped into the tray below. He grabbed one and sent a meaningful look to the olive skinned hottie. Walking back to the bar, he picked up his drink and began to sip it slowly. The man stood up, walked over to the machine, retrieved the second key and disappeared down the hall. The thrill of the hunt overtook Arty's sense of apprehension. Something about the man's walk was different but he couldn't put his finger on it. He didn't smell like a Were. Arty noted that the scents he had detected earlier were all over the man. His massive erection took over and his thought processes were derailed. He knew he was going to score and there was no man, gay or straight, that could handle him if they got out of line. Arty downed his drink, tipped the bartender and took off after his new prey.

Arty turned the key and opened the door. The dimly lit room smelled of that pheromone-laden cologne and intensified Arty's ardor. The man was sitting in the far corner of the room. Arty could barely see his face and body. Arty was about to flick on the light when the man's smooth voice stopped him, "No, don't turn it on. I like the mystery." The voice sent Arty's heart racing even faster. Arty took off his coat and proceeded to unbutton his shirt. The voice said, "Hey, slow down a little. What is your name?" Arty hesitated, "No names." he said with a hint of apprehension. The man asked, "Well, what name should I scream when we are getting busy?" Arty lost his sense and said, "Arturo." The man said, "Hmmm, nice Greek name.

How ironic, huh?" Arty didn't get it. He was confused, his passion getting in the way of his body's warnings. The hairs were standing up on the back of his neck. Taking a deep breath, he returned his focus to the man and asked, "What's yours?" The man stood, walked over to Arty, looked him in the eye and said, "My name is Prabal."

Arty began to sweat. The room felt as though someone turned the heater on high. The cologne was making Arty crazy and he grabbed Prabal by his arms and tried to kiss him. Prabal, stronger than he appeared, put his hand on Arty's chest and pushed him back. "Slow down, big guy," Prabal said coyly, with a hint of sarcasm. Arty did not appreciate the game. After all, everyone knew everyone was here for SEX!

Arty started losing his patience. He focused in the darkness of the room, looked at Prabal and said. "You know, I ain't got time for this. There are men out there, who are more than willing to get down to the nitty-gritty and not play games." Prabal smiled and said calmly, "You're right, there are. Tell me Arty, did you look at them? Did anyone look familiar to you? Did you notice that a few of the patrons were women?" Arty thought about what Prabal just said to him and in an instant, his memory flashed back. The door person was a woman! So was the bartender! The two large men in the corner, he had never seen before either! The towel boy was a blond, scarred and rugged man that he didn't recognize and the disc jockey was a handsome Japanese fellow. He had never seen any of them there before. They had infiltrated his secret place, quietly watching him. In fact, they were the only people in the bathhouse! "What the fuck is this?" Arty asked. Prabal looked at him and asked calmly, "Arty, have you ever heard of the Institute?"

Arty swung around and flipped the light switch. He wanted this fool, Prabal, to see the horror of his impending metamorphosis. Arty's anger flared, as did his temperature. His heartrate elevated quickly and his breath came in ragged pants. The pain in his bones signaled the onset of the change, which only egged on his rage. The werewolf hair felt like needle pricks growing from his skin, delivering fiery pain from inside out. Through the agony, Arty stared at Prabal and said through an animalistic growl, "You're in trouble now!" Prabal wasn't fazed one iota by Arty's warning and calmly stared back. That perplexed Arty. No one had ever had reacted like that before. The change had already reached the point of no return and Arty couldn't stop it now. Frankly, Arty wasn't capable of stopping it, not that he wanted to. As far as he was concerned, Prabal was going to die in that room at the claws of Arty's werewolf.

Prabal's calm infuriated Arty and he couldn't understand why the man wasn't afraid. Prabal pulled out a gun and pointed the barrel at Arty's chest. The threat of Prabal's pistol didn't affect Arty, and he neither saw nor felt any danger from it. Many of Arty's victims had tried to fight back. They had stabbed him, shot him and hit him with whatever they could get their hands on, but when it came time to die by Werewolf, nothing they did mattered. Arty was certain that nothing Prabal did tonight would result in a different outcome.

Prabal pulled the trigger and with the loud pop came agony beyond any he had ever experienced in his life. In moments his heart burned, fire coursed through his veins. Arty felt his heart slowing, and his vision blurred. He fell backwards against the wall and slid to the floor. He wouldn't be a werewolf tonight; he was going to die sitting there on the floor opposite Prabal. The blood was spurting out of Arty with each pulse. The thump of his heartbeat and the sound of blood spraying reverberated in his ears with an odd echo. His head and body frozen in place, Arty's skin became cold as he sat in the puddle of his blood and struggled to breath. He tried, but couldn't speak.

Arty looked at Prabal, disbelief clear in his expression. Prabal spoke just as calmly as he had before he shot Arty, "Hurts huh? You're probably wondering why you couldn't detect me. There are wolf pheromones mixed with our colognes." Arty, overcome with delirium, managed to register that Prabal had said "our". His breathing became even shallower. Though Arty hadn't said it aloud, Prabal said, "Yes ours. Oh, the metallic paint smell is silver mixed with Valium and morphine." Prabal reached into his pocket, produced a bullet and showed it to Arty. "These silver bullets splinter on impact, to maximize pain and the Valium and morphine mix slows you down.

The pain comes from your supernatural allergy to silver, which provides enough of a distraction to keep you from harming one of us. The drugs are a little insurance, just in case you are one of the few werewolves that aren't allergic to silver." Shaking his head, Prabal said, "I would be forced into beheading you if that was the case. Man Arty, you should have taken the Institute up on their invitation. You would've learned more about Globes Disease. It's much too late for that now. We have been watching you for a while now and you're far too dangerous and unpredictable. We ain't takin' you in big fella. You're not useful to us." Prabal took a deep breath and said, "Well Arty, it was a pleasure hunting you." Barely able to breathe and overcome by the pain, Arty struggled to look at Prabal. His last vision was of Prabal walking over, and calmly placing the barrel of the gun to Arty's left eye. There was a loud pop, a flash of light, excruciating pain and then, nothing.

THE PACK

Approximately a year after Vlad

Jodi arrived at the Ragnorocks home early in the evening. She was excited to see them, especially under less dubious conditions. She looked a whole lot different from her Rebellious-Goth-Skater-Schoolgirl days. She looked more mature and she was becoming a beautiful, less hateful young woman. Surviving certain death at the hands of a vengeful vampire will do that to a person. She was wearing a Céline Paris T-shirt, skinny jeans, a couple of silver chains and a new pair of high-heeled sneakers. Jodi stood on the porch and rang the bell. She scented her new family. Sal, Terry, Goldy, Quake, and Diana were all there. She smelled food and drinks and she could hear laughter, which made her smile, another new thing for her these days. Diana answered the door and grabbed her for a hug. They had all survived a catastrophic event and this felt a little like one of those reunions for the local news. Jodi chuckled to herself even as she cried tears of joy. Jodi was content, happy for the first time in a long time. She felt welcome, as if she had come home. This group was Jodi's family now, her pack.

The Vlad incident had changed everyone. Terry and Goldy moved past their shyness and decided to take a chance. They dated briefly, fell in love and quickly married. Goldy was glowing at 8 months pregnant and Terry beamed with pride. Between life with Goldy and a promotion at work, Terry wasn't as self-deprecating and unsure as he once was. He was slowly moving away from the Black man is victimized by society syndrome. He was no longer a victim; he was now an aggressive participant in life. They all had newfound hope. Jodi's perspective towards her own culture had changed. Sal's arm was slowly growing back, but his macho Italian bravado had all but gone away. Sal had realized he was wrong for prejudging those different from himself, so his outlook was far different than it had been. Quake, on the other hand, had not changed a bit. As always, he was booming-loud and loving life. Quake was working the grill; he called out to get Jodi's attention, as she made it through the sea of people. Jodi thought of her father and wished he could have been there. She sighed and grabbed the drink Terry handed her. Jodi noticed Terry's heavy demeanor was lifting; there was an odd feminine aura around him. She picked up a slightly different scent coming from him, but before she could focus on what was different about Terry, Jodi heard her name.

"Hey, Jodi, how're ya holding up?" Quake's voice bellowed above the music and crowd as Jodi made her way to the grill. "How are the classes Goldy's been giving? Are they helping?" Jodi responded quietly, "Uhm, yes actually, surprisingly well, thank you for asking." "Great," rumbled Quake. "Fuck vampires!" Quake chortled loudly. "It's been what, over a year?" Quake leaned towards Jodi, his giant face shadowing hers from the sun. He turned from jovial to serious. "Listen, things aren't right around here. You are not safe. This is 'the calm before the storm'. We ain't sure what's gonna happen, but whatever it is, it ain't gonna be good. For your own protection we think you should go on the road." Jodi gave him a surprised look. Quake answered her silent query, "Yeah, leave town soon Jodi." Jodi was wondering who WE was, but before she could ask they were all standing around her, Goldy, Terry, Sal and Diana quietly agreeing with Quake's advice.

Sal gave a knowing nod; something was going on at the Institute. He wasn't privy to all the top-secret information, but things were a lot busier from bottom to top. Sal felt something was amiss and whatever it, was, Jodi could see the concern in Sal's eyes as he spoke, "Things are different out there now. Security is tighter, projects more private, higher clearance levels are required more often. All access is determined by clearance level. I'm a level 3 and now there are places that I can no longer access. Listen to Quake, he is absolutely correct, something is definitely brewing." Terry chimed in, "We have all been Weres a long time and we were under the radar all that time, until recently. Because of our age and experience, we can handle ourselves, but Jodi you're still coming into your own and we want to protect you.

Remember, if there is one vampire, there are sure to be more. Knowledge of your existence makes you an easy target." Goldy interjected "One thing is for certain, we can't let what happened get in the way of a cure for any of us." Sal continued, "Cure or not, whatever is going on, we have to keep things as low key as possible." Diana put her arm around Jodi and continued with a softer, more motherly approach. "Didn't you mention a nice young man that you wanted to travel and explore the states with? Live baby, enjoy your life while you're young like Quake and I and Terry and Goldy are. Love isn't something you run away from, it's meant to be something you run to."

Jodi was scared. Scared to leave, scared to stay. She was afraid of the unknown. She worried about her new relationship with Pierce. She was fearful of opening herself up to anyone. Hell, she had only recently begun opening up to her new family. She was scared to make any decisions at all. Diana continued, "Courage is often defined by allowing those you trust to position themselves behind you, so that they can push you to succeed." Jodi understood that. She needed a second chance, and the opportunity to continue her own growth. Jodi wanted the chance to apply what she had learned to see if she could succeed, like those in her new family. Terry and Goldy had paired up and found their way. Jodi had begun to feel that she, too, should give life a chance. She longed to be a Lycanthrope with control over the disease and eventually be able to help others, as Goldy had. Deep inside Jodi was interested in a cure, but she realized that controlling the disease was the first step. She also understood that her presence could put her new family in danger. She was the only one that had been on TV, which made her easily recognizable by everyone, especially the Institute, the Hunters or possibly vengeful vampires. Jodi relented because of all their love and logic.

Jodi had hunted and killed perverts. They were humans. Jodi knew she was no match for vampires, at least not yet. "How many vampires are really out there?" Jodi wondered. "If they are out there, what are the odds they know about Vlad and seek revenge? Do we really want to know the answer to these questions?" Jodi shook herself from her thoughts and acknowledged the advice given to her by the pack. That night she laughed, drank and dined. For once in her life, Jodi was going to follow someone's advice instead of being rebellious. Jodi accepted their guidance, their money and the train ticket to ride out of La Mort Douce.

Jodi already had plane tickets to New York and Japan, if she was ever so inclined to go. She noted the train tickets were on dates carefully selected for when the lunar pull was at its weakest. She hugged them all as the evening ended. She cried, openly, something that was very difficult for her. These people loved and cared about her and Jodi could truly call them family. She didn't want to let them down; still, she wanted to be here for them somehow.

Jodi recognized the look in their eyes. None of them expected to live through whatever looming threat was waiting for them. They couldn't leave La Mort Douce; their roots firmly planted. They all planned to stick it out through the end. They knew it was up to them to take a stand. Jodi represented the future of their kind. She promised herself she would be a more mature and better-prepared werewolf. She also promised herself she would be a more knowledgeable and mature human being. She swore to herself that she would return to repay them all for their love. She didn't speak a word to them of her inner promise, she simply said "Thank you." Jodi knew she would return to save them all somehow.

PIERCE SHADOWHAWK

Pierce Shadowhawk was late getting to the Ragnorocks home. He was excited to meet Jodi's new family. Pierce was a tall, muscular, dark-skinned Native American man in his early 20s. He had thick black hair, which he wore just above his muscular shoulders. Pierce struggled to feel comfortable with his ethnic background. He often found himself trying to balance ethnic pride with professionalism. Pierce felt schizophrenic at work. He found it difficult having to act white so that others would view him as a professional and non-threatening. This type of subtle prejudice made him feel as if La Mort Douce remained trapped in the past. Controlling his temper at work was quite a challenge.

Pierce had to attend Anger Management, which, in his opinion, was complete and utter bullshit. It frustrated him that three white men could pick on a lone Native American and pay no penalty. Pierce, who merely defended himself, dispatched the bullies adeptly, and his reward for this self-preservation was an arrest and then anger management. What a travesty! It was like that at work as well. If Pierce spoke his mind on any given subject, coworkers dismissed him as the angry Indian. Men, with the same amount of time on the job spoke their minds, and were 'hilarious' or lauded as being forward thinkers. Sheriff Bray explained to Pierce that it wasn't his fault; Pierce was a victim of circumstance, but circumstance should not make him a victim. Bray spent hours talking with him, which many considered uncharacteristic for the oft-aloof Sheriff. He once told Pierce, "Play the game, long enough to find the means to change the game."

Pierce did just that; he played their game with secret aspirations of gaining an advantage. He changed his attitude, curbed his anger and miraculously found love. Eventually, he got his dream job, as a conservationist, and asked Jodi to come with him. She had refused at first, but later texted him that she had changed her mind. She said, "Let's start in New York." Pierce couldn't contain his excitement. He made the necessary calls and found an opening at the Wilton Wildlife Park in Eastern New York. Pierce couldn't wait to tell Jodi all about it.

Just as Pierce was about to ring the Ragnorocks doorbell, the front door swung open and Jodi jumped in to his arms, catching Pierce by surprise. "She must have scented me," he thought. Pierce thought it odd; he had the gift of insight with others, but had none about his own relationships or career. He sensed an ominous fate for the town and Jodi's new family. He knew Sal would sacrifice more than an arm to save them. He knew Terry and Quake were bright lights in the pack but soon would clash. Diana and Goldy would face the cruelest of trials. He felt the same about Jodi and knew he needed to get her away. Jodi was the key to her own well being and healing. But for that to happen, she would have to leave to discover her real potential. Pierce's own fate was a dark and blurry mystery. He hoped this adventure would help both of them mature and find enlightenment. He just wanted to be out of La Mort Douce so he could discover a new perspective on the world, see, feel and experience new things. His wish was to develop the ability to see his own fate, a skill his grandfather had mastered. He hoped to hone his skills enough that he might one day be useful to the world, to Jodi and her family, even to La Mort Douce.

OPERATION PACK MENTALITY – NORTH MOUNTAINS

The early morning sun had not come up yet. George, a middle-aged man with dark hair and greying sideburns was a marketing executive for the Douce Water Company. He looked a bit like George Reeves from the old Superman television show of the 50s. He was a lone bicyclist who often rode the northern mountains of La Mort Douce. George had taken the mountainous routes many times. He knew better than to go near Montagne du Loup. It was too close to the hunting grounds and the local news was never short of animal attack stories. Besides, it was too far from where he lived. He just needed a good sprint up the hill and then he'd return home, shower and get ready for work. Work had become more hectic with the growth of La Mort Douce in recent years.

George loved the crisp morning air and the cold evenings. He took it all in as he zipped past a clearing and headed towards a bike trail looking down the side of the hill. He couldn't resist getting a better view and possibly a photograph. George skidded to a stop and looked down at La Mort Douce, which was once a mining town with an ominous history. Now it was gradually becoming a modern town with an ominous history.

George pulled his camera phone from his jacket pocket and went through the menu. He heard a rustling behind him, looked around and saw nothing. He figured his presence had disturbed some small woodland creature. Once he'd selected the camera function, George raised his phone to take a picture. Behind him, he heard a low, guttural growl, which worried him a little. He rationalized that mountain lions were not common in this region and wolves were generally due east. George quickly took his picture and calmly decided he would leave, just in case. He turned and leaned onto his handlebars, so he could pocket his phone. He changed his mind and thought instead, "Maybe, if I use the flash, it will scare away whatever is in the bushes." George turned and flashed off another shot. It would be George's last photo.

What leapt out of the brush towered over George with a blunt snout and sharp fangs; drooling and snarling all over his scared, surprised and trembling body. George flashed the camera again, purely by accident, but the flash only provoked it further. The first swipe took off the arm holding the camera. George's arm fell to the ground while his convulsing hand continued to click off photos. George screamed in anguish. The second swipe took off George's head, abruptly ending his shrieks. As his head rolled down the embankment, the creature bit into George's torso and fed on his headless corpse, even as it remained on the bike. The beast devoured what was left of George, right there on the trail. The sounds of flesh ripping, the slurping of liquid and organs and the popping sound of tendons and bones were the only sounds left.

LE PARC DE MOYENS

Operation Pack Mentality had begun with Arty. The Hunters were in full swing and having a blast. This is what they were here for, what they lived for, what they'd sat on their tails waiting to do. No more training, no more hurry up and wait; it was go time. The Hunters had just come from investigating the headless remains of a bicyclist near the base of the North Mountains. They had found George's camera, analyzed the digital pictures and decided they would make a sweep of the mountains in the morning. Chuck told his team they would head for Central Park, Le Parc Moyens, for a priority intervention.

In the van on their way to Le Parc Moyens, they had already heard the local radio news reporting to the early morning coffee addicts, that there was a mountain lion in the northern mountains of La Mort Douce. "Sheesh! How do these ass-holes get wind of this stuff so fast?" Adonis groaned. "Shit, at least TMZ's crazy asses ain't out here," Low-Key's deep voice chimed in. Mack interjected, "If TMZ ever came out this way, I'd shoot Harvey Levin myself." They all laughed, except for Prabal and Chuck. Chuck didn't allow himself levity and neither could he allow his crew to lose focus, so he brought them back to reality. "Stay sharp everyone, we're here. Prabal, take the high point overlooking the tunnel, Low-Key and Adonis take those park benches, just in case it runs. Ray-Rae you're up." He barked orders and pointed in the direction of the park's infamous tunnel, "There's the tunnel, walk it from end to end, appear to be distracted and make it look real this time! I don't want this one to get the chance to run. Casanova, you're our eyes and ears, stay near the van, in case we need to make a quick departure. Mack, you get one end of the tunnel, I'll get the other; everyone clear?" They each acknowledged in the affirmative. "Okay, let's get to work."

Ray-Rae entered the tunnel texting Mack on her PDA. Mack laughed as she read message after message from Ray-Rae. Chuck cut Mack a look, but before he could tell them to cut their high jinx, he saw that the ruse appeared to be successful. Ray-Rae seemed distracted and something tried to take advantage. Not yet twilight, Chuck figured a Were would be looking for a last chance at a morning meal. Casanova had infrared binoculars and could see the Werewolf's heat signature, which stood out like a sore thumb. Casanova spied it, hiding in the bushes. This one read at least 20 degrees hotter than the Hunters did. "Hey y'all, we got company." Casanova drawled. Chuck whispered into his mic, "Stay sharp." Ray-Rae had walked 3 quarters of the tunnel, not looking up once. She was about 10 feet from the exit when the distinctive growl of a werewolf interrupted the quiet, dark morning. Ray-Rae stopped and looked up from her texting, her heart raced. The beast could hear her heart beat. It was a fatal mistake when the animal misinterpreted Ray-Rae's excitement for fear. The bushes next to the tunnel rustled and a werewolf boldly revealed its presence, tall and lean, with long claws, long thick grey fur, and a thin toothy muzzle. It attempted to intimidate Ray-Rae, growling continuously. Suddenly, the animal lunged.

The attack was a surprise to Ray-Rae. The lack of prolonged posturing to elicit more fear from her was a concern. Ray-Rae thought, "These animals thrive on the fear of humans. The endorphins and adrenaline make the kill tastier somehow." Ray-Rae dropped her PDA and reached for her pistols in her back belt holsters. She hit the ground and fired. The beast flew at Ray-Rae. She put two darts in its neck, one in its chest, another in its belly and before it knew what hit it, it fell. Landing beyond her, it struggled up onto all fours. Looking at Ray-Rae, the beast howled in confused, lethargic pain as the Valium, morphine and silver shards began to do their job. "It's on the move!" warned Ray-Rae as it tried to run. It was too late to escape. Prabal shot a dart to the back of its neck and Chuck blocked its path at the other end of the tunnel, firing a silver-lined net from what looked like a small bazooka. The animal went down. It struggled against the net, to no avail. When Low-Key and Adonis arrived, they pulled the net's ends together, tightening it around the creature and preventing it from breaking free. The silver threads in the net increased the werewolf's agony.

The crew stood around watching the female werewolf as she struggled, only trapping herself further. Her screams, barks and bites indicated she was confused and hurt. The net was damaging her body externally, while the darts did their job internally. The beast began losing consciousness and started changing back to human form as the sun started to rise.

Ray-Rae walked over and kicked the werewolf, "I friggin' broke my PDA because of you." Chuck scolded her, "Hey take it easy." Ray-Rae kicked her again. Prabal walked over to her and said, "Let it go Ray-Rae, I'm sure you have phone insurance". Before he could say more, Ray-Rae grabbed herself by the crotch, and yelled, "Insure this! It's not just a phone it's a PDA!" They didn't need civilians around to see this and Chuck put an end to the scene, Hunters were supposed to fly under the radar, it made for better hunting. "Okay team, great job. Now, cover her up and take her back to the Institute. We have a lot more work to do, this town is infested." Adonis and Low-Key high-fived and fist bumped one another and exclaimed at the same time; "...We are the exterminators!"

CHUCK'S KILL

Chuck was exhausted. It was early morning; only 48 hours had passed since the elimination of Arty and the Tunnel Were. Now the Northern Mountain Were was on their agenda. Chuck figured they would head north, handle that animal, go back to the Institute for a briefing and then move on to bigger fish. He had uploaded the Institute's collection of videos. They were to capture the last four beasts. Chuck knew it and his team knew it. They really didn't need another briefing to tell them that. If the Institute wanted the Hunters to continue in an expedient fashion, they shouldn't have to stop for meetings so often, it was unnecessary. "Don't kill the last four." That's all she needed to convey in his book. Dr. von Shelley usually ignored all the communication gadgets in favor of her meeting agenda. Chuck didn't get her she made him leery. She was off the beaten path when it came to chain of command. Her agenda vacillated between capture and experiment or kill and dissect. Chuck felt there was more to what they were doing; personal agendas were afoot. Not that it mattered; the Institute was still under military control. Chuck disengaged himself from his thoughts and barked into the radio. "Stay sharp, this one might want breakfast before going home. I will meet him at his address.'

Chuck sat in the dark coat closet of a townhouse. Light peeked through the cracks of the door. He gave roll call through his microphone, "Prabal, Casanova you got visual?" They acknowledged with the standard "Roger." Chuck continued, "Adonis, Low-Key, front seat of the van?" They acknowledged and attempted to adjust their large frames in the seats of the van's cab. They completely filled the space shoulder-to-shoulder. From Prabal's viewfinder, it was hilarious to behold. Prabal decided to add levity to the situation, "Hey fellas, try to look smaller, please." Ray-Rae and Mack were walking up and down the sidewalk in front of the townhouse, giggling.

Prabal interrupted the comic moment. "I see it..." A wolf-like animal was running through bushes and backyards, hopping over fences until it ended up in the back yard of the home Mack and Ray-Rae had just walked past. The wolf ran up to the back porch, stopped, sniffed and looked around. The creature stood up and reached for the door with its long paw. Prabal was on the radio, "I got visual and a shot." Chuck commanded, "No shot, this one is mine." Prabal responded somewhat disappointed, "Roger. He's going in." Chuck whispered orders to stay alert. The werewolf slowly changed to a human as it turned the doorknob. He was a, tall, thin male with long black hair. His clothes were tattered, what was left of them. He appeared to be dark skinned, possibly Native American.

The human entered the kitchen and immediately washed his face, blood coating the sink. Afterwards, he headed to the bathroom to shower. Next, he went to the living room in his robe, grabbed the remote and turned on the television. The man went into his kitchen to grab a drink, when he returned to the living room, he came face to face with Chuck, blond, scarred, intimidatingly calm and leveling a gun at him. The man shouted a warning, "You don't know who you're messing with, leave now!" Within moments, he began to change back into a werewolf. While he was in the process of changing, Chuck cocked his sawed off shot gun, calmly walked over to the changing werewolf and splattered his head and brains all over the living room wall and ceiling. Chuck watched the man's lifeless body quickly change back to human as it crumpled to the floor. Chuck dryly replied to the dead werewolf, "You don't know who you're messing with."

GOLDY

Goldy felt relieved as she hung up the phone. Jodi had just checked in to say she arrived safely in New York. It amazed her how a few shared moments and conversations can change lives so drastically. She had been discussing her most intimate feelings with a young girl who, a short time ago was La Mort Douce's youngest serial killer. Jodi refused to be a victim of Lycanthropy, though it had taken time before Jodi had learned to adopt that mindset. Jodi had purposefully executed certain perverts for their crimes. Goldy understood Jodi's position and agreed those Jodi had killed deserved their punishment. Goldy just wasn't sure it was their right to choose the fate of others? Would any of us choose to be werewolves? Would we willingly inflict this disease on anyone else? Would anyone choose this disease? Jodi had finally absorbed much of this new thinking under Goldy's tutelage. Unlike the books and movies Jodi and Goldy had seen this thing was not glamorous. It was painful, nasty and fraught with shame and torturous emotions. Lycanthropy was a dirty bloody affliction.

Despite the use of Chakra, Zen, African Mysticism and Ausar Auset, Goldy had some very ungraceful and often embarrassing moments. Goldy mastered those skills and excelled at teaching others to use them. Occasionally the instructor's control did not always work well for the teacher, which frustrated her. Goldy did not want to be the cause of someone being hurt or even killed. Like Quake and the others, when things did not work, she and Terry had a basement with silver lined cages and locks. Goldy believed each failure helped her get closer to success, closer to complete control.

Goldy thought of her present situation and condition and began to worry again. Any woman her age would be worried, married for a 4th time and with child on the way at this age. It was a wonderful new start for a person with a tumultuous past. Goldy was elated that Terry had jumped in with both feet, loving and marrying her. Terry was ecstatic about being married and was elated by the thought of being a father for the first time. A normal woman under normal circumstances would have many questions and thoughts like, "Will our child be healthy? How will my body recover after the child is born? How will this affect work schedules, us as a couple, travel, nannies, strollers, cradles, diapers, the whole nine yards? Will Terry still love, enjoy and look at me the same way? Will mother and child survive the pregnancy as well as the birth? How do you choose between breast-feeding and formula? Ugh, can these breasts even take that again?" Goldy asked herself.

A lot of her friends and associates expressed their opinion based on what they saw of Goldy. They would say things like, "You have the body of a 30 year old woman." One of Goldy's standard responses was, "Honey, you need glasses." Goldy had a head start on the hours of self-doubt. She often asked herself, "Are you out of your mind? My ankles hurt, my back hurts, and I'm sick in the morning and ravenous in the afternoon. I have mood swings and temperature changes. I don't feel like a 30 year old."

Goldy stared in the mirror; Terry wandered by and gave her the look. Dinner was wonderful, the dishes cleaned and Terry was beaming. Goldy wondered if Terry had even considered the other issues. After all, they were Lycanthropes. From the moment her test was positive, she panicked and tried to research with no success. She found nothing on the subject of Lycanthropes procreating. A werewolf impregnated by another werewolf? Women of Goldy's age were unlikely to conceive. "Maybe it's supernatural sperm and eggs," Goldy giggled uncomfortably to herself. "Maybe this disease heals all its victim's ailments. The only after effect is turning into a big giant dog that kills people." Goldy giggled and sighed as her feelings shot in a new direction. Will the child have this disease, like its parents? Will it be a hybrid? Will it survive?

The Institute was ecstatic, helping with her medical care along the way, monitoring and testing her. They accommodated her every need, took blood samples and took care of all her prenatal treatments and exams. Their enthusiastic assistance made her uneasy. According to Dr. von Shelley, they had no record of any Lycanthrope having a child or any human having a Lycanthrope's child. The fact that they were so helpful made Goldy apprehensive. Goldy's mind was going to buckle under the weight of her distress.

Goldy sighed again; she knew La Mort Douce anchored her new pack's roots in its foundation. Quake and Terry seemed confident they could handle whatever was to come. Terry's newfound swagger was refreshing. He convinced her that, as a team, a family, a pack, they could and would weather any storm. Goldy was hopeful, but women's intuition combined with werewolf intuition told her a different story. Goldy felt something was coming. This was the 'calm before the storm'. What would the price in casualties be? We are human first after all, mostly. We just want what all Americans want, a chance to flourish in this land of opportunity and live the American dream. Even if it only lasted a few fleeting moments, Goldy wanted happiness.

Now dressed, Goldy spun around once and looked at herself. She had on a purple and black teddy. "Ugh", she felt fat. "Look at those thighs and oh my god is that a basketball or my ass?" she thought self-deprecatingly. She didn't even bother looking at her stomach; she just rested her hands on it, rubbed the constantly moving child inside and took a deep breath. If the catcalls in the bedroom were anything to judge by, she was the only person that minded her condition. She smiled, glanced in the mirror one last time, turned around, stood in the doorway and posed as gracefully as any pregnant woman her age could. She left the light on long enough for Terry to get an eyeful. When Goldy saw his eyes had reached maximum dilation, she flipped the light off.

Goldy let the sudden darkness, accented by ambient light and the look in Terry's eyes chase away all her doubts and concerns. She wanted to enjoy this moment. This was bliss. Terry was insanely crazy for her. He had never been married; he'd worked, dated and traveled enough to know what he liked. He appreciated her completely, the good and bad. That appreciation made Goldy feel sexy, valuable and wanted. Goldy wanted to give everything she had to this moment, because she believed such happiness had a short shelf life. Bliss like this couldn't last. So Goldy would relish it, bathe in it and enjoy every second, minute, hour and day that Terry loved her. Besides, how could a girl in her condition resist the big night Terry had planned? Goldy wanted to enjoy it while she still could.

QUAKE

Quake rarely purchased gifts for family or friends. He usually left those types of things to Diana, but he was particularly proud of this one and wanted to deliver it personally to Terry and Goldy. Diana humored him and told him to go ahead, but to hurry back because she had something special planned for them that night. Quake liked when she said things like, something special, because he always knew what that meant. Married all these years and she still liked doing things for him, especially that.

Quake was crazy for Diana and would do anything and everything for her as well. Quake was of a mind that he had married his dream girl. Shoot, how many men could say that? From the moment he laid eyes on her, he was smitten. These years with her had only made his love for her grow, though, Quake's giant heart was no match for Diana's selfless sacrifice and devotion. Quake had recognized the same thing in Terry's eyes, his confidence was up, he seemed less of a victim and more like the type of man to overcome prejudice, slights and perceived slights to get his own piece of the American pie. Terry was finally finding his way. Goldy inspired Terry, and all of them to believe that Globes Disease could be controlled, conquered and defeated.

The night air was cool and calm. It was spring and some birds were still singing. The flowers filled the air with different scents day and night. Quake felt good, almost giddy. He walked briskly and when he had traveled a mile, Quake thought, "Shoot, I should walk more often." The town was becoming increasingly more beautiful. Maybe it was just a reflection of Quake's state of mind. Nevertheless, the city council had made strides to improve the landscape of La Mort Douce. The plan was to offset the industrial growth with a pleasing view. They had taken advantage of all the beautiful flowers that grew around La Mort Douce naturally. Quake didn't know their names, nor did he care to. He just liked that there were more trees, more plants, and that La Mort Douce radiated lovely fragrances. Once a mining town, it was now growing into something else. He just hoped that one of its newest residents would make good on their promise, The Institute.

Quake looked up from his warm and fuzzy moment, just a few houses down from his destination. What he saw infuriated him. There was a black Suburban and a black van parked in front of the Andersen's home. Two soldiers, dressed like ninjas and carrying weapons, while white smoke billowed from the Andersen's home exited carrying Terry. They tossed him, none too gently, into the van as another carried Goldy's pregnant, unconscious body and tossed her in as well. Her head appeared to be bloody. . One of them, a woman, was standing up in the back of the van holding a weapon. Four soldiers headed for the SUV. The last one headed to the driver's seat of the van. Quake dropped the gift he was carrying and began running, yelling, "No, No, No!" The rear of the van was still open and the woman in the back raised her rifle and took aim. Quake was in mid-stride, changing into his werewolf.

THE HUNTERS

Ray-Rae looked out from the back of the van to see the largest werewolf she had ever seen in her career, heading her way. Its fur was a reddish brown and it was nearly twice the height and size of a brown bear. She yelled up to Mack who was driving. "We got one trailing us!" She raised her rifle and fired three times as Mack slammed on the gas pedal. Ray-Rae screamed back at her, "Hold it steady, I only hit him once." Quake's werewolf galloped after the van with deadly intent. He was already at the bumper, even with a dart in his shoulder. He growled and took a swipe at Ray-Rae as the van pressed forward. Ray-Rae fell on her back just inches from Terry and Goldy's bound and unconscious bodies. She fired off five rounds, only two hitting Quake. One bounced off his head, but didn't penetrate him and the other stuck into his massive chest. He growled and attempted to haul himself into the van. He was half in and half out, his hind legs dangling. Holding on with one massive paw, he ripped out the darts with the other. Ray-Rae continued calling out to Mack, all of which transmitted over their radio, "Faster Mack, faster! Where in fuck are you, Prabal? You're 'sposed to be on point!" Prabal responded, "I can't be on point if you guys are moving away from my position. Hold on, I'm almost street level." "Ray-Rae!" Mack's voice chimed in, "I know he ain't suggesting we stop?" Chuck interjected, "Hey, you guys got this, or what? We are headed for the next target, but we can double back?" Ray-Rae shouted, "I think this is one of them. I think this is one of the Ragnorocks!"

Quake registered his surname, even in his feral state. They're after Diana and me! That realization made him go even more berserk.

He frantically pulled himself all the way into the van. Inside the van, he stood up bowing up the roof of the van with his head and throwing the van off balance. Ray-Rae continued to scream, 'He's in here! He's in the back of the friggin' van with me! Mack!" Mack had just reached back to fire her pistol when Quake stepped forward. His movement shook the van making it even more unstable. Mack blindly fired several shots, all of which missed. Quake continued to shake the van, eventually knocking the gun out of Mack's hand. Ray-Rae was frantically trying to reload when Quake grabbed her and dragged her close to him, hatred in his eyes. Instinctively, she drew the pistol from her belt and fired away to no avail. "This thing is not stopping, help me Mack! Help me!" The van swerved back and forth; as Mack struggled to reach for the gun she'd dropped. Prabal was in hot pursuit, behind them. He stopped occasionally to see if he could get off a good shot. "Help me, somebody help!" Ray-Rae yelled. Quake went to bite her, but the van swerved again and instead of her neck, he bit her shoulder. Ray-Rae let out a bloodcurdling scream.

Mack hit the brakes and the van slowed, as she screamed "Noooo..." Prabal stopped and yelled, "SHIT!" He settled himself and aimed. Ray-Rae continued cry out in pain and disbelief. Prabal fired six shots, all of them hitting Quake's werewolf in the back. Quake released his victim, reared back and fell out of the van. After a few tumbles he rolled to a stop, landing on his side, like a downed rhino in the middle of the street, breathing slowly and heavily. Prabal walked over to Quake and spoke into his radio, "Mack, get Ray-Rae and the cargo to the Institute ASAP. Chuck, head to the next location and finish the pickup. I'm transmitting my position so we can package this one to take back to the Institute when we're done." Prabal took a deep breath, looked around and then looked down at Quake. "Yeah big fella, we're definitely gonna need you. It would be a shame to kill you." Prabal's radio squelched with Chuck's voice, "Roger, we are on top of the last location. Prabal, can you confirm you have one of the two Ragnorocks?" Prabal confirmed, "Roger it's him, big, red and nearly impossible to stop. This is definitely the big guy from the video." Chuck answered. "Roger, we're sending another van to your location." Chuck's tone changed, "Mack?" She responded, "I'm on it! The Institute knows we're coming and they have a med-team waiting. In the background, Ray-Rae was screaming, "This sucks, this fuckin' sucks!" followed by Mack trying to console her as she was signing off, "Hang in there Ray-Rae, we've got a 24 to 48 hour window, just hang in there."

Prabal stood over Quake. He pointed his rifle at him. He thought to himself, "How many was that, six, seven darts? That would just about have killed the average werewolf. It seems we're gonna need a special dosage just for this guy." Prabal checked his weapon, reloaded it and looked down at the big red beast again. "Strange..." he thought, "... Usually they change back to human after being shot." Prabal poked Quake with the barrel of his rifle, considered shooting him again for good measure and immediately regretted his indecision. Quake jumped up and lunged, Prabal fired but hit a light-pole. The impact when Quake landed on top of Prabal on the hard asphalt was bone crushing. Prabal felt his pelvis break and his ribs crack. He was in insurmountable pain as the large werewolf stared at him slobber dripping all over Prabal. Quake's eyes rolled around in his skull, he was dizzy from the drugs. Prabal had difficulty breathing; the weight of the beast was suffocating. With his last breath, Prabal radioed, "This one is gonna need a larger dosage." Quake growled, it echoed through Prabal's microphone, the earpieces of those listening and the evening air. Quake took Prabal's head off in one swift, huge, bloody, bone-crunching bite.

Prabal's radio transmitted Chuck's voice, regularly requesting him to repeat the last transmission. All the while, Quake gorged himself on Prabal's entrails. A van turned the corner, headlights illuminating the gruesome scene. Quake turned towards it, the lights shining on his muzzle, dripping with blood, brains and entrails. Quake was lightheaded; the drugs had begun to take effect. Delirious and drugged, Quake stood over his kill and howled. Quake had new purpose. He had to save the members of his pack, and he especially needed to save Diana. He howled again and the lights of nearby homes began to come on, and a few doors opened. Quake ran off, leaving Prabal dead, headless and gutted in the middle of the street. The early morning darkness was highlighted by the van's headlights and the streetlamps all spotlighting the bloody spectacle. Prabal the Hunter was dead.

QUAKE

Quake's werewolf was in excruciating pain. His body was reacting to the silver-laced drugs and darts. Despite the pain and lethargy, he bounded towards home, weaving through backyards and shrubbery. He stopped to scrape the darts off his back against a tree, instinctively trying to get rid of the discomfort. In this state, the urgent need to get home was his only thought. He couldn't comprehend why the person he most desired to bite, taste, even kill, was now the one thing he wanted to preserve. Quake arrived home and found a black suburban already parked out front. Things were blurry and his head was beginning to fog. He stood up on his hind legs and dug at his stomach trying to extract some of the darts from Ray-Rae's gun. The burning had become too much and he needed it to stop.

Four soldiers, in black like the others he'd just encountered, exited the vehicle. Quake let out an unholy howl in an attempt to scare off his current adversaries; it didn't work. He'd scented Diana, when the doors opened, so he knew she was already in the back of the SUV. Enraged, Quake's werewolf lethargically charged the four men. They positioned themselves directly behind the doors, waiting for him as he plodded towards them. The men stood their ground, confident and fearless. The larger two were in front, battle ready, while the smaller two stood behind the human behemoths. The challenge was on.

This would be Quakes last act before succumbing to the drugs and silver coursing through him, possibly the last before he died. Quake increased his speed and was ready to leap. He was 20 feet away when the two in front sidestepped, exposing the two behind them. As Quake leapt at them, one fired a rifle, the other a small bazooka type device, with timed precision. A dart with a larger dose hit Quake in the neck. The pain was overwhelming and in mid-leap, there had been no way to avoid it. Quake yelped as a net engulfed him before he could make another move. The net tangled him up immediately and he hit the ground with such force, the whole block seemed to shake. The pain caused by the net was incredible. Quakes blood boiled, molten hot through his joints, veins, lungs and heart. The fire felt as if he were being electrocuted and set on fire all at once and his. The force of landing sent him tumbling towards the soldiers, who promptly moved out of his way. The only thing that stopped his forward progress was the SUV. His head and shoulders crushed the front of it, with the force of a semi. The bumper, grill and hood were an accordion-like mess. Despite the emergency brake, the vehicle skidded back some ten feet. There was no driving away in it now. At great cost to his own well being, Quake had temporarily succeeded in keeping the Hunters from driving away with Diana.

Quake's breathing was shallow and labored as he slowly changed back to human. The drugs and pain were too much and his body was succumbing. He looked up at the four men standing over him. They all took off their helmets and hoods. They began to talk amongst themselves. "You gotta be fucking kidding me!" exclaimed the Asian fellow with a southern accent. Quake's breathing was becoming ever shallower. A blond man with a scar said, "Let's get him to the Institute so the lab can save him before he OD's from all that shit we pumped into him." A large light-skinned man chimed in and said, "I sure hope they know what they're doing." A large Samoan guy asked, "How's the female?" The light-skinned guy looked up and said, "She's good, but the SUV is toast. We're gonna need a bigger boat anyway." The blond man, who was obviously the leader, began to issue orders. "Call for another van and more manpower, it's gonna take at least six of us to carry this monster."

Quake whispered something. They all looked at one another. The leader bent down and asked "What was that champ?" Quake repeated himself again before falling into a painful, debilitating, caliginous abyss, "If anything happens to Diana, I'm gonna kill each and every one of you." The last thing Quake heard, that angered him beyond anything he had ever felt before, was the sound of the Hunter's laughter as Quake succumbed to the darkness, that laughter sealed their fates.

BACK AT THE INSTITUTE

CHUCK

Chuck was extremely pissed off. He stormed down the complicated corridors of the Institute. He was itching to confront Dr. von Shelley. "That was bullshit!" he thought. He arrived at the door of her office and banged on it with his fist. Normally he could control his Canadian accent, but he didn't care about enunciating just then. He had a crew to protect. The ghosts of Massey still haunted him and the scars inside ran deeper than the scars on his face. He banged on the door again. "Ma'am, I need to discuss somethin' with you." Her response infuriated Chuck. "What is it about?" Dr. von Shelley sounded exasperated. Chuck responded to her tone, a tone that was instigating his ire, "You know exactly what it's aboot, ma'am! Open this door or I will use my boot-key!"

The door clicked with an electronic whir. Chuck thought to himself, "Didn't she use a key the last time I stood in front of this door?" He made a mental note to himself to ask Casanova to get a complete set of specs on the Institute. Chuck needed to know exactly where all the interior doors led and where all entrances and exits were, especially any secret ones, which were manually and/or electronically controlled around the facility, where all the cameras were located, and he specifically needed to know where the control room was. Chuck hated being at a disadvantage and felt it was high time he took control of things. No way would he be blindsided, as the Institute had been when Vlad showed up. Chuck already felt a lack of trust for Dr. von Shelley and recent events only served to increase that. He took a deep breath and tried to remember all his military training on diplomacy. Composed and ready to discuss his concerns, Chuck opened the door and entered hoping to iron things out, calmly.

"Are you out of your mind?" Chuck's diplomacy was already leaving him. "Why the hell haven't you given Ray-Rae the antidote? Our numbers are down too low as it is, so we have to have ALL of the team intact." Dr. von Shelley calmly replied, "I have every intention of making sure Ray-Rae remains a part of your team. The antidote is available and effective against the disease. There is a 24 to 48 hour window from the time she was bitten, but we need to collect some data before giving it to her." Chuck stood there and studied Dr. von Shelley. He calmed himself, again and steadied his breathing. He didn't believe her or trust her and now he needed to think in terms of protecting himself and his team, La Mort Douce was fast becoming a place Chuck wasn't comfortable being in. It was increasingly feeling like another Massey was looming. Dr. von Shelley kept talking, "I realize the importance of your team and I called Austin, notified him of the situation and told him we would need more Hunters. Will that team you have in training be ready soon? Chuck looked at her in disbelief. He knew the team she was asking about wasn't ready to take on anything like what his team had just faced. He knew they definitely weren't ready to cut their teeth in this hellhole of a town. "Well" he responded coyly, "I have to brief my team. I'm just waiting for Prabal to return so we can prepare for the next phase of Operation Pack Mentality."

Dr. von Shelley couldn't hide her reaction. "Prabal?" "Chuck, Prabal is gone." She said, in a calm voice. He was stunned and couldn't speak. He was frozen. Dr. von Shelley continued to speak. "Operation Pack Mentality is on hold until we can beef up our team. Chuck thought, "Our?" Dr. von Shelley continued, "We captured the pack leaders. Quake and Terry are definitely paramount to our experiments. The dosage of drugs for Quake will need adjustment. I have been looking at Valium, morphine and elephant tranquilizer combinations, along with the silver shards. The interface technology has improved, so our control will be greater than before. We are even considering creating integrated foot soldiers, if we can perfect the mind control process. I have seen the videos you uploaded, Chuck and have contacted the Canadian Security Intelligence Service. I have sent countless recommendations of commendation for your exemplary service, but we need to follow this through to the end. Can you do that? Debrief your team and be ready to finish this?"

Chuck was stunned. His existing anger and grief intermingled with new fury and contempt. He simply could not speak. He thought of Prabal and Massey and realized the Hunters were expendable to Dr. von Shelley. She obviously did not intend to follow a code of honor. She had an agenda and Chuck needed to find out what that was. He didn't care if Casanova had to charm every man and woman in the place. Chuck knew Mack's tenacity would get them ready for all-out war. Low-Key and Adonis were always ready for mayhem. Chuck reigned in his emotions. He looked at Dr. von Shelley and asked, "Ma'am, where's Ray-Rae right now? I would like to reassure her. After which, I will debrief my team ASAP." Her stern face changed. She had a flash of motherliness. Chuck thought, "You're not the only one who can manipulate." Dr. von Shelley spoke softly, "Thank you. I knew you would understand. I knew the Chiefs had picked the right man. Here's a key card to where she is. Use corridor "C", same floor as the observation labs. Afterwards meet me in the observation lab to see our efforts come to fruition, okay?" Dr. von Shelley returned to whatever task she'd been occupied with earlier and spoke again without looking up, "Oh, by the way, thank you Chuck."

Chuck exited the room and staggered in the hallway. He felt like a zombie. He traversed the corridors as if on autopilot, but his brain continued to work as he tried to work out this latest addition to his problems. He now believed Dr. von Shelley and the Institute were intent on jeopardizing the Hunters. He would never allow them to sacrifice his team. Mack, Adonis and Low-Key caught up with him. "Did you guys hear?" Chuck looked her in the eyes. She was shocked.

She hadn't worn that haunted look since Massey. "What are we gonna do?" Mack asked. Chuck continued walking, but responded, "We are gonna go see Ray and then I'm gonna make a call. After that, we are goin' off the reservation. It's time we watched our own asses. Screw Operation Pack Mentality. It's now us against Dr. von Shelley and the Institute."

The Hunters arrived at Ray-Rae's room. Casanova was already there. No one spoke. Chuck used the key card and they entered a room divided by a multi-layered wall of specially reinforced bullet-proof glass. They all stood in silence looking through the glass at Ray-Rae, curled up on a gurney, sweating and shaking feverishly in her hospital gown. Ray-Rae looked up and spoke. "Chuck, Mack, Casanova, Low-Key, Adonis…" she paused, shivered, "… Don't let her do this to me."

Chuck snapped out of his emotional, mental coma. He looked at Mack, "How long ago was Ray-Rae bitten, five hours?" Mack nodded. Chuck looked up at the cameras, "Huddle." They all stood in a semi-circle near the glass wall. Ray-Rae walked over to the glass to complete the circle. Chuck whispered orders, "Okay, at most we have 43 hours. Casanova I need Intel ASAP. Get all the information you can on Dr. von Shelley and this building; schematics, electronics, off record and on. I need to know who has access, how to get in and out of here. We'll need any keys or key cards you can get, though I'd prefer a master keycard and master key. We need to know what rooms can be locked and unlocked manually or otherwise. Mack, round up as much ordinance as you can find, then get belts, holsters, packs and backpacks so we can carry it all. Adonis, Low-Key, we are taking this to the street. If they ain't one of us then they're our enemies. When the shit hits the fan, we trust no one but ourselves. Low-Key, Casanova will find the escape areas, make sure transportation is at each one, cars, trucks, SUVs, motorcycles; whatever you can find. Mack, can you ensure transport at each exit is fully stocked with weapons, armor, and any gear you think we may need? Mack nodded. Adonis, streamline everything we have. Put it on USB flash-drives and have 'em ready, just in case we have to answer to our respective government agencies. Ray-Rae we are going to get you out of here and we're gonna cure you, even if I have to steal the antidote myself!"

Chuck was about to leave when Mack asked, "Where are you going?" He turned and looked up at the camera. He made sure his voice was low enough and positioned his head so no one could read his lips. "I'm goin' to the observation room to see what they are gonna do to our last captures. I need to see where the antidote is kept and how it works. We'll meet there when you all have completed my orders. I gotta make a phone call." Before they exited to tackle their assignments, each of the Hunters made sure they put their hand to the thick glass as if to touch hands with Ray-Rae, who pressed hers against the glass on the other side. They did this to show love, support and solidarity. Ray-Rae's face was glistening with tears streaming down her face.

Chuck was the last to touch the glass and leave. Chuck turned back and gave Ray-Rae one last nod. As he left the room, Chuck bumped into a one armed man. He excused himself and continued. Chuck had made it halfway to the team's quarters when the possibility that they might not all survive this hit him. Chuck entered the dorm, systematically pulled the power cords on every camera, and then went over to the computer. He logged onto an encrypted site with secret codes and passwords, and waited as the secure connection was established. On screen a message beeped, indicating the site was ready. His level of trust was zero and he would not be comfortable until he got the intel he'd requested from Casanova. Chuck leaned in close to the monitor, to block the view of any unseen cameras, clicked the mouse and spoke, "Hey Chief, it's me."

IN THE NAME OF SCIENCE

Dr. von Shelley observed Chuck and his team gathered at the thick glass of Ray-Rae's room. She was at her desk toggling through camera views and their congregation caught her eye. She couldn't tell if they were conspiring or holding a prayer circle. At this point, it was of no concern to her. Science was her priority. Albert Einstein once said, "All religions, arts and sciences are branches of the same tree." Dr. von Shelley wondered what that quote would be if Einstein had faced supernatural circumstances such as she was dealing with.

Dr. von Shelley stared blankly at her computer screen for a moment and determined that the Hunters meeting was a trivial concern compared to the wonderful prizes she had gotten in Mr. Ragnorock and Mr. Andersen. Those two were quite different from the last few subjects she had encountered. With a click of her mouse she was back to looking at the experiments of the past few hours on the pair. As horrific as animal and human trials could be, Dr. von Shelley felt justified in experimenting on them. After all, those two weren't either. Having no audio also assisted in alleviating any guilt.

Dr. von Shelley replayed each test. Her exemplary lab technicians had been following her orders perfectly. They were both strapped down to electronic gurneys with silver restraints. She watched as they cut out their eyelids, which grew back within the hour. She'd had the techs do it again and then pour acid in their eyes. She could see that they had howled and screamed, and was thankful again the sound was off. It was a terrible thing to hear, but not to witness.

This time the regeneration took a few hours as their hollowed eye sockets filled with an odd fluid that solidified to jelly and eventually eyeballs. Dr. von Shelley thought it odd how the eyelids grew back and closed over the socket when the fluid turned to jelly. Ragnorock and Andersen continued to howl and scream. After a few hours, the lids opened to show perfectly functional new eyes, full of rage. She shuddered in fascination.

Dr. von Shelley had ordered their tails chopped off, which grew back almost instantly, just as had happened when she ordered 2x2 inch plugs of skin cut from their bodies. Most curious was that the severed pieces returned to human form and the subjects stayed werewolf. Anything they detached, hair, ears; even limbs all became human immediately after removal. The larger pieces took 30 minutes to an hour, but were still quite fascinating to observe.

Dr. von Shelley knew that, if she lopped off their heads, that was the end of them, she had already discovered that with other subjects. She was extremely curious about their genitals. She wanted to know how much pain it would cause, if she cut them off, whether they would grow back and how long would it take, if they did. She had plans to determine whether reproductive elements existed when they were in werewolf form. It made sense that they could procreate as humans, but she wanted to see if werewolves could mate and procreate. She was aware that they eliminated. The Hunters used the tactic of finding werewolf waste as a means of tracking them. Her assumption was that all bodily functions were normal; so to speak, she just needed to prove it. She enjoyed having the luxury of time to examine and play with her curiosities. Dr. von Shelley quickly made notes, then looked up and clicked the mouse again.

During the discovery process, Dr. von Shelley realized that any silver based chemicals or tools caused physical damage and the subjects took longer to heal from exposure. In some cases, it had caused permanent damage and scarring. Some of the beasts had been set on fire, others drowned. Amazingly, though they struggled, fought, screamed and seemed to have died, they awakened and revived, almost immediately after being removed from what they were exposed too. These creatures seemed to thrive on feral rage and pain. They were the most primal beings she had yet come across and Dr. von Shelley felt that if she could somehow harness that for soldiers, they could overcome any torture and almost any climate.

Silver-based weapons, extremely high dosages of morphine based drugs and tranquilizers laced with silver nitrates were standard for controlling them. Beheadings were very effective, but too permanent. Extreme cold was a surprise. The creatures only seemed to die from drowning when the water was subfreezing, similar to the body of water surrounding the Institute's island. Currently, Dr. von Shelley's theory was that the cold slowed down their heart rates; tempered their rage and eventually they reverted to human form and drowned. Dr. von Shelley was having a sub-temperate water tank built, just so she could observe and confirm that phenomenon. Nevertheless, time was of the essence and all Dr. von Shelley was doing by watching these videos was psyching herself up for what she wanted to do. She was thoroughly geeked out now and ready for more fun. Clicking the mouse again, she shut down her computer, stood up, adjusted her clothing and swigged down the dregs of her energy drink. She checked her watch, as she often did; it was time to go back to work.

DR. VON SHELLEY

Dr. von Shelley walked into the observation room, recently re-modeled after the last fiasco, and felt her pride swell. It was still circular and bright with natural light from the glass dome above. Some of the improvements included blackout glass, used to electronically lighten or darken the room and block out lunar rays. This control strengthened or weakened the Weres as needed. The wonderful new mechanical tables and gurneys had multiple configuration options, for just about any position she desired with the touch of a button. She really liked that they were on tracks for ease of positioning them any place in the room. From the center, the track system was reminiscent of the line patterns on a basketball accommodated up to six gurneys in the middle of the room. She could work on patients and volunteers in any part of the room. The ceiling cameras and screens were on the same tracking system as well. Electronically she could record or observe any activity in the room or the Institute for that matter. Here, Dr. von Shelley felt most powerful. She was the Queen Bee.

Quake and Terry had their arms, legs and torso strapped to the gurneys. They wore neck braces to keep head movement to a minimum. They were back to back with monitors tracking above their heads. Dr. von Shelley nodded at the two tech assistants and the gurneys automatically moved from back to back of each other to an offset configuration, with their heads side by side. The gurneys tilted at such an angle that Quake and Terry could easily see their respective viewing screens. If not for the neck restraints, they would have been able to turn and look at each other eye to eye. There were tubes, patches, monitoring devices, blood pressure cuffs and numerous wires and needles connected, strapped and inserted throughout their bodies monitoring every body function imaginable. Mechanical helmets hung above them as well.

Dr. von Shelley circled the men like a proud hunter, marveling at them as they lay there. Both men had unique physical attributes and she planned to take advantage of them. Quake was a beautiful Nordic titan, strong with unlimited physical potential and astounding resiliency. Terry was a solid lean bodied specimen, built from hundreds of years of labor genetics wrapped around a seriously dedicated and cerebral mind. Dr. von Shelley believed she could use them both to serve her purposes. She walked around them and continued to relish in her conquest. She nodded again and the screens in front of them came to life.

The men slowly opened their eyes as the effects of the sedatives wore off. They watched as the doctor circled them. Dressed in hospital gowns they both looked extremely uncomfortable. The monitors showed continuous loop recordings of both Quake and Terry as werewolves. "Wakey, wakey boys!" Dr. von Shelley said cheerfully. "I find the Valium, morphine and silver nitrate usually cause interesting damage to my subjects. The combination of sedation and pain usually makes patients more compliant, but you two seem to be able to fight through it. Mr. Ragnorock, your physical attributes required major adjustments to your dosage. We actually had to add elephant tranquilizer to the mixture, so please don't give us a reason to use it today." A man with a tranquilizer rifle stepped up and looked at Quake. Dr. von Shelley walked around to Terry, "Mr. Andersen, the challenge with you seems to be your sheer will. Baffling, but interesting. The drugs get to you and you feel the pain, but something inside you just refuses subjugation. So, again, I've had to come up with a different approach."

Sal and Chuck entered the room at the same time bumping into one another. They were both horrified at what they saw on the screens.

Quake's screen showed his werewolf in a room, with Diana cowering in the corner; his Were attacking and biting her. Men entered the room before he could kill her and shot him with Tasers and tranquilizer rifles. The werewolf turned around and killed them all, swiftly and effortlessly. Blood, guts and screaming filled the monitor above Quake. He struggled against his restraints with tears streaming from his eyes. On the monitor, Diana was lying on the floor in the corner, bleeding and shivering, as soon as the beast had moved far enough away from her, while dispensing with the staff, a thick Plexiglas wall came down between them. She couldn't escape, but he couldn't get to her either.

The beast, once done with his distraction, turned and tried to tear through the Plexiglas to finish off Diana. Dr. von Shelley walked over to Quake and looked up into his furious eyes, "Having a hard time changing? The drugs still have you a little loopy. Well, soon you will be able to change and you could get loose to kill us all, but how would that help Diana? We have developed an antidote for those exposed to Lycanthropy Mr. Ragnorock." Dr. von Shelley motioned at a dispenser that resembled a vending machine filled with vials. "Lycanthropy has a 24 to 48 hour gestation window from when the victim is first infected." She glanced at her watch and said, "You have between 17 and 41 hours to make a decision."

"What do you want?" Quake asked through the tears, pain and rage. Dr. von Shelley said, "Well, the North American joint agencies have been working to build an incredibly lethal, elite military force. We have been testing ways to control a werewolf for solo operations or even to lead a pack of submissive werewolves to kill and/or capture enemies we cannot find through conventional means. Can you imagine how quickly an elite Special Forces team made up of werewolves could have found Hitler or any of our modern day terrorists? With a magnificent specimen, such as you, you could be used to hunt, capture or kill rogue werewolves." Dr. von Shelley stood there for a moment, sighed happily, and continued to speak. "Many of our test subjects have failed, we believe, because none of them willingly volunteered for our procedures. Therefore, I am giving you the opportunity to be different. I only have a few more options if this doesn't work and I really don't want to use them." Terry muttered through his hazy mind, "No, Quake, don't do it." Dr. von Shelley ignored him and said, "The clock is ticking Mr. Ragnorock, time to make your decision." Quakes pain and anguish were immeasurable. He would rather die than have Diana live with the monster he had been living with all these years. He looked Dr. von Shelley in the eyes, and said, "Yes." Dr. von Shelley nodded at a technician. The helmet above Quake lowered onto his head followed by the sounds of whirring machinery as metal tore into flesh and bone and Quakes screams of agony.

Dr. von Shelley sauntered over to Terry's side and nodded to another technician. A video began to play for Terry of Goldy on a table surrounded by medical staff. Dr. von Shelley appeared in scrubs, mask and gloves on the screen. The doctor watched Terry to gauge his reaction to the monitor. Dr. von Shelley performed a cesarean section on Goldy to deliver their baby. Once she had removed the child, the staff left Goldy on the table and focused all their attention on the child. Terry went berserk and fought against his restraints. As he screamed and cried out, Dr. von Shelley calmly said, "Don't worry Terry, you and Quake will heal from your procedures. Goldy, didn't fare so well, but the infant is doing nicely. Dr. von Shelley looked back at the screen and Terry's eyes automatically followed. His child, a boy, was in an incubator with tubes and needles all over him.

"The infant is a medical miracle. It survived the extraction and it looks like it may have some special traits of its own." On screen, the baby's body quivered as Dr. von Shelley administered a light electrical shock to it. The newborn began to transform automatically in an effort to defend itself, though the hair and fangs withdrew quickly. "He hadn't figured out how to transmute yet, but then he was only a few minutes old. He could barely cry but his instincts are impressive."

Terry went crazy and attempted to change into a werewolf. Dr. von Shelley looked over at the medical technician. “Don’t knock him out; just give him enough to prevent him changing.” Dr. von Shelley looked at Terry. “Now Mr. Andersen, for the sake of your child, will you volunteer?” Terry looked at her, eyes glazing over from the drugs, “Never,” he defiantly responded and then passed out. Dr. von Shelley looked at the medical technician and said, “What the hell?” The technician shrugged his shoulders, as if to say, “Who knew that amount would knock him out?”

SELF-PRESERVATION

Chuck's anger and contempt for Dr. von Shelley intensified watching her behavior. He hoped his crew would arrive soon. He spied the one armed man he had bumped into in the hall and watched him walk over to the electronic medical cabinet.

Sal had seen enough. He couldn't take watching any more of this travesty of medical privilege. He realized he needed to help the pack and decided to figure out a way to free them and help Diana. During the commotion when Terry passed out and Quakes operation, no one noticed him. Sal made his way over to the cabinet, waited for a technician to retrieve some medications and enter the code. When the technician walked away, he tucked the dangling shirtsleeve of his re-growing arm, in the doorframe. Though it sounded as if it had closed, Sal made sure it hadn't. When no one was looking, he opened the cabinet, grabbed one vial and one retractable auto-lock syringe; he surreptitiously concealed the items and then calmly made his way to the exit. Before he left the room, the same jerk he'd bumped into earlier bumped into him again. "Jeez!" he thought, "You gotta be fucking kiddin' me. Is this guy blind or what?"

Chuck took notice of Sal's demeanor, attitude and missing arm. Chuck, once scarred by a dangerous monster, decided to intercept the one armed man. He purposely bumped into Sal, and saw the vials and syringes he was holding. Right away Chuck knew he needed one of them to help Ray-Rae. Mack arrived and Chuck signaled her to follow the one armed man. Dr. von Shelley happened to notice the silent communication between the Hunters. Chuck loved his crew and felt a special connection with them all.

They were close enough to finish each other's sentences and really understood each other's quirks and moods. Chuck knew they all felt his sense of urgency for getting out of this place. Before that happened, all hell broke loose, again.

Dr. von Shelley had seen Sal leave with Mack following discreetly behind him. She turned her attention to the technician controlling Terry's functions. She instructed him not to administer any more drugs and notify her when he was awake. She needed Terry's compliance right away. She was about to leave the room when Chuck stopped her. "Hey, what's goin' on with Ray-Rae?" Chuck asked. "I am heading that way now, Chuck." Dr. von Shelley responded, sounding annoyed and impatient. "Really, without the antidote?" He pressed. Dr. von Shelley looked around and stepped closer so only Chuck could hear her. "Have you ever considered fortifying the Hunters with a supernatural genome?" Chuck was stunned. "Look, the Institute could build an elite special forces pack. With Ragnorock as muscle and Andersen for brains, the possibilities are limitless." Chuck knew he was right about her. "Are you fucking crazy? Go to hell Doc!" Enraged, he turned and stalked away.

TERRY'S ESCAPE

Terry had faked passing out in hopes that the staff would stop pumping drugs into him and it worked. The moon was not in its full cycle but it was close enough to draw strength. Terry began to feel the drugs wearing off and knew he would feel stronger within a few minutes. Terry was furious. He was hurt, too, but he refused to let anyone, especially this woman, victimize him ever again. Terry had been a victim most of his life, though usually of his own self-doubt and self-hatred. In the past, he'd clung to too many nonproductive ideas, using his humble beginnings, skin color and his dead twin as excuses to feel sorry for himself. He'd relished in the reactions he received when people learned he had grown up poor and until recently, he had been feeling sorry for himself over having Globes Disease.

Through his relationship with Goldy, Terry had finally come to realize that it didn't matter what you looked like or where you came from. All humans had to decide how they would live with a given challenge. Right now, it boiled down to Terry; deciding whether he would live with integrity and self-worth, would he be there for the people he loved and would he be dependable to those who had come to rely on him.

Terry feared the unknown more than anything, but he resolved to commit to taking a stand, even without knowing the outcome. Terry had defiantly refused Dr. von Shelley because he believed he could save his family, his friends, his pack. Terry realized that, by taking no action, the things that did occur may not affect him, but they would affect all those he knew. The people he loved and cherished depended on him and were suffering. The question was how much would they suffer and for how long? Terry knew inaction was not an option or he would lose all of them. His child, Diana, Sal and Jodi needed help. Terry wanted to kill that bitch for what she had done to them all.

Through the rage and pain, Terry began to change. Alarms went off, needles, catheters and tubes dislodged from his body, and the silver-lined restraints snapped. The neck and the torso straps broke first. The dark side was creeping in, but continuously Terry repeated, "Save the family, save the pack, kill the doctor," to himself.

Before Dr. von Shelley could even give commands, Terry was off the gurney. She turned to Chuck, but he was gone. The technicians had all scattered. Someone had enough sense to hit the general alarm. She watched as the enormous black Dire wolf tore through staff members like they were weeds, ripping their heads off, tearing them in half, shaking them like rag dolls and spitting them out. The screams, the ripping flesh and crushing of bones was nauseatingly frightening. He was coming for her and she knew it. She ran over to Quake's console and checked the screen. Panic welled up in her as she saw the operation was only 75% complete but she needed time to flee. The screen flashed a command prompt and blinking cursor. She frantically typed "QUAKE ENGAGE" and tapped the enter button, just as she felt the body heat from the dark creature that stood behind her. The Dire beast slobbered saliva and blood all over her and the console. Dr. von Shelley, fearing it was too late, closed her eyes and waited for an excruciating death.

Pop! Pop! Pop! Dr. von Shelley heard the sound of the gun behind her as she cowered in fear. Terry's wolf yelped and growled. Casanova had inadvertently saved her. She heard Chuck yell something and the gunfire ceased, giving her enough time to drop to the floor and crawl under a console. She was soaked with sweat, fear, flesh, blood, and werewolf saliva. She dry heaved, whether from fright or the stinking muck, she didn't know. Terry had turned to see who had fired on him. Chuck was at the doorway, beckoning Casanova to get the hell out of there. Casanova exited and holstered his weapon. Chuck yelled, "Are you crazy? We're outta here, don't save that bitch, leave her to die with her science experiments!" Casanova nodded his understanding. Chuck asked, "You find the plans, codes and keys?" "Yep," responded Casanova with his back to the doorway. He reached in his pocket and handed Chuck an envelope containing the USBs, disc drives with the plans, a master key and master key card. "Damn Cas, I don't know how you do this shit. You are amazing. We would be lost without you!" Chuck yelled in amazement. Casanova chuckled, "I do have a gift." They both heard roars, glass breaking, tables overturning and screams, howling and growling. The men looked at each other and agreed it was time to leave. Their first stop would be to get Ray-Rae and the Hunters would escape, as a team.

Chuck and Casanova had just turned to make their way down the hall, when the double doors flew open. Terry's huge Dire wolf bit into Casanova's neck and shoulders, lifting him off the ground as blood poured and sprayed everywhere. Casanova screamed pain and tried to reach his gun but his arms were now immobile. The fact that Terry's wolf was shaking him vigorously from side to side didn't help either. Chuck turned back, reached for his gun and yelled out, "Cas!" He kneeled, took aim, and yelled, "Screw this!" Chuck concentrated, ready to fire his weapon, loaded with hollow, silver-laced bullets filled with the stronger drug combo. Chuck was ready to blast the Dire beast right through the eye and blow out its brains, if he could just get the shot. Terry continued ravaging Casanova in the doorway, violence and terror emanating from them with blood spray. Chuck took a deep breath, trying to keep his cool. He would do everything he could to save his crew. He repeated to himself, "Not another Massey, not another Massey." Milliseconds felt like a lifetime. The trigger felt like a part of him. Later, Chuck would swear he'd heard the trigger spring. Chuck was prepared to kill Terry and Casanova if he needed to.

Unexpectedly Quake appeared. He was massive and towered over Terry who was inordinately tall himself. Quake grabbed Terry from behind and hauled him backward. Terry protested. Quake had the Dire Wolf and his prey in tow. Everyone still living watched in surprise as a fight over Casanova's limp body ensued. Chuck screamed, "No!" and followed the hairy pair into the lab. As they tore at one another, Terry's Werewolf turned, Casanovas' body clenched in his blood-spattered muzzle. Casanovas neck and shoulder nearly ripped in half; his ribs were splayed open exposing a collapsed left lung and a barely inflated right one. He was barely hanging on. Just when Chuck thought all hope was lost, Casanova's right hand flinched and he aimed again, thinking he still had time, but. Quake's wolf grabbed Casanova's lower half, severing him in two. Chuck realized it was too late for Casanova and he would be foolish to shoot at them. Redirecting their wrath onto him would put him at a severe disadvantage. He knew the wolves had decimated the staff in the lab and Dr. von Shelley was among the few left. She was shivering under a console, covered in blood and gore, her pleading eyes staring at Chuck. He stared back at Dr. von Shelley with contempt and hatred in his heart. He said, "I blame you Doc, I blame you." Crossing himself, he exited the lab and headed for the double doors, leaving Dr. von Shelley to the same fate as Casanova.

SHOWDOWN 2

Quake was out of his mind. He couldn't control his brain or body. As a Werewolf, he was already not himself, deeply savage and full of bloodlust. He was always on the edge of complete animalistic ruthlessness, yet Quake somehow knew he was not behaving how he normally would. Somehow, part of his brain had disengaged from his body and the instructions his brain was receiving from the electronic stimulation made killing Terry a priority. Quake's restraints had released and he was standing, but the operation was too recent and the pain was excruciating. He grabbed his head and let out a yell, his skull and brain were on fire and all he could think of was slaying Terry. This awakened his beast and he began to transform.

Terry had gone to a place he tried never to go. He was enraged and berserk. He wanted to and nearly did kill all those in the lab. If he could have, he would have killed everyone in the Institute, especially that bitch, Dr. von Shelley. Unbelievable pain in his back, from bullet wounds, interrupted his rampage and further ignited his mania. His mantra, save the family, save the pack, kill the doctor, still echoing in his head urged him as he fought to overcome the silver and drugs working their way into his system. He was distracted, briefly, by Quake waking and stumbling off his gurney. Through his pain, Terry witnessed Quake yell, clutch at his head and then transform into his werewolf. Terry followed the shooter through the double doors, surprising Chuck and Casanova. Terry's dire wolf bit into the shoulder and neck of the nearest man, fully intent on incapacitating and killing his catch. He lifted the man who had shot him and shook him.

Once Quake was mobile, he was on a mission to engage Terry. When Quake's werewolf had completed his change, he saw Terry tearing into another human. Quake attacked and pulled them back through the doorway. Quake had to fulfill his overwhelming need to kill Terry, but his blood lust was just enough more powerful; He had to get some of the kill as well. The squish, squash and crunch of blood, flesh, bones, and entrails echoed through the lab. Between Casanova's screaming and his blood spilling out of Terry's mouth, splatting on the floor, the temptation was too much to resist and sent Quake over the edge. Spinning Terry around, he too bit into the human. Together they tore at the body like two dogs fighting over raw meat. The screaming stopped when the body gave way at the waist. Quake now had a share in the kill.

Terry had nearly finished with Casanova when Quake attacked him. There were only tattered bloody scraps left. They hit the floor, cracking it from the impact of their combined weight, sliding in human blood and guts. Quake bit at Terry; Terry clawed back. The air filled with the sounds of gnashing teeth, claws, pained howls, barks and growls as flying bits of flesh and fur billowed out from the skirmish. Terry was looking for any opportunity to get his hands on the gadgets overriding Quake's brain. Terry dug his claws into Quakes ears and eyes and squeezed the soft tissue. Quake, further infuriated by the excruciating pain stood up, with Terry hanging on tenaciously. Terry's determination to get the advantage over his larger opponent paid off as he managed to get himself around the back of Quake. There were metal bits, micro-cameras and miniature computer parts attached to Quake's skull. Tubes and wires were weaved into his ears and temple. Somehow, the Institute had found a way to jack into the brain and take control of its subjects using ears as microphones and eyes as cameras for their organic technology. Terry tore and ripped at the parts wildly, causing Quake to pause in confusion. Quake's Were quickly went back to slashing at Terry on his back.

In his mind, Quake somehow understood that Terry was trying to free him from his psycho-electronic shackles, but he still had no control. His instincts were to be in control of his own body and mind and he knew he needed to stop fighting. As Terry ripped away at the foreign objects in his skull, Quake felt himself transitioning from organic robot to werewolf to human. Nonetheless, Quake also realized that anyone left, who might be watching, needed to believe he had carried out his last command to exterminate Terry. Quake's first consideration was preservation of the pack. He needed to get free, find Diana and regroup so he could make the bastards at the Institute pay. He let Terry continue tearing away on his back until he heard and felt a high-pitched ping followed by a screech that dropped him to the floor. Quake could feel his human struggling against his werewolf; he was losing the thinking part of himself, slipping back into a destructive, mindless killer. Before completing his transition, Quake commanded his feral side to wait out the urge for self-defense. Once the seconds passed, Quake was ready to battle again. He let out a horrific howl, reached behind his head, grabbed hold of Terry and flipped him over his shoulders, slamming him to the floor. It seemed as if the whole building shook from the impact. Knocked unconscious, Terry ceased fighting and Quake promptly stepped on Terry's chest and howled in triumph. Then Quake's wolf bent down and bit Terry's werewolf on the neck and shoulders.

CHAOS & DISORDER

Chuck was chasing Mack, who was in hot pursuit of Sal, as alarms continued to blare. "Screw von Shelley, screw her agenda," Chuck said to himself. His focus was on saving the rest of his team and hightailing it out of there. He had to shake off all thoughts of Casanova's annihilation. Otherwise, he wouldn't be effective. Chuck caught up with Mack at a corner of one of the many hallways, as she was peaking around it. Chaos was evident everywhere in the facility with staff and security making every effort to gain control of the patients and respond to the alarms. There was yelling and howling coming from every direction. Chuck looked over Mack's shoulder and they saw Sal enter Ray-Rae's room. He exited quickly, as if he had entered the wrong room and went in the next door. He reappeared with an older woman who was injured and shivering; much like Ray-Rae had been earlier. Diana was hot, sweaty and in pain, she looked up at Sal, "P-please get my new friend Ray-Rae out as well." Sal hesitated briefly before running back and getting Ray-Rae. Sal asked Diana, "Where's Goldy?" Diana struggled to answer, before she managed to say, "I-I don't know." The women each leaned into one of his shoulders. Sal told them, "I will get you out of here and then go back to find Goldy. Mack and Chuck looked at one another as if to say, "Now what do we do?"

Chuck said, "Mack, you go and find Adonis and Low Key, they should be waiting for us with transports and additional weapons by now." Before she could get moving, Mack stopped and handed Chuck a master key card and a master key. "Hey, when did you get these?" Mack winked at Chuck. "You 'ole pick-pocket you. You could steal a guy's cock and he wouldn't notice." Chuck said with a smile. Mack responded with a quick, gentle kiss to his cheek, "You're such a charmer." Chuck continued to speak, this time with authority, "We'll meet at the rendezvous point." Chuck looked into Mack's eyes and grabbed her by the shoulders; "We are not Hunters right now. We need to focus on salvaging the team. Got it?" Mack nodded and responded, "Roger, I got it."

Dr. von Shelley was relieved that one of the Hunters had saved her. She was even more pleased that Terry and Quake's werewolves were preoccupied with fighting over the body of that same hero. She neither knew nor cared to know his name. All that mattered to her was that his sacrifice had given her time to crawl out of the lab. She needed to get control of the situation, collect, catalog and protect the information she had accumulated. The American and Canadian government bigwigs weren't going to take kindly to yet another incident at the Institute. They would shut them down and erase any traces of the program she'd worked so hard to keep afloat. If she could get to the control room, she could take charge, put the Institute on lockdown and initiate a kill order for all the Weres loose in the building and on the grounds. If she could get a look at the cameras and get a better feel of what was going on, she would be able to make decisions that are more effective and regain order. Dr. von Shelley repeatedly radioed the control room, but there was no answer to her calls; this seriously annoyed her. Catching sight of Chuck, she followed him, soon realizing he was following Salvatore Dario. She knew Sal had absconded with some antidote vials earlier and she was not happy about one of her own successful volunteers being a turncoat. She decided she needed to get to her office, secure her records and get to the control room. Dr. von Shelley would deal with Sal soon enough but first damage control was paramount.

SAL'S NOT-SO-GREAT ESCAPE

Sal took Diana and Ray-Rae out through one of the many double door exits that led out of the east side of the building. They made their way into the woods, crossed over a creek and went to a little known cabin. Sal figured Diana and Ray-Rae could hide out there, temporarily at least, until he could safely get them back to La Mort Douce. Though Sal knew how the damage to the cabin door occurred, he said nothing. He figured that no one would be worried about the place with everything else that was going on. Showing them the basement, he pointed out all the basic supplies, a first aid kit, non-perishable food, bedding and explained that it served as a safe hideout as well. Sal handed Diana the syringe, bid them farewell and headed back to the Institute. Once inside he went straight to the control room. Amid all the chaos, he was certain that his lack of security clearance would not be an issue. He intended to lock the place down, with the large, red Werewolf inside, locate Terry, preferably alive, and then find Goldy.

Once he was within sight of the control room, Sal watched from a nearby doorway as staff ran hither and yon. He figured it was just a matter of time before someone needed to use the lavatory. Time seemed to pass very slowly, though it had only been a few minutes. "Jeez, ain't someone gotta pee in there?" He mumbled exasperatedly. His patience paid off, and Dr. von Shelley exited the room, giving orders as she left. Fortunately, the end of the hallway was only a few feet away. When she turned the corner, Sal caught the door before it closed. He quietly walked in and found one man working at a computer. The console was straight out of a sci-fi movie. The technician had on a headset and was speaking continuously into the microphone, and never noticed Sal's presence.

Sal knew he had to be quick. Transforming in to his Were would have been fun and easier, but it would have been a lot messier that way. Besides, he wasn't entirely sure that he could completely control his beast as Goldy had been trying to teach him. He snuck up to the technician, grabbed him in a headlock, jabbed him with a tranquilizer-filled syringe and dropped the man onto the floor.

Sitting at the computer, Sal went to work looking for details about von Shelley. He discovered she'd grown up in Geneva, educated at the University in Ingolstadt, Germany. After which, she returned to Geneva to marry. Eventually she took over research begun by her great grandfather of five generations prior. What Sal read made his mouth drop. He thought, "I shouldn't be surprised, since my own life has stretched the limits of what people accept as reality." A Werewolf had bitten Sal and a Vampire had ripped his arm off, so he hadn't thought anything else could surprise him, until now and it spilled out of his mouth in typical Sal fashion. "You gotta be fuckin' kidding me!"

Sal was distracted from copying the information into email, by what he saw on some of the other monitors. A POV camera from Quake's implants showed him carrying Terry and the baby in the direction of the cabin. "Scratch containing the big red Werewolf." Sal mumbled sarcastically. Another was replaying of a fight between Terry and Quake. Yet another screen showed a room with Goldy in it. He reacted quickly and released the electronic locks to her room. Getting back to business, he typed in the email address of his intended recipient. That was as far as he got.

Sal had experienced a lot of pain in his life. He'd endured numerous altercations hanging out at the Italian clubs and hot spots in the old neighborhood. He had been in plenty of fights with idiots who dared to come to his part of town. He'd torn a bicep once playing sports. The bite that had made him a Werewolf had been excruciating, and the pain had been blinding when Vlad ripped his arm off.

This trumped everything he had ever experienced. It was like a sledgehammer and a burning hot poker simultaneously crashing into him. Sal heard a pop and saw a flash, but when he opened his eyes, only one was functioning. The other felt as though it was on fire and hot liquid was flowing down his face from it. He saw the gore on the screen in front of him and smelled the silver nitrate burning through his blood stream. He felt like he was cooking from the inside out. Before Sal could comprehend what had occurred he saw Dr. von Shelley's reflection in the monitor. She stood behind him with a grin, a gun and his blood splattered all over her. His final act, completed through sheer will power, was to press the enter button on the keyboard, sending the email with all the information he had gathered. Sal's last thought was, "God, I hate that woman!" Dr. von Shelley stepped in closer, and fired her gun again, exploding Sal's skull through his face.

WHAT NOW?

Chuck and Mack followed Sal and the two women out of the building. Wary of a possible ambush, they were heavily armed. Giving the small group a wide berth, they tracked them through the woods to a cabin. Sal left a short time later and as soon as it was clear, they rushed into the cabin to find Ray-Rae and Diana, both still in pain from their injuries, talking. Diana administered the antidote to Ray-Rae as she was talking. "You're young; you still have your whole life ahead of you and now you have a second chance. You have to stop ruining people's lives and taking pleasure in their deaths. You must learn to nurture, preserve and give life. Then maybe you'll be as lucky as I have been. I've experienced the greatest love any woman could ever hope for, from the most loving and caring person ever to walk the face of the earth." Chuck and Mack were astonished as they realized Diana had made huge a sacrifice using the syringe Sal left with her on Ray-Rae. Diana startled at their presence and was immediately afraid. She stood up, faced the Hunters and thought, "What now?"

Recognizing her fear, Chuck was quick to reassure Diana that they meant her no harm. Low-Key and Adonis arrived just then and the tension grew. Unsure of what they had walked in on, the two giants with the Were-baby simply stood there. Diana ran over and held out her arms for the child. Chuck gave a nod of assent and a relieved Diana backed away clutching the child. She was wondering how they had come to have Terry and Goldy's baby and asked what had happened and if they knew where Goldy, Terry or Quake was. Before anyone could answer, a booming thud shook the cabin. Diana knew it could be none other than Quake. He entered the cabin, part man and part Were, with tattered electronic parts hanging from his bleeding skull, covered in flesh, entrails, blood and a body flung over his shoulder. He unceremoniously dropped Terry to the floor and a shocked silence fell over the room. The Hunters stood between Quake and Diana, still holding the Were-baby.

Quake looked around the room, taking stock of the scene. He said, "This looks like a stalemate. Diana, take care of the baby and Terry. I am going to look for the antidote, but I've also got more killing to do!" He let out a maniacal howling laugh and leaned into the room. Fixing a glare on the Hunters, He snarled, "You all got a problem with that?" Chuck looked around the room and said, "As far as I'm concerned, you take care of your folks and I will take care of mine." Quake stood to his full height, bumping his head on the ceiling. He said, "Great, happy hunting." With that, he turned, lumbered off the porch and headed back towards the Institute. Chuck looked back at Diana with concern on his face, and asked, "Are you gonna be okay?" When she nodded in the affirmative, he turned to his team and said, "Grab Ray-Rae and let's get the fuck outta here."

DR. VON SHELLEY

Dr. von Shelley entered her office, escaping all the commotion. In her private bath, she washed her hands and face, fixed her hair and changed her lab coat. At her computer, she sat down, confirmed her file backup, ejected the discs, removed the flash drive and took a deep breath. The gun she had used to kill the turncoat, Salvatore Dario, was still in her pocket. She thought, "What a waste!" She'd been waiting for his arm to grow back so she could enter him into the program. Sal would have made a great werewolf soldier. She thought, what better way to hunt prey than to use its own kind? The bedlam outside her door was distracting and frustrating, but it was beyond her control. Unfortunately, she was going to have to abandon the facility. The cooperating governments would have to come in and scrap the project and after that last videoconference with Austin, it was more than likely they would erase any trace of the Institute.

Dr. von Shelley knew she would have to take whatever she could carry and seek out private sponsorship. She sighed as she considered her selling points. First, she had an antidote, and recorded how to duplicate the process. Second, she had Vlad and Oksana's DNA. Third, she had recorded enough damning material that if the bigwigs tried to defame her she could strike back. Knowing the Generals and the Chiefs, they wouldn't want to play that game; elimination would be their agenda. As far as von Shelley was concerned, she needed more time for tests and research to prove she was on the right track. The project really needed to be smaller and more personal. Right now, time was not a luxury. Surely the government's would send a cleanup crew and everything she'd worked for would be taken from her if she didn't get everything she could beforehand.

Dr. von Shelley considered the possibility of a contingency program. If she could find someone newly infected with Globes Disease or even find a 'willing' human to infect with both types of supernatural DNA she possessed. If she could do that, perhaps she would have a chance to tie up some loose ends here in La Mort Douce and minimize some of the losses. She just needed to avoid the angry Weres, disgruntled Hunters and government officials she had recently failed. She could go to the cabin and hole up there for a while. After Harold's escape, she and a few others had decided to outfit the basement bunker with supplies, just in case there was ever a need and this situation certainly qualified. It was time to leave before the cleanup team arrived. The cabin was off the books and hardly anyone knew it existed, making it the perfect sanctuary.

GOLDY'S ESCAPE

Goldy awoke strapped to a gurney, groggy, nauseated and in excruciating pain. As she came to a bit more, she remembered and wondered what they had done to her baby? The aching, cramping and bleeding in her abdomen accentuated her overwhelming grief, gruesome reminders that her child was missing, maybe even dead. This heartbreak was different from any she had known before, because this time she had been happy beyond anything she had ever felt before. Goldy sobbed as heartfelt tears stung her eyes.

As she lay there in agony, a video began to play of Dr. von Shelley; a tall, thin lipped, tight jawed, strong-shouldered woman, with blonde hair pulled back in a severe bun, wearing her usual lab coat. Dr. von Shelley was performing a caesarian on Goldy. Watching the screen intently, Goldy's rabidity ignited and burned deep within her. Dr. von Shelley extracted the baby, and her staff immediately began prodding him with electric shocks and poking needles into his tiny body. This filled Goldy with hatred such as she had never known before. She fought against her restraints; enraged she couldn't concentrate on her breathing and began to lose control.

Goldy screamed, "Where is Terry, where is my husband? Why did you take my baby?" The video changed and Goldy watched as Dr. von Shelley made her ridiculous offer to Terry and Quake and all that followed.

Goldy howled hysterically, nearing the brink of change as she fought against her restraints. Just when she thought she couldn't go on, the electronic doors clicked open. The sound gave her renewed hope and she ripped and tore at her restraints with even more resolve.

Werewolf or not, Goldy knew she would never heal from the suffering that Dr. von Shelley had inflicted on her or from the damage she had just inflicted upon herself. Eventually Goldy fully completed the transformation and managed to break free. She landed hard in a puddle of blood. Frenzied and crazed, she let out a high-pitched wail, calling for her newborn child, hoping that either the baby or Terry would respond. As Goldy's wolf bounded through the hallways of the Institute, she killed every human in her path. She'd lost husband, child and now her mind. The killings were merely retribution for all she'd lost. As she ripped through human after human, headed for the exit, it was clear Goldy was on a mission.

THE DEN

THE HUNT

The mid-September chill of La Mort Douce's evening air bit at the exposed skin of a young hunter in his early twenties. He was walking south to the hunting grounds, near the Montagne du Loup (Mountains of Purpose) and Le Petit Lac de Vostok, fully dressed in winter hunting gear. An orange balaclava covered his blond hair, blue eyes and angelic face, though his gloves weren't as thick as he normally would have liked, but he needed to shoot accurately. He had lost track of time chasing down a medium sized wolf and hadn't anticipated being out so late. Wolf season had begun and he wanted to bring home one that he could carry on his own to impress his father and three older brothers. He felt confident, having been out with them numerous times before, enough to bag one on his own.

The young hunter was a star athlete and the first of his friends to get a job, even if it was with the construction company where his father and brothers worked. Things generally came easy to him. He would follow his family's path, like those before him and was eager to do so. He knew and understood a life of hunting, fishing, working, and making children. It is what being a man is about.

The young hunter saw her at the southern end of Le Petit Lac de Vostok. She was tall and thin, with a long, thick sable coat that was silky and un-matted. Such a beautiful wolf would make his first solo kill even more special. He aimed and took a shot; but it only wounded her and he realized immediately that he should have moved in closer. When she jumped up and headed off towards the mountains.

He briskly made the 300-yard trek to the other side of the lake and followed her footprints to the base of Montagne du Loup. The closer he got, the more excited he felt. He was in shape, but he was aware that the elements had bested men ten times his measure. He knew he would have to finish off this wolf soon and get her home, so his family could help him skin and prep her.

The tracks led to a grotto at the base of the mountain. He stopped and looked at the setting sun. Something was nagging at him but he pushed it away, intent on completing this task. He kneeled down, got out his flashlight and immediately spied the female lying about 15 feet in, against the end wall, whimpering. Several cubs were hiding behind her. The young hunter looked at her long and hard. He didn't like that the feeling he had suppressed was rearing up again. Standing, he turned off his flashlight and decided to leave her be.

He suddenly had the feeling that something was behind him, so he turned around cautiously. He could see nothing but the lake and the tracks the wolf and he had made. Shaking it off, he turned to thoughts of home, warmth and the meal waiting for him. Shouldering his rifle, he began to head back when a thought struck him. His brothers would wonder why he hadn't finished off a perfectly good adult wolf, puppies or not. He had been the baby all his life and he couldn't take the thought of that. One thing he excelled at was succeeding beyond all their accomplishments. He broke more records, scored more points and out fought all his opponents trying to keep up with them. Ultimately, he could not give away this chance at victory. He turned around, walked the few feet back to the mouth of the cave and kneeled on the ground. The wolf was growling now and he changed his mind again. He really didn't want to crawl in there to bring her corpse out. Besides, just the thought of leaving the cubs orphaned left a bad taste in his mouth. He walked a few feet away before he stopped once again, as thoughts of his brothers lambasting him for being a wuss invaded his mind again.

Lying down on the rocks and dirt, he set his flashlight on a rock next to him, shining into the cave. He positioned the rifle, taking aim at the wolf. She growled with more ferocity and the sounds reverberated around him, making it seem as if there were more than one animal. It was unsettling and her snarl gave him chills. He closed one eye and positioned his finger. He was a heartbeat from firing when the wolf stood up, filling the cave and casting a huge protective shadow over the cubs. The young hunter got another good look at her and he realized he had made a fundamental mistake that could very well cost him his life. She wasn't bleeding and he had followed footprints to the grotto, not blood. Judging from the sounds behind him and the sinking feeling in the pit of his stomach, he was the prey. Moments later, he felt the excruciating pain of teeth chomping down on his legs, yanking him from the mouth of the cave.

He was on his stomach and utterly vulnerable. The ripping and tearing at his legs and back immediately trumped the initial pain. The yips, howls and growls of his attackers completely drowned out his screams and before long, he was exhausted from fighting against the agony. His bones broke, ligaments popped, muscles tore, sides sliced open and viscera ripped out. His coat shredded, the down feathers floated in pools of red with bits of his flesh on the cold ground in front of him. His eyes couldn't help but focus on it. He was delirious, but in his final moments, he looked back at the cave and saw what looked like a human shadow. Before he could look around, the wolf he had so diligently hunted launched out of the cave, instantly ripping at his face. The young hunter could cry out no more, he could only hear his last breaths gurgling. Soon, pain ceased to matter. A chorus of wolf howls and gnashing teeth ushered him into the abyss of death.

VIKTORIA & OKSANA

Viktoria Mary von Shelley was irritated. She hated videoconferences, especially when they were with the two government agencies to which she was beholden. These North Americans had a sense of entitlement that irked her and yet they were essential to her plans, so she tolerated them. At present, Canada and America had the money and means to help her accomplish what she wanted to achieve.

Viktoria preferred to do things as she saw fit, without the interruptions that came with having overseers. Nevertheless, she continually made compromises in order to pursue her experiments. She liked to delegate uninteresting duties as much as possible, reserving her brainpower for her own 'special projects'. The current state of things made it impossible for her to avoid getting her hands dirty. The mysterious visitor sitting in her office irked Viktoria. Her cadaverous guest was looking for answers, thus making things even more complicated and intense for Viktoria. The pressure from the constantly beeping call screen, compounded by the impending danger she felt from the striking alabaster creature sitting in her office, weighed on her. The woman was tall; broad shouldered, with strong features, angled eyebrows, jet-black hair and dark glossy red lips that starkly contrasted her skin. The woman's upper body was an inverted triangle, with ample breasts giving shape to her hipless frame. It was obvious she was Russian.

Russia was over 1800 Kilometers from Ingolstadt, Germany, where Viktoria went to college. Russia and Germany, two super-power enemies in World War I, had become modern day energy allies. The two countries had a long and sordid history older than the United States itself. The General expected the doctor to answer the video call, and despite this dangerous woman sitting before her, Viktoria felt it vital to do so.

"Forgive me Oksana, this is a very important call and I really must take it. I do hope you understand." Viktoria delivered this in her most polite voice. Oksana was as gracious as any cold-hearted bitch could be, nodding and waving her off, as she would a mere peon, while she replayed the video of the Vlad massacre. Viktoria didn't like it. In fact, the flagrant dismissal was the deepest of insults. Regardless, she pushed down her fear of Oksana in order to attend to business. Besides, it bought her time to determine her advantage, assuming she had one. The call did not start well. General Austin's face loomed large on the screen before her and he didn't look happy, at all. Austin was a gruff, bulldog faced, African American man with an air of strength. It took considerable effort not to let him shake her countenance.

At some point Viktoria realized that General Austin could not see Oksana and had to hide her surprise. "You really screwed the pooch this time doctor," rumbled Austin, "I hope we don't have to come down there and clean up your mess. That would cost a lot more money and we would be forced to take over your little project; maybe even shut you down altogether." Viktoria's stomach clenched, as she understood the implication of Austin's words. The last thing she needed was officials from two governments descending upon La Mort Douce. The town, more like an asylum run by its inmates, was perfect for what she needed; the organized chaos allowed her control. She responded, "Look General, we have a good plan, it just needs more time and work." Austin interrupted, "Personally, I want to see a plan to eradicate and cure this shit, not this genetic, DNA, chip merging crap you proposed. I don't think using those freak animals as soldiers, spies or factory drones for that matter is a good idea.

What I have seen on the videos doesn't indicate much progress. These dogs ought to be put down." Oksana chimed in and said, "I agree," in her thick Russian accent. Viktoria was briefly panic-stricken, but the General continued speaking as though he hadn't heard.

"What the hell is with this new name for Lycanthropy anyway? A werewolf is still a God-damned werewolf, right?" "Because General," Viktoria interrupted, "Globes Disease is a global phenomenon, hence the name. This is not something that just affects one fabled town, nor is it a horror movie, an old wives tail or a curse. It is a disease and if we give it a global connotation, it will help bring global acceptance. In some cases, it doesn't have to be night or a full moon. If so inclined a werewolf could change anytime anywhere on this planet. Remember, the effect of the moon on a Lycanthrope occurs whether it is visible or not. The intensity of the disease fluctuates based on the tug of war between the moon and earth. It is the same as how tides are affected." Viktoria paused and attempted to simplify her explanation, she spoke slower this time. "The moon is a big round bright globe in the sky that's highly visible when it's full. "Globes Disease" sounds a lot better than "Full Moon Disease" and is easier to say than Lycanthrope.

Austin stared at the screen blankly, realizing he was debating an issue he had no control over. Orders were orders, no matter what he thought. "Look, do what you have to do with your research. Take your killing machines and turn them into obedient soldiers. Grow spies from embryos or whatever voodoo you do. Ultimately, they are nothing more than furry four legged sharks. Once they taste human blood, they will want more. Just know that when that happens, I will do anything and everything to protect American voters and taxpayers, the Canadians be damned. Besides, they don't have nearly the funding we have." Austin smiled at the sarcasm in his diatribe, "Listen Doctor, you are on very shaky ground and one misstep away from having the plug pulled on your little operation! Make no mistake, we will come to La Mort Douce, shut you down and take out all known supernaturals if we have to. You have the means to cure some of them; we have the means to kill them. Fix it or we will!" With that, Austin disconnected.

Viktoria's annoyance grew as she realized that Oksana continued to replay the video of Vlad's demise. She took a deep breath, turned around and smiled. "Nice trick you have there. How come he couldn't hear or see you?" Without looking up, Oksana responded, "The same reason this video shows an invisible man fighting and killing. It is known as Obfuscation" Viktoria immediately understood. She thought to herself "Of course, when you are dealing with anything outside the realm of conventional science, everything is possible, even folklore and superstition." When Oksana finally got bored with looking at the recording, she stood up with grace and purpose. She leaned in close to Viktoria and looked deep into her eyes with the intensity of a true hunter. "I will deal with the dogs my way, the Institute can deal with them your way and the government agencies you work for can handle things however they wish. I am here for one purpose and one purpose only, to avenge my lover Vladimir Romanov and eradicate the mutts responsible from this earth. Are you going to help me?"

Viktoria's fear was instantaneous but the scientist in her reared up and savored the moment. Viktoria hadn't been able to collect enough useful DNA from Vlad. She quickly walked around her desk, opened a drawer and pulled out some blank blood sample slides, a syringe and some vials. Viktoria was always prepared. Turning to Oksana, she said, "I am more than willing to help you. You can use anything I have that might assist you in your quest for revenge. Would you kindly give me something in return?" Viktoria displayed the items from her drawer, "Would you donate some blood samples to my research?" Oksana looked curiously at the items as Viktoria continued, "I am, after all, a scientist." Oksana shrugged her shoulders and said, "Why not."

GENERAL AUSTIN

General Austin was not happy about the news he'd received about that shitty little town, La Mort Douce. He briefly considered blowing it off the map, but there was no justifying that, yet. A missing town and multitudes of dead civilians, no matter how insignificant, would not be good PR for the military. Between camera phones, email, texting and social networking, it was damn near impossible to go 'deep cover' with anything nowadays. Austin wanted to keep the operation under US Military control. As far as he was concerned, the Canadians had screwed the pooch and their Hunters had failed—again. He'd read the report on Massey and didn't want the town known as "Sweet Death" to become the scene of yet another massacre. He wanted to hang on to Dr. von Shelley, though he would settle for her files and notes, if he had to. He needed to eliminate all traces of the Institute. Austin wanted to sequester all the Weres and quarantine the entire godforsaken township, but he would have to do it under the guise of an industrial accident. After all La Mort Douce was an energy resource town.

General Austin's priority was damage control. He would and send in the Long Range Reconnaissance Patrol, Team Red Riding Hood, to cause the 'accidental' destruction of the bridges and railways into La Mort Douce, and then he could declare Martial Law. After that, he could set up a base of operations and depot on American soil and present it as a Military relief effort. Providing the town with aid, supplies, water, and food would give the appearance of good will and paint the government in a good light. He wanted nothing more to do with this "U.S.-Canada joint venture crap." It was time he took charge and got some semblance of control over this situation. Austin needed to know who was human, who was supernatural and whether an infestation existed. Until he had those answers, he had no clue whether to the situation called for control or annihilation. Whatever swam over the border would be Canada's problem.

His next order of business would be to contact the Hunters for a full briefing about what exactly had happened. It occurred to him to take command of them, send them in to demo the Institute and bring him Dr. von Shelley. Then it would be time to debrief, decommission and deactivate the Hunters altogether with an offer of asylum to the non-Americans on the team, if they wanted it. Austin attempted contacting Chuck again, without success. He tried Dr. von Shelley as well, with the same result.

Once he'd calmed himself, he called Major Bazzo, confirmed the secure line and proceeded with their videoconference. Bazzo was a strapping, blond, steely-muscled man with powerful hands and enormous shoulders. He was model handsome and construction worker rough, yet somehow managed to remain youthful, give or take a few pounds. They'd met in boot camp, years ago. Austin thought to himself, "Mother nature can be so unfair and unkind." The two had risen through the ranks together and he trusted Bazzo. He was the kind of man who would always follow through, dependable, a good friend and a great soldier.

"Hello, General." Major Bazzo greeted Austin. "James, I need to reassign you, so I am emailing you all the information about the Institute, including all the locations in North America they occupy. The priority is in La Mort Douce. You need to get on this ASAP, so delegate all your current assignments. You will provide recon, decon, containment and control of the entire town. I don't care how you keep them in. Blame it on an industrial accident if you need a scapegoat. Even if we have to make them a separate country and force them to use passports, something definitive needs to happen. If possible, wait to see if LRRP Team Red Riding Hood is successful first. If not, have your contingency at the ready." "Roger" Bazzo affirmed.

Austin continued, "I am declaring Martial Law. Set up a relief base nearby. We will control all passage in or out of that mountainous death trap. Listen Bazzo, if there is any interference, human or supernatural deal with it using extreme prejudice, without fail. Eliminate, bribe or reprogram anyone in the way to prevent information leaks. We are dealing with werewolves and vampires and God knows what else on the loose in La Mort Douce. I don't care if it's a Unicorn, a witch or a faerie; if it doesn't cooperate with the U.S. Government, take it out!"

"If we have to, we will not only shut down the Institute, we will bomb the site and blame our 'industrial accident' for it. I hope that option is the last resort. That should just about cover all we need. Got it?" Bazzo nodded, "I got it General, consider it as good as done."

Austin loved military hierarchy. There was no emotion to the process, just efficient use of resources based on probability and cold hard calculation by the best and the most qualified. Emotions were set aside to achieve a common goal for the betterment of the country. Austin sat back and sighed, that was bullshit. He just needed to tell himself something to take his mind off the human contingency. His orders would undoubtedly affect innocent people, but as far as Austin was concerned, the Institute, La Mort Douce and Globes Diseases were nothing more than thorns in his ass and he needed solutions to eliminate the irritation. Austin just hoped Team Red Riding Hood was the solution.

JEB HOGSCLAW

It was late and cold. Jeb had just sat down after working his farm all day. He was cranky, dirty, hungry and too tired to take a shower. It was only September, but the uncomfortably cold nights had come early this season. Hearing a commotion outside, Jeb thought, "What now?" The animals had suddenly become agitated; horses were stomping and neighing, sheep were bleating, dogs were barking and the cows were lowing. "Darn wolves," Jeb mumbled. He went to the window and looked out into the darkness. He squinted and stared, but saw nothing. Realizing he needed a better view, Jeb sighed, slipped into his loafers and walked to the door. Putting on his boots would have taken too long and now Jeb was in a hurry to see what the ruckus was. Something didn't feel right.

He took a deep breath, opened the door, grabbed his rifle and stepped out into the crisp air. Looking at the crescent moon, reminded him of when the Institute had eradicated the town of another wolf problem. Still, Jeb knew he couldn't be too careful. He had hollowed out all his bullets and laced them with silver and garlic. He wasn't even sure if it would work, but he figured it was better than nothing was. Slowly and quietly, he worked his way past the barn and to the fields, his rifle up and ready. He heard growls through the racket his livestock was making. "Darn it, it is wolves." His eyes finally acclimated to the dark and what he saw before him was like nothing he had seen in his lifetime. Jeb's jaw dropped as he caught sight of a pack of wolves that had corralled a large lamb near the gate. The largest of the wolves pushed through the circling pack and approached the panic-stricken lamb. Towering over the poor creature, the wolf gently lifted the screaming creature by the nape of its neck and pranced away with it. A mother cat with a kitten wouldn't have been any less delicate.

Jeb couldn't believe his eyes. "What the heck!" he muttered, raising his rifle again. The pack looked up in unison; first at Jeb then at the crescent moon. Jeb peeked over his rifle and saw a shadowy, feminine, silhouette. She raised her hand ever so slightly towards him, as though giving an instruction. Returning his attention to the pack, he found their focus on him. Jeb's heart began racing and he steadied himself, taking aim at the large wolf trotting off with the lamb. Gripped by fear, Jeb was too slow and his shot missed. The pack was on him in seconds, toppling him over with a bone-jarring thud. The lamb continued it's bleating as the pack ripped at Jeb's flesh, his own screams echoing in his ears. The rifle hit the ground and went off. Jeb felt his organs yanked out of him. The pain and terror were mind numbing as Jeb was ushered towards his last gasps of life. The smell of Jeb's last meal, bile and blood combined with wolf saliva assailed his senses. He knew he was dying when he could no longer cry out and the pain started to dissipate. Jeb thought he heard a howl from the direction he had seen the silhouette, in those last agonizing moments before slipping into oblivion.

GOLDY

Goldy had never made love with any man the way she and Terry made love. It was like classical music, starting slow and tender; a little teasing, a lot of pleasing, building to the edge of satisfaction; just enough pleasure to stoke the fires of desire. Gradually, the fervor built until suddenly, as if directed by a conductor, they reached magnificent peaks. The rhythm of their bodies and thrumming of their hearts pounding away to the melody of blistering hot sex brought her to sweet release, repeatedly. Just when she would think she had nothing left, Terry could always elicit more from her, before their symphony achieved final crescendo, bringing Terry to such an explosive orgasm she could feel it crashing deep within her. They'd only been married a few years and it still felt titillating, as though they were secret lovers. Goldy had never been in love like this before, ever!

When Goldy exited the bathroom in a beautiful, flowing, sheer, purple and black teddy, Terry smiled at her and told her how beautiful she was. Those words made Goldy feel wonderful and sexy. She was in her third trimester and needed all the praise she could get. With both hands, she rubbed her stomach. "Sheesh, how in the world did this happen, forty-five and pregnant?" Goldy had been certain she couldn't have any more children. This was no less than a miraculous blessing. She had never been more in love than she was with Terry and she was elated to share something so wonderful with a man like him. She climbed into bed and they began to kiss, her protruding belly no hindrance. The electricity of Terry's touch connected his kisses like a conduit to every part of her that he caressed, permeating her with lust. She was ready before he was. Maybe it was the hormones or the fact that she was euphoric. She didn't care; she was completely in the moment, mind, body and spirit. Goldy only knew she longed for him to be inside her.

Being a nearly middle-aged woman and pregnant was a huge challenge, and the logistics of lovemaking made it even more of one, and they gladly met that challenge. Terry was thrilled that they continued to be intimate. He had heard stories from guys at work about their wives rejecting them in bed during pregnancy. For some reason, apart from a few weeks of morning sickness, Goldy seemed to be immune to that side effect. The contrasting sensations he felt while roaming her body were heady. Firm, heavy breasts, hard stomach, skin taunt along the muscles of her arms and thighs. Her bottom was pleasingly full and round; he hoped she wouldn't lose too much of it after the baby was born. They kissed deeply and their passion built again as they lovingly reconnected. They breathed as one, their souls aligned, the rhythm of their hearts beat in unison as their bodies began to sync. Abruptly, a loud boom interrupted their passion as their bedroom exploded with activity. Goldy screamed as a smoke bomb crashed through the window and armed men in black uniforms and masks rushed in through the doors. Three darts hit Terry before he could even think of transforming into his werewolf. Goldy's terror turned to rage that she couldn't act on. She would risk losing her child if she tried to transform. The raiders didn't shoot her with darts, since they knew she was pregnant. One of them whacked her on the head, knocking her unconscious. As she was fading, she heard a muffled voice say, "What's your problem idiot? She's pregnant! SHE is the precious cargo! The male is the expendable one, asshole!"

Goldy awoke suddenly. For months, she'd been having some variation of the same dream almost nightly. They consistently began with Terry making-love with her and ended with the attack by Hunters. Goldy felt warmth against her body and looked around to find herself surrounded by her pack, answering the question of why she was warm. Indian summer had passed and winter was methodically creeping into the area. Their collective presence kept the cold at bay.

Le Parc Moyen's flowers, plants and trees, once lush and brilliant, would soon go dormant. The peaks on Montagne du Loup were turning whiter and blew down a cool breeze in the mornings and evenings. The pack occupied a baseline cave as their den. The Le Petit Lac de Vostok, just east of the mountain, had already claimed its first victims of the season. A couple of young anglers hadn't heeded an old man's warning about when it was and wasn't safe to fish and it had cost them their lives. The lake claimed lives and fertilized the flowers, plants, trees and animals with its cool, crisp, sweet water bolstered by the town's human sacrifices. Those things no longer concerned Goldy, she was emotionally, mentally and physically in a different place and consumed with the preservation of her den.

Goldy had moved beyond the classy, socialite, Cosmo model look, now her thick mane of hair hung down her head and around her face, now covered with layers of dirt, blood and who knows what else. Beneath all that muck, her natural beauty still shone through, enough to rival most models, but her mind had disconnected from reality. Wild eyed, angry and feral, she had become matriarch to about 25 to 30 wolves.

The pack slept snuggled in tight around her, like puppies. She was the center of their focus and they did her bidding faithfully. Each of them would willingly protect her with their lives. Goldy yawned and looked up, all of their heads turned and focused on her. If she moved, they moved. If Goldy needed something, a pack member provided it as quickly as possible.

Goldy wasn't ready to rise, so she laid her head back down and the pack did the same. Goldy had distanced herself from La Mort Douce's society and created her own civilization. Le Parc de Gevaudan, mostly known as the hunting grounds, was her territory. It was a forgotten land preserve, which stretched for miles east of town, along the base of the mountains. The attack that had infected Terry occurred less than a mile from Goldy's lair. Goldy felt completely at home in her den and she wanted to sleep so she could get back to that dream. She needed that dream to remind her of why she couldn't forget that she chose this life for good reason. Her den of wolves could be trusted far more than any human. Humans only failed her. The nature of wolves was clear and simplistic. Hunt, feed, protect, mate and raise the little ones to perpetuate the cycle. Human purpose, often convoluted and treacherous, made them untrustworthy and extremely dangerous, in Goldy's opinion.

SHERIFF BRAY

Sheriff Bray pulled up to Jeb's farm and McNamera got to his patrol car before he could even put it in park and turn it off. That annoyed him to no end. He had a routine that included finishing his coffee, re-checking the computer, grabbing note pads, pen, pencil, gun, cuffs, and clipping his keys to his belt. It was 10:00 am, but his day had begun much earlier, which contributed, to his malaise. Keeping the window up, he did his best to ignore him, hoping McNamera wouldn't tap on the window and break his concentration. Bray had to complete his checklist uninterrupted.

McNamera either didn't get the hint or couldn't read the body language, so he kept trying to talk through the window even though Bray continued to ignore him. "Jeez," thought Bray, "What a freakin' busy body. The crime scene ain't going nowhere. What's the rush?" Bray took a deep breath and proceeded with his mental checklist while the deputy continued nagging outside the car.

Bray opened the door and, as McNamera was in his way, he couldn't exit his vehicle unencumbered. Bray put on his hat and glared over the top of his sunglasses, as if to say, would'ja move? McNamera got the hint after a few seconds, allowing Bray egress from his patrol car. "What have we got?" drawled Bray. "Well, Sir…" McNamera responded, somewhat excited, "It's… uhm, best you see firsthand." Bray hated TV cop show talk. Everybody here already had a gander, so it ain't no secret. "Look boy, I don't much like surprises and I am starting to get aggravated, so why don't you calm down and tell me somethin' useful." Bray cut a look of seriousness at the deputy. McNamera responded, without even realizing he was getting on the sheriffs nerves. "Well sir, what we have is another wolf attack..." Bray stopped at a tarp-covered carcass to find a pair of coroner's assistants standing ready to receive their instructions.

"So, lemme get this right... I'm here 'cuz of some slaughtered livestock? If it was a wolf, just shoot it. In fact, ain't it wolf-hunting season? Listen up, do Jeb a favor, get your hunting license and come back up this way. You and Jeb can wait for the hungry bastards to show up again and blow them away." McNamera, even more nervous and agitated than before, said, "That ain't the problem, sir." Bray popped a toothpick in his mouth as a distraction; he had recently given up cigars. Looking around he asked, "Well, what's the problem? Where the heck is Jeb, anyway?" McNamera's strained expression made it difficult to be delicate, but no one had ever accused Bray of ever being delicate. He grumped, "Well, spit it out dammit!"

McNamera nodded to the two men standing by the tarp. They uncovered what Bray had assumed was an animal, but was Jeb, or what was left of him anyway. His body was shredded, throat torn out and his face just chunks of meat, with one eye that looked like a drippy wet egg hanging from the socket. Jeb's limbs, torn off to bloody nubs and his bowels, still oozed black, sticky, goo across the ground. The tailbone sat amid left over bits of organs and feces. The scene was consistent with what a pack of wolves followed by scavengers could do to a human body. Jeb's body may have looked like it had been through a *wolf tug of war*, but Jeb's heart, obviously torn from his chest, was missing.

"Weepin' Jesus," Bray said as he crossed himself. McNamera nodded his agreement and plunged ahead with the remainder of his report. "This is the only carcass left behind. Whatever livestock the wolves got was carted off without a trace; no blood or signs of struggle." Bray spit out his toothpick and promptly pulled out a cigar. He bit off the tip, never mind a friggin' cutter. Bray spit out the tip and looked at McNamera. "And, what else?" "Come on...isn't it obvious, Sheriff? You've been here long enough to know the M.O. of the wolves here in La Mort Douce." Bray grabbed McNamera by the arm and propelled him away from the mutilated, stinking carcass. "Shush boy! Keep your crazy speculations to yourself. We don't need any more of that hysteria shit we had awhile back. The Institute eradicated those rat bastards, remember?" Bray wasn't happy and the way he moistened his stogie made that apparent.

McNamera replied, full of conviction, "Well I am telling you my gut feeling, which is telling me that those boys at the Institute ain't on the up and up. We never get to go to their building, don't know whose jurisdiction they are under and the fire department hasn't been up there for building inspections, medical calls, fire alarms and no one has gotten a speeding or a parking ticket over yonder. Why do you think that is? If the werewolves were eradicated, then what the hell do you call what happened to Jeb, Sir?"

Bray knew the truth. He just couldn't discuss it. He lit his cigar and turned his back to the wind so the smoke wouldn't get in McNamera's face. "Well son, that's private property and those boys got government ties and top secret projects, and I do mean secret, as in I Spy, burn after reading, this tape will self-destruct type stuff. I don't need to know and frankly, I don't want to know. In fact, I hope I never know what goes on over on that little island between the borders." Bray paused and took another puff, hoping to calm himself through the smoke. "Look, get your huntin' gear, rifle and a few silver laced bullets, but keep it to yourself. You and your boys go do some huntin' and get rid of the four legged and two legged sons a' bitches out there, threatening the lives and welfare of this fine town and its residents." Bray reached in his uniform pocket for his pen and pad, but they weren't there. Completely exasperated by his interrupted routine, now he didn't have his gosh darn pen and pad when he needed them. Bray let his irritation show, "God Damn it!"

"Shoot, I gotta get my pen and pad." McNamera offered him his own. Bray barked, "Keep it!" As Bray walked back to his vehicle, he wondered how he was going to explain smelling of cigars to the missus. He opened the door, sat down in the driver's seat and grabbed his pad and pen. He puffed furiously on his cigar, to the point of making himself dizzy, he then radioed in a request for CSU. Even though the population had grown significantly over the past 10 years, he still knew most of the folks that lived here. Jeb had been a schoolmate and friend, and he wasn't sure he could tell the man's parents the bad news on his own, when the time came. Bray cursed through the cigar smoke billowing around his head, "Damn! Damn! Damn!"

Despite the advice he had given McNamera, Bray really didn't want to see any Were-hunting parties. He knew he wouldn't be able to stop the citizens if that's what they decided to do and given the town's history and all, it was likely they would. Besides, they had a right to protect themselves and their property. He watched the two boys, who'd zipped up Jeb's remains into a body bag walk by. Bray was definitely not happy. He'd thought he was back to just dealing with human weirdoes. He didn't have the resources it took to take on any additional supernatural goings-on, which left him feeling helpless in this situation. He had the authority to serve and protect the citizens here in anyway humanly possible. "But what do ya' do when what you're up against ain't human and defies human logic or ability?" Bray didn't like the feeling of being between a rock and a hard place. For Bray, the law should be straight forward, but when the normal rules no longer apply, then what? He was there to serve the public's interest no matter how absurd the situation. Bray surmised that trusting the Institute to have eradicated the "Werewolf problem" may have been foolish, but it had been out of his control.

La Mort Douce's sheriffs, past and present, had seen more than their fair share. Each had encountered problems with dubious choices made by those in higher authority. Like it or not, it was their job to uphold the laws. Each generation, duty bound to the next, from dealing with the slaughter of Indians, to witch-hunts, to slavery and the numerous lynchings that followed. None of it added up to an honorable legacy to inherit. His father had endured the ugliness of the Civil Rights movement, together they had served their community amid the fervor over gay rights and now he had this on his plate. He imagined it wasn't too big of a stretch that werewolf liberation and equal rights for all bloodsuckers could come next. However, judging from Jeb's body, 'kill or be killed' was the backstory. "Would it really come to that?" Bray wondered?"

Bray's family had a long line of law enforcement members handcuffed through time and its changing perspectives. "Why in the heck do I do this?" he grumbled to himself. This is comic book come to life crap. On his watch, he'd had the unfortunate commission of dealing with real people who'd become victims of the lycanthrope population. TV programming and movies made out this disease to be merely a curse, sometimes even a gift. Like rabies, though, it is a disease causing those who survived an attack to be infected thereby perpetuating the cycle. Surviving by killing off and devouring humans and occasionally infecting people, it moved on and on, spreading throughout time and history. As with any crime victim, those poor folks didn't choose to be what they had become. Like his ancestors before, he was just one sheriff in a heavily populated town of rightfully paranoid people. He couldn't really leave this place, after all, he'd been born and raised here, he was married and working towards having a third child. Bray just felt stuck. Like those before him, he observed and did what he could do to keep the peace. Bray sighed. At least one of his boys would very likely end up continuing the Bray family tradition of law enforcement. "God, help my son when the time arrives for him to take over," Bray prayed, silently. Brays thoughts returned to worrying about the here and now. "Gosh darn it, this just don't feel right, at all." Bray lamented to himself. Shaking it off, he ran through his checks, and realized his keys were still in the ignition. Bray sighed, started the patrol car and cussed a blue streak through his cigar smoke as he pulled away.

JODI

Jodi exited the charter bus in La Mort Douce and thought the morning sun seemed brighter than she remembered. She took a long, slow, deep breath of the fresh air. She'd visited New York and Japan, places where the buildings seemed to shield their residents from the benefits of the sun, clouds, wind, stars, and clear skies. City life had dulled her senses. Everything in La Mort Douce was fresh and crisp. The residents were proud of their nearly non-existent pollution. Generally, it blew beyond the mountains to the southeast. Jodi often joked that any pollution in La Mort Douce blew back to New York, where she could smell the lingering odors of death.

Jodi noticed every little noise. The sounds of traffic, sirens, voices, wind, rustling leaves and children playing had all seemed to rise up in her ears equally, instead of being individually present as they had in places she had visited in the past. All of the city noises had combined to create a constant murmur, like what you might hear during a school play. All the familiar scents were back. The people, the blood, the history; it was there as well. Jodi smiled, happy to be back home.

Jodi had gone to Japan to reconcile with her father after Vlad's attack on the Institute. She had been making plans to be in La Mort Douce to see the birth of Terry and Goldy's child, when she lost contact with all of them. She didn't know what to think, so she mustered up enough funds to get home. She was excited to see her fellow pack-mates and she wanted to show how much she had matured from the sullen girl dressed in Goth garb. Now a rehabilitated and sophisticated young adult, Jodi sported new look represented as well. Tight blue jeans and colorful, flowing blouses now complimented her body. "Yeah" Jodi thought with sarcasm and a hint of defiance, "I have an amazing figure." She chuckled at her newfound self-confidence. She now had a family who loved her just the way she was and Jodi was thrilled to be back home to see them.

Jodi was worried about the pack. She hadn't heard from Goldy or Terry for too long. She knew only too well that Lycanthropy could cause altered thinking, insanity, wild and savage behavior; all detrimental to one's mental stability. Jodi had once experienced that all-consuming emotion and knew first hand it was nearly impossible to return. Globes Disease almost sent her to the electric chair and instigated a full-scale war on the werewolves in La Mort Douce. She knew if Goldy or Terry fell into despair or depression that the disease would take advantage of them. Jodi hoped she had not taken too long to return.

Jodi suddenly realized she was still standing at the bus station, deep in thought. Jodi caught herself staring when she thought she saw a woman that looked a lot like Terry board an outgoing bus. With a blink of her eyes, Terry's twin apparition was no longer among those boarding. Still, Jodi thought she could smell Terry, and vaguely remembered noticing it at the Ragnorock's. So focused on pondering her own life, she couldn't discern whether what she'd seen was real or not. Eventually she diverted her gaze and refocused her attention to her mission.

Thanks to her dearly departed mother, Jodi had never learned to drive and a skateboard just didn't fit her new image. Jodi decided to walk to the Ragnorock's home instead of taking a bus or cab. The west side of La Mort Douce was where the nicer homes were and the Andersen's lived that way as well, so she would head over to the Andersen's place after. Jodi worked her way through the increasingly busy town, outgrowing the terra firma it rested on. As she made her way, Jodi felt an overwhelming need to see the park, to feel what she'd felt before her arrest. She wanted to remember everything, feel the power that had driven her there to hunt. Jodi inhaled the clean, crisp air; enjoying the cool burn from it. A stroll through the park would be a good start towards getting her head back into this place and all of its surprises. Most importantly, Jodi needed to stay sharp.

Jodi stopped and surveyed Le Parc Moyen, noting the changes and what had stayed the same, before she crossed the street. It was lush and full of beautiful flowers. She eyed the play area before making a beeline for it. Oddly, she didn't have any horrible flashbacks. Instead, it all seemed like a distant memory. Jodi was happy about that, though she knew memories could resurface with jarring force when least expected. Jodi preferred mental preparation to tap into for that type of emotional assault.

When Jodi sat on the swing set, it all came back. Jodi saw it as clearly, as if she were watching her younger self on a large screen. She was wearing her trademark Goth outfit of black and gray with red ribbons accenting her pigtails. Oddly, it was the perfect lure for the middle-aged Japanese man. With mind numbing clarity, she watched as the pervert put his hand on her thigh. The change was instant, possibly because she had contracted Globes Disease at such a young age. The pain of transforming didn't slow her down as it did most others. She welcomed it and the anger it spawned; both gave her power. In the vision, she watched as she changed to her werewolf and knocked the man to the ground. He never got a chance to scream for help with Jodi's werewolf tearing vigorously at his throat, before he knew what was happening. His blood sprayed her face and her eyes; her nostrils filled with it, which ramped her rage even higher. She watched as her wolf gulped the flesh and bones from his neck as the body was convulsed. Jodi's wolf moved on to the man's chest, ripping at the ribs and chest plate until she reached the fleshy heart. It squished and splattered in her mouth like ripe fruit as she feasted. The pleasure was immeasurable, and her werewolf's purpose was now complete. She went for the man's groin in the same vicious manner as her final act of vengeance.

The sound of children playing pulled her back to reality. Instantly her impeccable hearing tuned into the sounds of life happening around her; horns honking, an airplane overhead, laughter, bouncing balls, barking of dogs. Jodi was surprised that she was happy to escape the memory of that night. She wondered what happened to wanting to use the memories as fuel. She got off the swing so that a child who didn't have one could swing with his siblings. Three little waifs were playing joyously. The two little girls and their slightly older brother were tan, curly mop headed kids, obviously of mixed lineage.

Jodi smiled; she enjoyed watching La Mort Douce's evolution, steadily moving past traditional ways. La Mort Douce housed every type of indigene and immigrant at one time or another. No matter how they arrived or what the circumstance, this isolated place was able to provide opportunities, probably the small town charm. Isolation had advantages and disadvantages. With Canada bordering the area, some of their views on diverse cultures and segregation had to rub off. It helped influence La Mort Douce from being the typical "hicktown" that the USA was often accused of habitating.

Jodi continued to converse with herself while the siblings kept playing, barely giving her notice except to navigate around her. The kids were still at the age where they obviously loved one another, no petty sibling rivalry, yet. Jodi extended them all a friendly smile, plodded through the sand and headed for the tunnel. The tunnel reeked of numerous deaths separated only by the distance of time. Jodi thought she could smell two, maybe three other Weres. She even felt the presence of Vlad tickling the hairs on her neck and sending shivers down her spine. It made her uneasy that his essence still lingered. Something inside her told her she should leave and heeded the warning. Jodi walked past a car with a couple inside making out. She overheard them giggling and hinting to one another about what they were going to do once it was completely dark. Jodi shook her head, thinking, "Who in the world would even consider being out late at night here in La Mort Douce?" With that thought, Jodi was ready to reunite with her pack family.

OKSANA

When Oksana Tameira Gavrilovich finally made it to La Mort Douce, she found good eating. She also acquired plenty of good information about her lost lover, Vladimir Romanov. Oksana slept all day in a cabin that reeked of death and her lost love. Once night had fallen, she followed a lead that took her to the Institute. There, she questioned a woman doctor who was the head of operations. Oksana spared the woman's life after she had kindly provided the information Oksana had travelled a great distance to obtain. Besides, one never knew when a doctor might come in handy. After viewing the recording of Vlad's demise, Oksana was angry, heartbroken and disturbed. The doctor may not have been sure of what she was looking at because of Vlad's Obfuscation, but Oksana could see it all and she wasn't pleased.

Oksana was hungry again and needed another meal, soon. She left the Institute and followed a path southwest through the woods and into the city. The cover it provided would be an advantage to Oksana in the event she had to return to the cabin. The evening air was crisp and perfect for her. It wasn't home, but the cold was a comfort all the same. Oksana wasn't much interested in keeping track of time. She paid attention to night and day and if she really needed to know, she read a calendar and calculated. Time was a blur. . The knowledge of possibly living forever blended many moments together. Oksana didn't need to keep track, she was going to live forever, so why bother?

Oksana was devastated after completing the arduous trip to America in search of Vlad only to discover his destruction. Oksana had never known that her kind could perish so easily, she sought retribution. She had chased her memories of Vlad all the way to the States and now the dogs that were responsible would pay for her loss and inconvenience. Once she'd fed and fortified herself, Oksana would hunt them down.

The night Vlad appeared in Oksana's room, all those years ago, she'd thought him a beautiful pale angel. After he made her a vampire, she'd wanted no other man. His touch was cold and dangerous, yet strangely gentle. Vlad's alabaster skin hadn't alarmed Oksana and at that time, she'd attributed his coolness to the cold weather. After many visits to her bed Oksana began to ache for him and in between their liaisons, she missed him greatly.

Oksana hadn't much cared that he was never warm, however odd it seemed. She believed she harbored enough heat for the two of them. She would become moist just from longing for him. He had a steady methodical touch that made her feel timeless. Oksana was blind to any details outside of his presence. When he was inside her, the passion, love, and pleasure were immeasurable and illimitable. Through simple ignorance, she was unaware that vampires could even have sex. That combined with her lust for him; convinced her he wasn't undead.

If Oksana was being truly honest with herself, she could admit that she had known on some level what Vlad was, she just didn't care. She had basked in his blood soaked tears and sweat, even the blood stained semen that pleasantly spilled out of her was a clue. Oksana reveled in Vlad's seductions. Never was Oksana as completely satisfied, as she had been on what turned out to be their last night together. Oksana lived that night and she died the next day. When she awoke as vampire, she wanted, needed and ached for more of Vlad. She reflected on the other things she'd chosen to ignore. Vlad's strange discolored nails, the hint of death on his breath and the sharp teeth that he'd nipped her with to infect her. She had not realized that he had done it until she was dying and she'd been searching for Vlad ever since she'd risen. She wanted her maker as her mate.

Oksana had felt Vlad's essence within ever since that moment, trailing in his wake for decades, searching for him the world over. Even now, Oksana was still deeply in love with Vladimir Romanov.

Arriving at the town's central park, quicker than she had anticipated, she observed a young couple in a parked car. It was evident they had been passionately groping one another for quite some time. Eventually they exited the vehicle and ran hand in hand across the parking lot to the grass, stopping often to kiss and fondle along the way. They looked around for witnesses as they reached the tunnel and Oksana heard them speaking the words of lovers. Once in the tunnel, as if it hid them from view, they were all over each other. In great contrast to the way Vlad had touched her, there was no true romance or passion in what this couple was doing. They were animalistic and uncivilized. Vlad may have been methodical and mechanical, perhaps to simulate what he remembered of human lovemaking, but at least he'd cared enough to take the time to please her. His kiss was passionate, as was his hunger for her. Vlad willingly kissed her all over, appreciated her and brought her to new heights of ecstasy, fueling her desire and love. What she was witnessing in the tunnel was barbaric and uncouth. Their grunting, spastic movements, lack of rhythm, flow or connection seriously disgusted her. Oksana hadn't made love in many years, so why should she let others have that pleasure? Humans like this couple did not appreciate the gift and beauty of love and mutual pleasure. They only sullied its purity with their behavior. They irritated Oksana, but she was also hungry and their carelessness provided her with the perfect opportunity to feed.

Oksana approached the otherwise engaged couple in stealth mode, though they were so engrossed they wouldn't have noticed her anyway. Oksana salivated. Her contempt for humans who did not appreciate life or death fueled her hunger. She despised those who meandered through their existence, never noticing or caring about their surroundings. She loved frightening humans and this couple deserved a dose of reality. Fear seemed to make them taste better, and she derived extreme pleasure in giving them the experience of terror. The last moments before death often caused her prey to appreciate life, at least once before they died. She got off on that. , Oksana had learned over the years that all vampires have crazy quirks and tastes. She never preyed on those who behaved as if their lives were worth living or had something useful to contribute to society. Any fool who took life for granted was doomed in her eyes. This couple obviously cared nothing for others, society, decency, children or the parents of children who could stumble upon them mating like wild animals and she was just the one to show them the error of their ways. When Oksana reached them, they were in the final throws of their wild, loud and passionate gyrations. Their moans and primal grunts echoed from the tunnel. She could smell their sex well as the faint essence of past deaths. The couple was sweaty, hot and panting. Sensing her presence, the couple turned and looked at Oksana simultaneously. Both smiled and the man said "Hi" by way of acknowledgement. The woman raked her gaze slowly up and down Oksana, as if she were considering offering an invitation to join them, "Did you enjoy the show?" She asked with a smirk. "What's your name?" Oksana replied, giving them her complete name while sizing them up. They looked at each other and giggled. The man drawled, "Hmmm, we've never had Russian before." The woman all but purred, "Well Oksana, our car is right over there. We live nearby. Why don't you come with us so we can all get to know one another?"

Oksana followed the couple to their vehicle. They were still all over one another even during the ride to their home. Oksana originally thought to have her meal in the tunnel, but realized she would need shelter. Their invitation was the perfect solution. Oksana followed the couple into their neo-punk decorated home, paused, looked around, and decided the place was suitable enough. Her hunger was causing her temples to throb and she could barely hear over it. She wasn't interested in the refreshments they offered to her, she just waited for an opportunity. They presented her with one when they disrobed and headed into the bathroom containing a large tub with a shower. They slid behind the curtains and invited her in. Her fangs grew as her hunger deepened. One fang pricked her bottom lip. By the time Oksana disrobed and joined them, her breathing had become a slow deep pant.

As Oksana stepped into the shower, blood trickled from her bottom lip. She hardly noticed the horror in the couple's eyes as they took note of her pale, veiny, white skin and the dark blood dripping from her mouth. She focused on their blood-engorged veins, their skin flushed from sex and the heat of the shower, until they started screaming. She didn't want anyone else hearing the squealing, since she needed to stay there without the risk of detection. Oksana reached up with each arm, grabbed their necks and lifted them off the tub floor; squeezing until their eyes bulged. Pivoting her body until her back was under the spray, she bumped the faucet off with her buttocks and effortlessly engaged the tub stopper with her foot; all while the couple squirmed and writhed. Oksana enjoyed they're struggling; it made their blood heat up. The warmer the blood, the more delicious it was. She liked the fight or flight response instigated by terror. Using her thumbnails, she punctured their carotid arteries, sliced their necks and popped their heads to the side. Their searing blood spewed into the stopped-up tub, mixing with the water. Oksana gorged herself drinking from their twitching bodies. Oksana tossed aside the male first. His body hit the toilet with a sickening thud. The much smaller woman landed with a duller splat on the floor. Blood and water slowly trickled into puddles on the floor.

Oksana's pallor slowly brightened as the hot, fresh, blood permeated her system. Still in the tub, she rubbed it all over herself and basked in the carnage. Eventually she slid down onto her belly and began to drink from the slightly diluted hot nectar until she had gorged herself well beyond her limits. She sighed, belched, turned onto her back and bathed in the remaining liquid. She ran the hot water occasionally to keep the blood from coagulating and to keep the bath warm. Her skin was pink and her body was warm and toasty, all Oksana had to do was to relax. She liked killing this way; with no worries about her garments being soiled and being able to dispose of the bodies at her leisure.

Sated, Oksana napped in the hot bloody water. She opened her eyes and continued to lie there and relax. She was fully satisfied and feeling energized. She reminded herself that she needed to seal the place off from daylight soon or else she would have to find a safe place to sleep. Oksana felt a twinge of sadness and loss. She had been looking for so very long and now, here she was in the place he loved most and had lived the longest. After years of searching, though she could feel and smell his presence, she realized he was no more. She would never have her long lost true love again, and retribution would have to do. Oksana had caught the scent of the girl, Jodi Sakarui, at Le Parc Moyen. Making her suffer was the first priority and then she would deal with the behemoth known as Quake.

JODI

Jodi arrived at the Ragnorock's home, inspecting the perimeter before entering the grounds. As she walked onto the porch memories flooded her mind. Jodi's 'gifts' from Lycanthropy included the ability to see, feel, and smell things long past. Jodi got a flash of Goldy coming to this door. Then another flash of men from the Institute, she smelled gunpowder and chemicals. She was no chemist and she wasn't at the Institute long enough to know all the tools they used, but Jodi recalled this combination all to well. Silver shavings caused enough pain to distract a human and keep a werewolf transformation at bay, giving the narcotics time to kick in. The doses were fast acting for Weres, but lethal to average humans.

Jodi backed off the porch and followed Goldy's path through her vision, around to the side of the house. Jodi checked the newly repaired backdoor and found it unlocked, which seemed odd to her. She peeked in through the window and thought, "I sure hope I don't have to transform today, I really like these jeans." The door hinges screeched shrilly as she pushed it open. Her feet echoed on the kitchen floor. The breakfast nook table was gone; Jodi noticed a few splinters on the floor under the counters and gouges on the new cabinet doors. Jodi stood in the kitchen for a while, scrutinizing everything, Goldy's claw marks, which were too deep to buff out completely.

Jodi continued to sniff around, caught the musty scent of the basement, and eyed the door. The air pressure throughout the house made it creak. Jodi wasn't scared; she was curious but cautious. She took a step forward and got a flash of Goldy demolishing the door,

Diana's fear and Quake's rage. If Jodi hadn't learned to take control of her enhanced abilities, she could easily have lost herself in those memories. Having learned to control the animal had really helped her become a better human. Jodi was grateful to Goldy for helping her learn to use her skills. She had often struggled with her beast, but Jodi desired to keep her freedom for as long as she possibly could.

Jodi took a deep breath. Goldy had taught her some deep breathing exercises, to help her control urges and rage. She could smell the Hunters in the house. She forced herself down the steps where she saw the cage, its broken lock, and a dart gun on the wall. There was dried blood on the floor. An unused silver lock sat on a nearby table. Jodi couldn't take anymore, and had to leave. Outside, the setting sun was a perfect distraction from her uneasiness. Being at the Ragnorock's had given her an idea of what happened to them. Unfortunately, her visions lead back to the Institute, a place she did not particularly want to go.

The sun had almost set when Jodi walked up to the Andersen's home. Surrounded by hedges, the structure largely camouflaged from the street. She slipped through the front gate, and entered an open foyer facing a beautiful wooden structure of Nordic lumber and glass. The grounds, landscaped with fountains and endless elements of Zen décor, brought a smile, as she recalled countless hours of shopping with Goldy. Jodi knew how Goldy liked to dress and how she like to decorate. After Goldy and Terry got together, Goldy constantly looked for, bought and wore gauzy, flowing gowns. Those hedges provided much needed privacy, as Goldy liked to look sexy for Terry but she didn't have any desire to give the neighbors a show.

Jodi chuckled, thinking about how she had resisted the traditional ways of her family. Goldy found a way to make Jodi's heritage seem magical and serene. Goldy's enthusiasm was immeasurable, especially when she spoke of Zen teachings. Jodi thought, "Now that's a way to learn about a culture. Immerse yourself and become one with it. Goldy had studied many spiritual cultures, through which she believed she could teach suppression and control of Globes Disease, beginning with the most basic principle of mind over matter. Goldy felt strongly that only in the most extreme cases, when all else had failed, should anyone turn to science.

Jodi entered the house, which reeked of the Hunters and she shuddered; she had noticed it outside as well. Jodi proceeded cautiously. As she walked through the house, she noticed that everything seemed to be intact. The Hunters had done a good job of not disturbing anything, but their scent signatures tainted Goldy and Terry's home.

The bedroom door had damage, and she shivered. What she smelled unnerved her and the fine hairs on her body stood up. She opened the door and the sight brought her to her knees. The bedroom, Goldy's most sacred room of all, was in mass disarray. The windows were broken and her sheer silk curtains fluttered in the breeze. The walls still had darts in them, as did the bed and the floor. Goldy's Hida Oak Japanese bed was a disheveled tainted mess. Jodi recognized the Egyptian cotton sheets from one of many shopping sprees. What affected Jodi the most was the visions triggered by all the smells and seeing blood splattered everywhere. She couldn't help but think of Terry and Goldy's unborn baby and wondered what those monsters had done to the three of them. Jodi thought of the innocence that may have been lost and of her own childhood. "Damn, the callous violent nature of humans. They have nerve calling us animals." Jodi stayed there for a while and did something she hadn't done since riding in the back of the police car, handcuffed and humiliated. She cried.

THE PACK

GOLDY

Once upon a time, I was human...
Once upon a time, I was feral...
Once upon a time, I was in love...
Once upon a time, I was...

The pack was hungry. Goldy had done all she could for them, but the harsh winter coupled with hunting season had reduced their odds for wild game. The pack gathered around her, licking her. Rough as it was, she accepted the pain. It kept her focused on denying her humanity. She felt the scratches of the many cubs trying to honor her with licks to her mouth, though she knew they were also begging for food. She allowed the unruly behavior until her smooth chocolate skin began to purple with bruises. Then she partially transformed to her werewolf. It was just enough to be on all fours and thought of as wolf.

Goldy ruled over them with the loving care of a true den mother. They gave honor to her in the order of their newly established hierarchy. The last member of the pack to do so being the battle scarred previous matriarch. The injuries she bore were nothing personal, in Goldy's view.

Memories are the only thing personal to Goldy anymore. Memories of vile humans, who invade, steal and destroy for their own selfish whims and pleasures. Her pack did what they needed to do to survive. Tonight her pack was telling her that they needed food. Mothers needed protein to nurse; males needed it to keep up their strength to protect and hunt. She'd been reluctant to step into the leadership role, because she was concerned about backlash from humans. It had only been a few days since they had last fed well. Though she wasn't completely comfortable with the idea, Goldy thought they ought to go back to the farm where they had gotten the tasty lamb.

JODI

Jodi had composed herself in her motel room and as she trekked through town, Jodi realized she had changed into her casual sneakers and a warm coat, but had forgotten to change out of her favorite jeans. "Damn," she thought. On her way back to Le Parc de Gevaudan, Jodi came upon a cordoned off farm. She was about to continue walking when she caught some familiar scents. A wolf pack had recently absconded with a cow. Curiosity piqued, she concentrated and noted the same pack had taken a lamb some days ago. She paused when she realized they had killed a human as well. This was not the work of an ordinary wolf pack. Goldy's scent intermingled with theirs. This concerned her but Jodi quickly realized it wasn't a good idea for her to be anywhere close to a crime scene. Casually, she followed the scent trail to the pack.

She went east, past the residences, around Le Petit Lac de Vostok to the base of Montagne du Loup. Once there, she followed the foothills to the north just before Le Parc de Gevaudan. Jodi was so deep in thought, she had lost track of time. She reflected on her friendships, and contemplated the Institute's true intentions. She felt remorse for not staying after Vlad's attack but she had followed Quake and Terry's instructions and left town. She trusted her Lycanthrope family more than her own biological family and Jodi rarely trusted anyone, which spoke volumes. Her loyalties to them had brought her home. She couldn't ignore that she had lost contact with them. Jodi detested the feeling that something was amiss and not knowing what was happening had become too much.

Jodi could scent that the pack was near, as was Goldy. Jodi moved slowly and purposefully, using her body language to convey she was no threat with every step. Eventually she transformed, just enough to give off the scent of a fellow wolf. Jodi spotted the cow carcass as her eyes adjusted to darkness. Looking around, she couldn't believe what she was seeing. At the edge of the group, Goldy was squatting in the brush in full human form. She was definitely not the woman Jodi remembered. She looked wild and unkempt; her hair like a lion's mane, her clothing tattered. Her scent, fouled by filth, was more appalling than her appearance. This Goldy barely projected a hint of humanity, which was totally out of character, definitely nothing like the woman Jodi remembered. Overwhelmed with disappointment, she knew she had to say something.

GOLDY

Goldy sat like a Queen Bee as her pack doted on her like drones. She'd grown comfortable with the scenario. Goldy countered everything Jodi said. She was angry and filled with hatred for humankind. She'd lost her job, lifestyle, child and the only man who truly loved her. Jodi wasn't there when these horrific events had occurred and she could never understand the loss or pain. Jodi had been a taker for most of her short life. Conversely, Goldy had been a giver; right up until everything in her life was lost. She was tired of being Zen, hated being victimized and had exhausted her ability to love and forgive. She wanted retribution, but more than anything, she just wanted to be alone. Goldy resolved to accept her destiny as an animal.

Goldy transformed between human, wolf-lady and werewolf throughout her tirade; as she ranted about humans, raved about the Institute and swore she would eventually amass a large enough pack to retrieve her child from their clutches. She ignored Jodi's points about the flaws in her plan. Jodi believed that they could accomplish more than the pack was capable of, if their Were family were reunited. Goldy could feel herself toggling from angry human to wild animal like a lunatic, but she couldn't control it. At some point, she decided she didn't care. Stopping, she looked up at the moon, so bright in the night sky, its halo made it center stage and the sea of stars easy to ignore. The human in her wanted to enjoy the beauty of it, but the Lycanthrope wanted to use its energy to spill human blood. She buried the human side of her deep within herself, the Queen of Wolves.

Goldy suddenly stood up, walked over to Jodi, hugged her and told her she loved her as a little sister. Turning, she gave the pack a silent signal and they hastily responded. Being out in the wild gave her an edge over Jodi. Goldy had heard the mob and scented their gunpowder and beer when they reached the northwest side of the lake. Jodi realized the pack was moving their young to safety, in preparation for an attack as the mob reached the foot of the mountain. As Goldy transformed into her wolf, she heard Jodi cussing about the imminent demise of her favorite pair of jeans. Jodi transformed just as gunfire erupted around them. There was definitely no changing Goldy's mind now.

THE MOB

Deputy Josh McNamera had tried to persuade the mob to disperse. He'd made every effort to reason with the group, not because he feared for the wolves, but because he wasn't sure what type of wolves they were dealing with. The mob was justifiably angry about Jeb's death. When they discovered that the wolf pack had returned and taken one of Jeb's cows, they'd had enough and followed the bloody trail from Jeb's farm to the southeast woods of La Mort Douce and on to Le Petit Lac de Vostok. All attempts to raise Sheriff Bray on the radio went unanswered, so he'd followed the group. Along the way, he had realized none of them had prepared to do any real hunting. They all had jackets more suitable for running around town, not this bone chilling cold. No one had binoculars, GPS, spare bullets, ropes, first aid kits and McNamera was the only one with a radio.

McNamera's concern grew when the low battery indicator began to beep, making the darn radio screech like crazy. He knew it was too late to stop this brazen foolishness. Most of these assholes had been at the pub until 2:00 am when he'd run them out of Coltrane's Tavern. Liquored up and chomping at the bit for vengeance, it hadn't taken much for them to get riled up when they saw him. The early morning wind was pushing at their backs and the chill was numbing, though the angry crowd probably didn't feel it yet; too much adrenaline and booze. McNamera looked out over the calm, cold lake and thought he saw someone about 300 yards from him, but the mob trekked on, ignoring his observations. By the time they arrived on the other side of the lake, it was close to 4:00 am but the men were undaunted. Hunting was no good under these conditions. The mob was too noisy in their stupid bravado and McNamera was sure any nearby creatures could smell the stench of sweat and booze from at least 100 yards away.

Suddenly, McNamera's radio came to life. Bray was irritated and cussing up a storm. A regular occurrence, but there wasn't much anyone could do about it. No one else was willing to take the job. Besides, not much ever changed in La Mort Douce, aside from the size of the population. The mentality and its dubious reputation stuck, including the fact that every sheriff ever appointed in La Mort Douce had been a Bray. McNamera tried to explain everything, but his radio went in and out repeatedly, so he wasn't sure how coherent his transmissions were. He was walking away from the raucous crowd, many of whom were pissing all over the side of Montagne du Loup, when he stepped on something. McNamera bent down to find tattered clothing and an ulna. Before he could tell the sheriff what he just found, all hell broke loose.

McNamera stood quickly and spun around when he heard the first shot. It had come from the northeast side of the mountain base and judging from the screams, it was apparent their battle had been lost before it had begun. Wolves appeared from every direction, catching the men at the front of the belligerent mob off guard, tearing at arms, shoulders and throats, preventing them from firing. Many of the men, crouched in the dirt with their rifles, had hit quite a few wolves, but ultimately wolves overtook them in the most ferocious way. The screams and sounds were deafening, the men behind those dying on the front line continued shooting. Standing their ground to no avail, a flurry of wolves ripped them to shreds. Blood and flesh mixed in the dirt, grass and leaves. There would be plenty for the scavengers when this ended. The onslaught was overwhelming and surprisingly organized, as wave after wave of wolves took down men in unmerciful droves.

The bloodcurdling screaming was more than McNamera could handle. He grabbed his radio. "Fuck! It's dead! Damn it!" He reached for his revolver, even as he realized there was little he could do from so far away against animals that large and fast. The sight of the slaughter was paralyzing. The pack had easily overtaken well over half the men. Many, who thought they were getting away, met a savage death. The few that stood their ground paid an equally deadly price, as the wolves incapacitated them. A few of them retreated, firing at the same time, unsuccessfully. Methodically, wolves trailed, ambushed, and ripped them apart, straggler's legs torn as they ran. The wolves loped along behind them until they collapsed and bled to death. Their shredded muscles and flesh hobbled them leaving them vulnerable to mastication.

It was not a good skirmish. It was folly to be out in the dark on two legs. The men had no advantage, no speed, no strength and they were ridiculously outnumbered and unprepared. A few survivors were heading McNamera's way. Leading the charge to catch them were two wolves that were significantly larger than the rest. McNamera didn't need anyone to tell him these were dire wolves. His heart began racing, he couldn't breathe or speak, but his survival instinct compelled him to run.

THE CHASE

Jodi was a more mature looking werewolf than the last time Goldy had seen her. With long, silky ears, she was still sinewy, but now she was almost as large as Goldy. The pack was all sporting thick winter coats, which made them appear much larger. Jodi remembered Goldy as tall and lean with a beautiful coat. What she saw when she found her today had been surprising, but now Goldy was a sight to see. She had effortlessly torn apart at least half a dozen men on her own, though she stopped short of chasing McNamera. Goldy had made her statement. She growled and howled, making herself appear ominous and larger. That act put fear in the remaining men, including McNamera, who scarpered.

Goldy looked at Jodi one final time before turning back to tend the wounded. Jodi chose to press on; her drive to seek prey had kicked in. McNamera was nearing the other side of the lake, zipping through the trees and plants in a zigzag pattern that amused Jodi. She never altered her pursuit; his scent was deep in her nostrils. Suddenly she was feeling her old rage. The need for revenge coursed through her beastly blood stream and there was no one to reel her back in, no Institute to calm the vengeful side of her and Goldy was too far away to help bring her out of this blood lust. All the old emotions about her fractured family life and Vlad's victimization resurfaced, allowing the disease to take over. Jodi was once again eager to dispense her brand of deadly justice.

Jodi's werewolf stopped at the north side of the lake, her ears moved as she listened intently to the low thump of McNamera's heartbeat. It was like a beacon and when McNamera attempted to catch his breath, it was not in cadence with the wind so it tickled Jodi's senses. She would find him soon and the fact that his fear had caused him to pee himself would make it even easier to find him. Jodi felt enraged by the massacre; many cubs trampled in the panic and quite a few wolves shot, some killed. Jodi believed the man she was chasing was responsible for stirring up the maddened mob. The emotions of her feral side were ablaze with contempt, her wolf resolved to kill him, right up until Jodi caught him.

When McNamera peeked around the tree he was hiding behind, Jodi was waiting for him. Snarling, she pounced on him with both paws on his chest, slamming him to the ground. She was salivating and ready to kill. McNamera screamed and begged for his life. He looked into her eyes and pleaded, "I tried to stop them, really tried! I uphold the law, and preserve the peace! Please don't!" She looked down at him and as a wolf, she understood his intent, but her fury overtook her again and she reared back to finish him. The sound of gunfire preceded a searing pain in Jodi's shoulder. She yelped and turned to see one of the stragglers pointing a rifle at her. He was dirty, bloody and trembling. The smoke from his rifle and the fog from his breath seemed to blend. The man cocked his rifle and stood his ground. Jodi turned her attention to the new antagonist. Blood poured from her wound, the pain was incessant and Jodi had begun to feel dizzy. "There must have been silver on that bullet." Jodi thought. The man yelled something, possibly a warning as Jodi stood and advanced towards him on her hind legs. He fired again and missed, barely. An explosion of shattered tree bark flew all over McNamera and the back of Jodi's head. She growled a warning and was about to lunge at him when the man's head was completely ripped from his neck. Jodi stood there lethargic, confused and astonished. McNamera peed himself again and promptly passed out.

Jodi didn't realize how weak she was until it was all over. After reverting to her human form the pain was still there and she was bleeding profusely from her shoulder wound. She fell to the ground and sat on her legs. When she looked up, Goldy; wild eyed, half-wolf, half-woman stood there as blood and brains dripped from her long, clawed fingers, covered in fur and skin, her hair a disaster and still Jodi couldn't take her eyes off her. After a long stare, Jodi joked, "Damn Goldy, at your worst you still look better than I do, in the morning without makeup, a shower and teeth not brushed." She hoped it would pull Goldy out of her feral state. Jodi looked at the unconscious deputy. She didn't want Goldy committing murder. Self-defense Jodi understood, but not outright murder. Jodi laughed at the notion of a werewolf worried about murder. Goldy walked over to Jodi in her half-and-half state. "This is gonna hurt," she warned with a growl, right before she dug into Jodi's shoulder. Jodi screamed. It echoed through the woods, across the lake and off the mountains. Lord only knew what the town heard. Jodi was shaking; she felt cold and was most likely going into shock. Before succumbing to unconsciousness, Goldy's voice penetrated enough to keep her from passing out. "You have to transform; it will help you heal faster." Goldy grabbed Jodi's shoulders looked deep into her eyes and forced Jodi's focus onto her. Goldy transformed into her full werewolf and Jodi did the same. Though her breathing was heavy, she followed Goldy's lead and lay her weary frame down.

BRAY & MCNAMERA

McNamera came to with a start. He was frightened out of his mind and instinctively drew his weapon. Judging by their muzzles, the two enormous wolves sitting in front of him were female. They looked at him in unison, but did not otherwise move. They sat; taking long, slow, measured breaths. If he didn't know, better he would have thought that they were doing some form of werewolf yoga. McNamera closed his eyes and shook his head in the hope he was only hallucinating.

McNamera slowly rose; still pointing his gun at the wolves, and was immediately both reminded of and embarrassed by his wet pants. He toggled side-to-side with his revolver unsure of which target to take down first, whether to shoot at all or if he should just run. While he was hesitating, he noticed one of the wolves was bleeding. He blinked twice because the wolf's wound was slowly healing as he watched. Before he could react, the other wolf magically transformed in front of him. She had appeared like a genie from a bottle. She was the most beautiful woman he had ever seen, even in tattered clothes, covered with dirt and her hair gone wild. McNamera was so taken by Goldy's beauty he lowered his weapon. He startled when Goldy spoke in a gentle voice, "We mean you no harm. We are just as afraid of you, as you are of us." McNamera blinked again, "Wow, what a wolf woman," he thought. McNamera figured he was in either shock or suffering from Post-Traumatic Stress Disorder.

It all seemed unreal and McNamara was certain no one would believe his account of what had occurred. "These things; these animals, they are supposed to be savage." McNamera thought. Goldy's voice interrupted his confused thoughts, "We just want to take care of our wounded and be left alone. No harm will come to you or your surviving friends if you all just go!" Goldy's voice was soft, almost hypnotic. McNamera thought to raise his weapon again but couldn't, instead, he walked away and never looked back. He didn't want to believe it, but he wasn't convinced it was a dream. During the trek back, he talked himself through several possible actions from planning his resignation to retirement or psychiatric disability. The closer he got to town, the more he thought he should move to another town; one with no snowy winters, no werewolves, no weirdoes; maybe California. By the time he had reached the station, he was ready to turn in his badge, equipment and type his resignation letter. Inexplicably, his previously dead radio chirped to life. It was Bray, his voice loud, as usual. "Deputy McNamera, this is Bray. What in the hell is going on out there? Do you fucking copy? Dag Nab It!"

GOLDY & TERRY

Jodi became human again after she'd healed from the bulk of her injuries. What remained was tolerable now. Twilight was waning and they would soon have to get out of sight, especially with all the corpses lying around. Jodi and Goldy watched McNamera in the distance get into his patrol car and drive away like a mad man. Jodi looked into Goldy's eyes, the ache in them apparent. Jodi knew instinctively that they would return to the den, and assess the damage and rebuild their ranks to return to the Institute.

Jodi was unsure if she was completely on board with the plan. The pair hugged and Jodi told Goldy she loved her. Jodi agreed to help find the others, do some recon at the Institute and promised she would return. After she'd cleaned up, rested and was fully healed, she would be ready for battle, in a different pair of jeans, of course. Watching her walk away, Goldy was sad, but she knew they both had tasks to accomplish. Jodi turned into her werewolf again and took off running. Goldy watched until she was gone from sight, then crumbled to the ground and wept.

Her anguish was fierce and she had not cried this way since her parents died. She knew what she planned was nothing short of suicide, but Goldy didn't want to live. She wanted to die; she just couldn't do it herself. Putting herself in a situation where some formidable force would take her life was the only solution. Maybe the Hunters assembled at the Institute would do the job or another vampire, possibly even another Were. She didn't care anymore. Goldy only knew that if there were still a reason for living, she would find it at the Institute. She hoped, for her sake, that Terry and their baby had survived and then she would have renewed reason to live. The sun had come into view over the horizon of the mountain but she didn't care. Goldy set her mind to assisting her pack recover and transformed.

Goldy slowly made her way to the other side of the lake. When she arrived at the lip of the mountain, she heard a distinctive howl. Standing between the full moon setting in the western sky, and the sun rising in the east, was the silhouette of a large dire wolf. Silhouette or not, Goldy recognized him. She reverted to human, stood there, tears in her eyes, butterflies in her stomach and overwhelmed by relief. "Some Wolves mate for life," she thought, "I guess I truly am one of them." Her face brightened with the colorful sunrise as she squinted in Terry's direction. As Terry's wolf began his approach. Goldy was stunned to see a large dire cub trotting along behind him.

RETURN TO THE CABIN

QUAKE & JODI

Tattered, bloodied and exhausted, Quake lay in the dirt, slow to recover from his battles. Super-naturals seemed to do significantly more damage to one another and their injuries lasted far longer. The humans fought well but it was child's play killing them. Quake was angry and distraught; the killings were his means of venting. Poor Diana, why did the Institute try to make him do such terrible things to his wife? Were any of the experiments even done to find a cure or was it all just for their entertainment value? He stood up; his hospital gown was in shambles and he was cold. The dewy grass chilled his feet and monstrous calves. He was weak, his skin itched, he was seriously thirsty and he could hear moving water. The night was getting the last of the full moon. The sun would be rising soon. Quake stumbled over to the nearby fresh water stream and drank deeply from the icy water. It was nirvana and his eyes rolled up into his head as he consumed enough to fill his belly and numb his tongue.

Quake surveyed his surroundings and realized he must be south of the Institute. He needed clothing and he wasn't sure if heading home would be safe, but he didn't care. Quake was willing to destroy anything and everything that got in his way, in his current mood. He would go find Goldy as soon as he got clothes. He was certain he'd scented Goldy from the direction of Montagne du Loup, she had a very distinctive musk. If he could find her, they could go back and help the others. With luck, they would also discover the Institute's true intent. Quake's resolve suddenly failed, his face contorted with pain and his eyes welled up with tears. He fell to his knees in the wet grass and sobbed, "Oh, Diana!"

Quake's breakdown was interrupted by something moving in the distance. Unsure of what it was, he dropped to the ground. The blood and mucus in his nose from fighting and crying had dulled his normally keen senses, putting him at a disadvantage. Unable to catch a clear scent, he crouched down, hiding his large frame among the bushes. He soon realized it was Jodi, the clumsy little girl. Well, she wasn't so little any more, she was quite the adult nevertheless, still clumsy.

What was she doing? What was she looking for? Was she headed to the Institute? She couldn't go there alone, it was too dangerous. Quake was seconds from standing up and calling out to her when he noticed a very pale, tall, powerful looking woman trailing her. She was very quiet, the mystery woman. Her footsteps made no sound and she had the purposeful, smooth movements that screamed vampire. Quake hated vampires.

Jodi systematically worked her way through the grounds around the Institute looking for clues. Eventually she spied a cabin. Upon entering, she recognized some very familiar scents and warning bells went off in her mind, but her need to rest and get cleaned up overrode them. She knew she could handle anything but she wanted to be at her best. Vlad was long since dead, so she didn't think she really needed to be worried about anything else. Jodi crept onto the porch of the well-worn cabin and looked around. She felt uneasy, but the sun would be rising soon. "Daybreak was imminent. What could possibly happen?" she thought, as she stepped into the cabin through the broken door.

The place was a mess; Jodi looked around and decided the basement would be the perfect place to rest. It was evident this place had not been lived in for a while, despite its chaotic condition. She equated the damage to vandals or fighting supernatural beings. Jodi opened the door to the basement entrance and turned on the light. All seemed clear, so she headed down the steps and looked around. She was surprised to find it so well stocked with supplies like canned food and soups, blankets, and even a first aid kit. Suddenly, she felt uneasy. Without warning, the basement door slammed shut and a woman's voice echoed into the cellar. "Hello child. My name is Oksana Tameira Gavrilovich. I am looking for the animals responsible for Vladimir Romanov's death. Tell me, Sobaka. Are you Jodi?"

Jodi spun around and knew immediately that she was the underdog in every way. Oksana was a tall, beautiful, chalky white, broad-shouldered Russian exuding an intimidating fierceness. Jodi growled, but before she could transform to fight her, the basement door shattered. A pair of clawed, hairy arms reached through and grabbed Oksana by the throat. The sight of Quake's arms, crushing the graceful neck of the creature paralyzed Jodi. Seconds before Jodi had been certain she would die at the hands of that dangerous woman. Oksana scratched, hissed and struggled violently to no avail. Overpowered by Quake's strength and the hatred that fueled it, blood poured from Oksana's mouth, nose and ears and she went limp, twitching every few seconds.

Quake's voice rumbled through the basement, "No, Oksana, I ain't givin' you time to heal." Quake's Were, continued to hold on to Oksana with one hand and grabbed the hair on top of her head with the other. The tearing and popping sounds of skin, bone and blood would have caused a normal human to heave. Oksana's head finally detached with a loud, sickening pop. Quake released her body, which tumbled down the stairs and landed at Jodi's feet. Dark blood, that reeked as though it fermented for hundreds of years, sprayed everywhere. Quake stood there looking down at Jodi through the large hole in the door, gagging on the miasma. His battle-scarred body was slowly changing back to human, though he never let go of Oksana's head.

Quake tossed Oksana's head. It thudded down the steps like a hairy bowling ball. Finally he said, "Damned, freaky, two-legged mosquito." The words spewed out with blood and spittle, were spoken with utter disdain and revulsion. Seeing Jodi was still somewhat shocked, Quake broke into a wry smile and said, "Well, I tell ya one thing, my feelings ain't changed. I still fucking hate vampires!"

DIANA

Diana left the cabin in search of Quake, Terry and the child. Quake left to make sure there were no imminent threats. Terry had awakened, grabbed his child and gone in search of Goldy. They told her she would be safe there, but she certainly didn't feel safe. She found no trace of them. Scared and alone, she returned home. Scenes haunted her from the night of their abduction. Their home largely destroyed by the Hunters.

The anger and the urge welled up and tempted her, but Diana refused to transform into a werewolf, even if it would help her track her husband and friends. She knew there would be no return from that and she wasn't about to give up her humanity. Thank God, she'd sat in on Goldy's classes.

Diana explored their roomy basement, rebuilt after Goldy had saved her from Quake. The back door and the kitchen redone as well, but the Institute sent the Hunters, who destroyed the rest of the house. The basement had numerous rows of shelves with non-perishables and all manner of supplies. As much as Quake ate, they kept a well-stocked pantry. The silver lined cage was still in the corner; a shiny new silver lock sat on a table nearby. Quake had converted their basement into the perfect cave for their pack. Most every basement in La Mort Douce had a similar set-up, minus the cage. Many went to the extreme and stockpiled weapons, ammo, blankets, first aid kits, additional food, and paper goods. After all, the winters in La Mort Douce were long, hard and deadly, especially if one was not prepared.

Diana had gone out for some much-needed fresh air but she wasn't ready to revisit her nightmares. She'd hidden undetected long enough and had no fear the Hunters would return. They had what they came for, especially given all that had happened at the Institute.

Before the chaos at the Institute, there had been hints of things brewing. The preparations, extra men, arms and military vehicles were all noticeable to the observant. When Diana returned home, she scented that someone had been there, for the first time since she had escaped capture. Who could it have been? That unknown frightened her. Diana didn't know what to do. She wished she could just find someone from her pack. She was beginning to feel anxious and something was nagging her, a niggling feeling that she had been waiting in the wrong place. Perhaps it was her intuition telling Diana to return to the Cabin.

RAY-RAE

Ray-Rae left the Hunters when she realized the antidote hadn't worked for her. She returned to the Institute in hope of retrieving more of the antidote. She prayed she would find something amid the ruins and chaos. Ray-Rae felt guilty; she didn't want to be selfish so she'd returned to the cabin to give Diana a chance at a cure and repay her kindness, but Diana was not there. Ray-Rae decided to look for her.

Ray-Rae and her team discovered quickly that the antidote had not worked as they had anticipated. The antidote had diminished effects of her Lycanthropy, but it was not a complete cure. Most likely, her exposure timetable had expired.

Whatever the cause, the Hunters had been aback when Ray-Rae transformed into a werewolf, well after the antidote's administration. Even more surprising, was how quickly and easily they were able to subdue Ray-Rae. Either the antidote was not what Dr. von Shelley claimed or it had been too long before Ray-Rae received her injection. Regardless, it created a diminished version of a werewolf, leaving her vulnerable and scared. Ray-Rae was mortified at having turned and to be so weak made it even worse. She would give anything to be a plain old vulnerable human again. Ray-Rae wanted answers, without them, she couldn't close the door and forget the wretched experience.

Ray-Rae ran away from the Hunters, distraught over their failure to cure her. She roamed the wilderness of La Mort Douce, considering her next move. She knew they would have to come for her. Chuck wouldn't want to, but it was their job to hunt werewolves. She would not let her friends and comrades kill or capture her for experiments. Before the escape, Ray-Rae suffered some humiliation at the Institute. Nothing like what the others went through but she could see it would have built up to that. They micro-chipped her, took blood, examined her and observed her. She knew what all that would lead to, as she had already witnessed all that had gone on there. She was leery of being part of something like that.

Ray-Rae empathized with the werewolf victims. The irony was that if it weren't for her exposure and infection, she would never have thought twice about the plight of werewolves. Ray-Rae thought, "Well it is, what it is." She realized she had to play the cards in her hand, but true to her nature, Ray-Rae was not going to accept her situation without a fight.

Ray-Rae searched La Mort Douce for Diana. She went back to the Ragnorock's home and walked through the place. Remnants of Ray-Rae and her team's raid were still evident. Ray-Rae wasn't proud of that. Something had begun to nag at her senses as she looked around the Ragnorock's yard. Someone had been here recently and judging from the size and depth of the footprints, it was most likely a woman. Of those the Hunters had captured, many had escaped, but where would they go? La Mort Douce was a difficult place to traverse. Besides, she knew the joint government bigwigs would not let them run free. Ray-Rae considered the cabin. It was right under the nose of the Institute. Who would think to look there? Ray-Rae made up her mind; she would go back and scout around the cabin.

When Ray-Rae arrived at the Institute, she walked around taking stock. Quite a few Lycanthropes were still imprisoned, she made a mental note to return and free them. Very little of the staff remained, making it easy to bypass detection. The dead and dying were still in evidence. Ray-Rae suddenly had an idea. Holding her hands up, she concentrated on controlling the transformation; her fingernails began to grow and her hands became claw-like. She reached around and extracted the tracking chip from her neck, feeling triumphant as she tossed it. She rested for a few moments while her neck healed and her hands returned to normal.

After exploring, Ray-Rae found nothing useful, not even in the lab Quake and Terry had destroyed. She headed for the cabin in hopes that Diana would return there. The basement supplies would sustain her while she waited. If Diana returned and the antidote didn't work on her either, she wanted to discuss their potential options. Maybe Ray-Rae could join their pack, and help them succeed against the Hunters.

JODI & QUAKE

The spring air was thick with the remnants of violence. Jodi could smell it everywhere. It was akin to that sulfur smell of road flares. The sunlight slowly cut in to the cabin, permeated by death. Some of it shone through the damaged door like a stage light. Oksana's decapitated body had already begun to sizzle and turn to ash. It was rough on the olfactory system. Jodi sat on the floor of the basement across from Oksana's remains, with Quake's head in her lap. She'd gathered a towel and some bandages and was cleaning his wounds as best she could under the circumstances. Jodi thought to herself, "I knew I shouldn't have worn these jeans." They were now tattered, bloodied and well beyond salvaging. She thought, "What if I started buying those fancy, stretch jeans? Would they survive the transformation? What would that look like, a long sinewy wolf traipsing through the woods in stretchy jeans?" Jodi had to withhold a snicker imagining that visual.

Quake's head was a complete and utter mess. Though he was slowly healing, she was still peeling quite a few mechanical parts, slowly, from his bloodied skull. Some of the wounds were going to take extra time. Jodi recognized some of the bites and claw marks were from another supernatural, possibly several. "Quake, what the heck happened here?" Jodi wondered aloud.

Dr. von Shelley's voice cut into Jodi's self-conversation from above. "More has gone on here than you will ever know. Your large friend there, along with Terry, was a catalyst for a lot more damage to the Institute than imaginable. They triggered an escape, chased off the Hunters, pissed off the government and killed almost everyone left in the Institute. It was all I could do to retrieve my back-up information and escape." Jodi immediately began to transform, with one thought in mind, "Kill von Shelley". Jodi had no moral compunction when it came to killing, especially when she killed for a good reason. Von Shelley was a good reason.

Dr. von Shelley shouted, "I wouldn't do that if I were you." She lifted a crossbow normally used by the Hunters. "I am not one to be trifled with, and neither your kind nor hers scare me." Von Shelley nodded at Oksana's ashes before stepping through them as she approached a partially transformed Jodi. "I am truly the Neo-Dr. Frankenstein, looking for the bigger better version of what my great, great, great-grand father attempted. With combined DNA's I believe I can make the ultimate creature, a servant of war, messenger of mayhem, and one helluva pet."

"You see..." Dr. von Shelley continued, "The Canadian and United States Governments were the perfect allies." Jodi was having a hard time holding back her fury, but she managed to say, "I-I don't understand, what is your purpose? Why are you doing this?" Dr. von Shelley continued her clichéd monologue, "Discovery for profit. I will be the first to own the patent and trademark rights to various research results and sell those to the highest bidder. Don't you get it? Military applications eventually become business applications that eventually become available for public consumption. Consider digital watches, cell phones and PDAs, just to name a few. Do we really need all that junk? Not at all, but Batman and James Bond make us believe we do. Celebrities, superheroes and spy movies make us want to have the latest and the greatest. It's a consumer's arms race out there. Everyone trying to come up with bigger, better gadgets, appliances, cars, computers and TV's, that we have become slaves to, all time wasting instruments we really don't need. We look for chemicals to help us run faster, lose weight, become stronger, be smarter, even have more sex. You name it; we're never satisfied with just being human."

Jodi was immensely irritated listening to the tripe that Dr. von Shelley was spewing, but she realized it was giving Quake more time to heal, so she remained. Dr. von Shelley pressed on. “Power and money, militaries and governments need power and I need money. To achieve those, I need to figure out how to control the uncontrollable, fix, cure and use an untapped resource like supernatural creatures to my advantage. Look at all the kids who consume this stuff as if it were real. Goth kids and fans of movies, TV shows and books have covered the genre for so long and they don’t even know that it actually is real. For those of us who know the truth, well baby, it’s an unexploited resource. Imagine a soldier with the ferocity of a werewolf, the cloaking and cunning of a vampire combined with technology, it would be Supernatural Super Soldier Cyborg!”

“I could be the next person to create and perfect the first wristwatch, PDA, MP3 player of this era.” Dr. von Shelley’s laugh seemed maniacal to Jodi. She was annoyed with her mock levity. “See, the purpose of the Institute was all about innovation and breakthrough. The military had their agenda and I had mine. They wanted to build an elite Special Forces pack, with Quake as the field leader and Terry as the General, all of whom would be under our control. They insisted on a cure, some type of anti-venom, just in case someone went “off the reservation”. Their fear was that the not-so-domesticated Weres would infect someone. They were foolish in thinking there might be a major infestation and believing we had to control it. This disease has been around for thousands of years. A supernatural infestation would have happened long before now. Most people attacked by vampires or werewolves were food, only a few become infected. Unfortunately, I haven’t figured out what circumstance decides whether that will happen, but I am close. Right now, my theory is some form of Supernatural selection. We hadn’t cracked that code yet but we would have.”

Jodi scented two different presences nearby. One was completely unfamiliar; the other Jodi hadn’t smelled in a quite some time. Both seem to be Werewolf. One made her think of Diana. Quake was healing and hearing it all, but Jodi continued to keep him from getting up by applying light pressure to his blood soaked head. "Quake, wait and heal." Jodi cautiously whispered. Jodi recognized Dr. von Shelley's narcissism and she stalled her even further. "So, tell me doctor, why is Quake so special?" Dr. von Shelley's oration was unrelenting, "Well, I believe one of the things that drove Quake, and others like him; to ferociously go after certain individuals was the need to perpetuate. Like rabies, Lycanthropy has to survive and it does through pathogenic transference. Quake loves Diana, but Quake's werewolf wants Diana to be just like him. Vampires do it, so do werewolves. Vampires seem more calculated with their choices or possibly, they use some supernatural logic when they decide to turn someone. Werewolves seem to pick their heirs purely on visceral instinct. To sum it up, they both make whom they want, when they want and how they want. Somewhere in the delivery system, they bite and give the right dosage, like insemination or venom. A supernatural either kills or makes another in their image. Save for the occasional accident or anomaly, there is usually a process to creating most new supernatural creatures. Can you imagine tapping into that power? So far, I have only been able to use my theory to counteract the werewolf's bite and its effects in an anti-venom drug that seems to work within 24 to 48 hours of infection, mostly. There is still more to be investigated."

Dr. von Shelley continued on, Jodi cut a knowing grin. "Do you know how difficult it is to activate Institutes in large cities AND keep things quiet? Towns like these are perfect for this kind of work. La Mort Douce's reputation ultimately made it better than any other place in the country." A new voice cut off her diatribe, "That's all very nice, but your anti-venom doesn't work." Ray-Rae stood in the doorway with a rifle pointed at Dr. von Shelley.

Ray-Rae had heard voices from the basement and approached quietly. Once she'd heard enough of Dr. von Shelley's monologue, she spoke. That was Quake's cue. He stood up, dead flesh and loose mechanical parts fell off him, and he lunged forward so rapidly that Dr. von Shelley and Ray-Rae froze in fear. He grabbed the doctor by the throat with one hand, lifted her in the air. Dr. von Shelley dropped her weapon, her feet dangling inches above the floor. Quake peered past her head, looked at Ray-Rae and snarled, "What do you mean the cure doesn't work?" Ray-Rae swallowed her fear and managed to say, "Um" as Jodi stood and yelled, "Quake, NO!" The calmer, familiar voice of an older woman came from behind Ray-Rae, grabbing the attention of the whole room, "Quake, my love, please don't..."

QUAKE

Quake's heart lurched and he released Doctor von Shelley. She fell abruptly to the already tainted floor. From the corner of his eye, Quake noticed Ray-Rae had approached close enough to kick the doctor's gun away as Jodi swiftly grabbed Dr. von Shelley. Quake ran, with surprising agility, to Diana, hugging and lifting her up off the floor. Their embrace was like nothing else in the world. Quake was overjoyed and overwhelmed. Diana couldn't control her sobbing and clung to him with all her might. The tension that had filled them during the time spent waiting and searching released in this joyous reunion.

The euphoria was short lived. When Quake spied the healed scar on Diana's shoulder, he wondered, how long they'd been prisoners, subjected to the Institute's experimentations? "How long has it been since we escaped?" With all the chaos and killing, it was unclear how much time had passed. Quake struggled to recount the time and became visibly frustrated. Diana could feel his body tense. Her feet on the floor again, she began kissing him all over his face in an attempt to calm him. She recognized the feral fury entering his eyes as he started to remember the lab, the table and the video! The pain in his temple was now slow and steady, throbbing to the beat of his heart, instead of the sting of an open bleeding wound. He could still taste the metal. Quake ignored it all in order to change back to his wolf and kill the doctor.

"Wait", Ray-Rae's voice cut across the tension-filled cabin. "The antidote works, sort of." Jodi scoffed, "Well, that's great, but none of us have the antidote!" Jodi paused and looked at Ray-Rae and asked,

"What do you mean, sort of?" Jodi tightened her grip on Dr. von Shelley. Ray-Rae replied gently, hoping to prevent Quake's wrath from fully taking over. "Sal stole a vial, which Diana used on me just before the Hunters found us. The Hunters hightailed it out of here, worried the two governments believed we caused the problem or went rogue. Chuck and the others went into hiding to regroup. I came back here because of Diana's kindness. I couldn't let her suffer and I figured if there was a chance that I could help, then I should try. Ray-Rae looked at Quake and Diana holding one another. "It's selfish motivation. An opportunity for redemption and hopefully we can find a way to cure both of us." Quake stepped towards Ray-Rae, even as a human he towered over her. He was still skeptical. She smelled like a Werewolf. Her scent was altogether different and new, not half-and-half like the rest. More, wolf like, with a hint of human. Quake peered down at Ray-Rae, "What's the catch?"

Dr. von Shelley interjected, struggling to speak and plead her case. "The drawback is exactly what we were afraid might happen. The results are not universal yet. They seem based on the individuals themselves. There are mitigating factors of age, time of infection, how long infected." Jodi squeezed more tightly around Dr. von Shelley's throat, "Do tell?" "Some people may have complete recovery, others may be diminished as werewolves, humans in wolves clothing so to speak."

Quake didn't like what he heard at all. "What?" Quake thundered. Ray-Rae stepped forward. "I get it", Ray-Rae said. Now that she had everyone's attention, she cleared her throat. "For example, I'm diminished, not completely cured. I turn into a wolf but I have no supernatural strength, powers or senses. When I am human, I am just a human. When I turn to wolf I am just a wolf." Before she could catch herself, Jodi briefly reverted to her old self, "Well that freakin' sucks!" Diana looked up at Quake, "It doesn't matter. I cannot be this, diminished or otherwise. I like, no, I love what we have. I love being in love with you, but Quake I love being human only. I cannot handle the beast as you have. I am not emotionally strong enough." Quake attempted to reason with her. "Diana, if I've done it, you can too. You have supported what I am all this time you can do this. You can learn to control it just like I have learned to do." Diana spoke, "Listen Quake, some of us are better in our supportive roles and others are not equipped to endure adversity directly. Some people don't have the personalities for battle. Some people, Quake, are like me, long-suffering. Like Penelope waited for Odysseus in the Iliad and the Odyssey. The same journey Odysseus survived would have killed Penelope, would destroy who I am, even kill me. I wouldn't be the woman you love. I wouldn't be Diana anymore. Do you understand?" Quake acknowledged her and responded sadly, "You had me at Odysseus. I understand."

Dr. von Shelley choked out more theories, "Perhaps the concentration was too low. Maybe the supernatural constitution of Lycanthropy is too high. Possibly we miscalculated." Jodi, her patience wearing thin, yelled. "What the HELL are you talking about?" Dr. von Shelley responded, "Maybe one shot was enough to be a 24 to 48 hour intervention, but not enough to complete the cure. If Diana has not yet turned into a werewolf, she still has a chance, but she is not out of the woods yet. Rare cases go past the 24 to 48 hour window. I am not sure exactly what happened with Ray-Rae." Ray-Rae cut in, "I have already turned into a wolf, so the possibility of a cure for me is slim. It is why I had to flee my crew and another reason I returned here, to warn, maybe even help you Diana. You see, now that I am a werewolf I am a target. Friends or not, we made a pact as a team."

Quake missed having Terry around; he could rely on him. The pair often bounced ideas off one another and this whole cure thing was getting too complicated for him. Quake knew he had to act without Terry's voice of logic. Diana was emotional, scared and clearly not thinking straight. He recognized that time was a major factor in this equation and he didn't want to take it for granted. Maybe it wasn't the time, but the amount like Dr. von Shelley said, but Quake couldn't trust the doctor. He lumbered over and snatched Dr. von Shelley out of Jodi's arms, surprising them both. Again, Dr. von Shelley found herself gripped by the throat, as he lifted her close to his face, fangs emerging. "Tell the truth!" Quake growled.

Dr. von Shelley swallowed past her fear and answered, "The truth is there are a few vials and syringes left. We could give her a dosage based on her age and weight and time exposed. Perhaps we were wrong about the infection time. There must be factors we haven't considered. H-Have you changed into a werewolf yet Diana?" "N-No! I already said I hadn't!" Diana replied. "That makes sense," Ray-Rae muttered. Dr. von Shelley continued Ray-Rae's thought, "Yes, because if you have changed, even once, the antidote may have diminished effects. Though I am curious as to how you accomplished this?" Diana replied matter-of-factly, "I paid attention to Goldy's teachings. She is one of the few who can control it. She'd been teaching Quake and the others, how to do the same. I paid attention." Quake gripped Dr. von Shelley's neck a little tighter; he had lost his tolerance for all this talking. He wanted action and results. "Where is the antidote?" Quake demanded. Dr. von Shelley again had to contend with being choked and speaking at the same time, "The lab where I had you and Terry sequestered." Ray-Rae cut in, "I was just there. I didn't find anything." Dr. von Shelley continued her choked response, "Large drawer, main desk, you'll find more there." Quake looked at Jodi, "I don't want you taking any unnecessary chances. Change to Were, go to the lab, grab as many syringes and vials as you can carry in those torn up jeans and get back here, fast. Dr. von Shelley has work to do."

They all trooped up the stairs into the cabin. There was an uncomfortable moment of silence as a universal contemplation permeated the cabin. Quake could smell Diana's fear, his eyes softened and his snout slowly withdrew and dissipated. He looked deeply into her eyes and said. "I love you Diana." Quake's pain returned, partly due to changing back to human and partly because his injuries were still healing; the most obvious pain was in his heart it ached.

Transforming to werewolf is often very painful, causing additional rage, but Quake was never afraid of that pain. His emotions were another story, they were difficult to deal with and control. Quake could transform at will. He'd practiced what Goldy taught him. She also trained him to have focus; fixate on the task you want the beast to perform most. Quake was good at that. He stood there for a moment and considered the options. He wracked his brains about how to get someone like von Shelly to cooperate. Before anyone in the cabin could realize what was about to happen. Before anyone could say anything to stop him, Quake changed back to werewolf, lifted Dr. von Shelley up to his face, looked her in the eye and then bit her shoulder.

DOCTOR VON SHELLEY

Dr. von Shelley expected that she would face death one day. She knew she'd pay for the things she had done eventually. She even believed that Chuck would come back and shoot her. Not in a million years did she ever consider that her experiments could backfire on her. She was a scientist, not a participant. She was a facilitator, not a victim. She believed she would just walk away, as she had always done. To be infected was not an outcome she ever considered for herself.

The bite from Quake was like nothing she'd ever felt before. It burned, as if two hot knives stabbed her and melted into her flesh. Her body immediately became hot and her blood felt thicker, like molten lava. Her heart started to pound and her chest developed sharp piercing pains with each thump. Her ears had a numb underwater feeling with each heartbeat. She became lightheaded and the room began to spin. She tried to control her breaths but the pain wouldn't let her. The effort was laborious. The booming ethereal growl of the voice of the monster that bit her, struck further heart pounding fear into the room. "Now, when Jodi returns, you will have a vested interest in making sure there is a cure for my Diana."

Fear rose in Dr. von Shelley as he spoke those words. She couldn't escape Quake's grasp, she couldn't struggle even if she wanted to. She felt feverish and nauseated, as if someone had pumped adrenaline into her system. She was mere rubbish to all those watching and that is how Quake treated her as he calmly walked over to the basement doorway and unceremoniously tossed her down the stairs like an unwanted toy. Von Shelley could only lie there shivering in a heap of pain, contemplating this change in circumstance. Quake turned and looked at Ray-Rae as he began to change back to human. When he was done, he said. "Take the doctor's equipment, everything she had with her and anything else you can find that might be useful and put it down there with her." Quake's expression softened when he looked into Diana's beautiful face and said, "When Jodi returns, the doctor will cure you. You will get your wish to be human again and then we will get out of here together. If not, well, I will take care of things."

That statement, that minuscule change in tone sent a chill through the cabin. Everyone knew what he meant. No one wanted to admit it but for some odd reason, even for these experienced killers, it sent chills down their collective spines. Quake turned, looked down at the sick and shivering Doctor, and spoke with intensity and sarcasm, "I am anticipating, when all is said and done, if you don't have a cure by the time Diana can no longer keep herself from changing, you will experience your last experiment. If I return before that occurs, the results will still be the same, death by werewolf. Were-mano a Were-mano, so to speak."

TEAM RED RIDING HOOD

The sound of helicopters in the distance added tension to the mood in the cabin. Ray-Rae spoke up. "We may have to go. My colleagues are on their way. I'm certain they have a new directive for complete eradication." Quake calmed himself, sighed and walked over to Diana. . He embraced her as if they were alone and kissed her long and deep. He didn't care who knew how much he loved this woman. Diana was the one and only person who'd stuck by him all these years. She was both the love of his life and his reason for living with what he had suffered through all these years. He looked intently into her eyes and promised Diana, himself and God that he would return.

Just then, Jodi appeared with a metal case full of vials. Her arrival interrupted the sentimental moment and jarred the room back into survival mode. "Is that helicopters I hear?" Jodi inquired. Quake took charge. "Jodi, take Diana down to the basement and give her and the doctor half the vials. She can remake or replicate what she needs. There should be enough supplies for two women to spend at least a month hidden down below. Then take the rest and get it to Goldy and Terry, just in case. Let them know the side effects, limitations and benefits. We will split up from here. I will take Ray-Rae and you head through town, in public view, so nothing should happen to you. Jodi gave Quake an inquisitive look. Quake answered her silent query, "They ain't gonna hurt a young girl in front of cameras and witnesses, makes them look bad."

After you meet up with Terry and Goldy, we will reconvene at Le Petit Lac de Vostok." Jodi escorted Diana into the cabin's bunker, hugged her and promised they would return when all was resolved. Quake and Ray-Rae's hasty exit was accented by the sound of helicopters getting closer. Jodi left, but headed to the Institute to look for more vials, just in case.

SHERIFF BRAY & DEPUTY McNAMERA

Josh McNamera never looked back after the wolf attack in the woods. He didn't want to face the truth. That morning, after he barely escaped he made up his mind, "No more!" He went home, washed up and took some time to reflect. He didn't know how long he was home. He knew he had called in sick and he had reached his limit. Josh thought long and hard of what his strategy would be. How he would break the news to Sheriff Bray.

Josh headed to the southwest side of the La Mort Douce to the station, in order to turn in all his equipment and type his letter of resignation. Josh pulled the squad car into the parking lot when his radio squawked. It was Bray. Josh didn't know why he responded. Maybe it was a Pavlovian thing. Whatever it was, he picked up the radio and clicked the button. Before he finished acknowledging Bray, he heard him say, "Stay put, I am on my way."

Sheriff Bray and Deputy McNamera's ride to the Institute seemed like a long one. Though Bray was McNamera's boss, he was also family in many ways. Bray had helped raise him and was like a big brother to Josh often there for him when he needed guidance. Bray had lobbied for him to take the deputy job, back when he was a gangly kid who didn't know one end of a gun from the other or what a billy club was. Bray had seen tenacity and determination in McNamera. No matter what Bray did to him, Josh persevered. If there was something to accomplish, a challenge to face, something he didn't know, then McNamera did it, met it, studied it or figured out whatever information or answers were required. Drive was something Josh got from his mother. That steadfast Irish blood was undeniable.

Despite all he had gone through to get this job, the current circumstances had him ready to quit. Josh had heard the centuries old stories circulating through the town. What he witnessed was something he would never forget. Although Josh didn't expect Bray to believe his story, he nonetheless recounted every detail of the event.

On the way in, the men noticed of the condition of the Institute. Windows were shattered and smoke billowed from the structure as the sound of helicopters thrummed across the horizon. The pair pulled in front of the gate and sat there for a while. On the other side was a long driveway leading to the Institute's main entrance. They both suspected the Institute was the catalyst for all the recent unrest, but had no concrete proof. Maybe today that would all change.

As they sat there considering their options, the long silence broke when Bray spoke, "Yeah, well I heard stories over the years. My understanding was, as long as them sons-a-bitches kept to themselves and the citizens stayed in town then there wouldn't be a problem. Werewolves, vampires, shit, government agencies or not, this is our town. We need to let them know: you leave us alone, we will leave you alone."

Josh was speechless. He exited the squad car and watched as Bray disposed of his soggy brown mess of a cigar and produced another. Bray would never admit it, but Josh could see his stress and his demeanor shook Josh. Why else would he risk the wrath of his wife by smoking two Stogies in one sitting? Josh cut a smirk, Sheriff Bray may run this town, he may be the King of La Mort Douce, but Mrs. Bray rules their household. The Sheriff certainly seemed glad to surrender it to her too. If I had a woman, who took care of me the way she does him, I would surrender too. Hot meals every day, spotless house, every sports channel a man could imagine. She runs their household as a finely tuned operation. After having a litter of kids, she still looked highly desirable. That sentiment may not be perfect for the rest of the world but in La Mort Douce it was heaven.

Bullets whizzed by McNamera's head and the distinct sound of slugs pelting the squad car abruptly interrupted Josh's thoughts of heaven. The sound was akin to metallic popcorn. Bray yelled, "Hit the deck!" They both sprang into action, drawing their guns and hiding behind the car, as low as possible. Adding to Josh's surprise was seeing Jodi running their way zigzagging like a wild canine, though she was in human form. Her clothes were tattered and she obviously hadn't changed them since he last saw her. She wasn't a werewolf, at least for the moment. Jodi seemed to have more blood on her than the last time Josh had seen her. She was carrying a metal case and it was obvious that whomever was in the building was firing at her, not them. "This ain't gonna be pretty." Bray shouted; words that mirrored exactly what McNamera was thinking.

THE HUNTERS RETURN

Major Bazzo gave his orders before veering off with his helicopter squadron to handle the only two entrances to the town. Mack, Low-Key, Adonis and a bunch of Canucks were with Chuck to secure any remaining Weres at the Institute. Secure…? HAH! Why couldn't the military just be honest and say, KILL? Chuck had his own motives. He planned to let Low-Key, Adonis and the new crew handle cleanup of the Institute. Chuck wanted to find Ray-Rae. She was still part of his team and he believed that if they tracked down Dr. von Shelley they could still cure Ray-Rae. The wild card in this would be whether Ray-Rae's perspective had changed. "Would she still want to hunt werewolves, would she be sympathetic to the animals, or worse, join them?" Chuck had to find her, see Ray-Rae was OK and give her a chance to choose. His team couldn't afford to lose any more assets.

Chuck was lost in his own thoughts when the squad landed on the Institute's helipad. They all exited and they looked to Chuck who wasted no time getting down to business. "Adonis and Low-Key, lead the troops and search the facility. See who is alive and not infected and take care of any strays, if you know what I mean? Mack and I got a GPS signal on Ray-Rae from in this building. I suspect she has removed her chip, but I've got an idea where she may be. We're gonna head that way." Chuck and Mack took off. Mack seemed extra quiet of late. Chuck wasn't sure how all this had affected her. He figured he would address it when the time was appropriate. Many had accused him of being a hard-ass, but no one ever accused him of not caring for his team. His team had been to hell and back with him, and Chuck was determined to return the favor at every opportunity.

As far as Chuck was concerned, no one could understand that mentality, unless they had been there and only the Hunters had. The Massey massacre was still recent enough to warrant his apprehension and concern whenever they embarked on a mission. He used those emotions to stay sharp and careful. Massey remained his one and only nightmare. Chuck blamed himself for that incident and now he carried the burden of the loss of Prabal and Casanova. He would not stand idly by and let anything happen to Ray-Rae. What kind of leader would he be if he didn't go to bat for his team, what kind of friend would he be for that matter?

Once again, Chuck's deep thinking had distracted him enough that he didn't even realize he was practically on top of his target. Chuck gave himself a quick pep talk. He needed to get it together, stay sharp. Right now, he was an unfocused leader; a leader who'd led Mack right into danger. Coming back to his senses, Chuck saw something very curious. They had made their way, a mile or so from the back entrance of the Institute, headed towards the cabin. They watched as Ray-Rae and Quake exited the cabin and headed towards them. Chuck and Mack snuck in closer to the cabin, keeping to the brush. The standoff with Quake was one of the few things in this world that gave him pause.

Before Chuck could devise a plan, Mack jumped out guns drawn. Chuck had never seen a werewolf transform so quickly. Quake's werewolf was a remarkable sight even to a werewolf hunter with Chuck's experience. He resembled a tall, brawny, red bear with long ears. "This freakin' thing could pass for a flaming Yeti!" Chuck thought. There was a tense moment and it seemed that nothing in the woods moved or breathed. Mack she cocked her firearm, breaking that silence. Two voices rang out in the woods. Birds flew away, startled up into the noontime sky. "Mack, No!" Both Chuck and Ray-Rae yelled in unison. Ray-Rae stepped in between Mack and Quake's wolf. Ray-Rae called out again, "Mack, wait!"

SHERIFF BRAY & DEPUTY MCNAMERA

Bullets were flying everywhere. The sounds of breaking glass and shrapnel hitting concrete and metal were deafening. The two officers fired at two large bodyguard types flanked by many others with rifles trying to kill Jodi. One of the men had a rocket launcher. Josh yelled over the bedlam. "Sheriff we are seriously outnumbered!" Bray yelled back, "Cover the girl!" They returned fire, forcing the two back towards the building. The others with the rifles continued to spray bullets in their direction, avoiding gunfire themselves, while Jodi raced away, dodging her attacker's fire. She was trying to get out of the open to take cover at the bullet-riddled squad car. Jodi had just made it when the man carrying the rocket launcher fired. It fizzed, popped and launched. The torpedo barely missed Jodi and the car detonating just beyond them, spraying debris everywhere. Jodi shouted, "Shit!" Josh shouted, "I agree, we need to hightail it outta here!" Bray looked her over. Jodi was bloody and dirty. Several bullets and darts had nicked her, but no direct hits. She was trying to catch her breath. Jodi yelled out, "They're Werewolf Hunters!" Bray crawled in the driver side of the damaged squad car and turned over the ignition accidentally activating the emergency lights. Bray yelled over the firefight, the engine and the siren using the public address radio. "Get in!" Jodi and Josh heeded his command. They had barely closed the door when Bray peeled away from the Institute's driveway. The building exploded behind them, raining another round of shrapnel down upon them.

FACE OFF

Mack stepped closer to Ray-Rae, who was still in front of Quake's werewolf, telling her not to shoot. Quake's growl vibrated all around them, a reminder of his nickname. Chuck was unhappy and uneasy. Slowly, he moved his hands and reached for his weapons. His intentions were completely different from Mack's. He just needed to be prepared, in case things went sideways. Mack finally spoke up, "We can't let you go Ray-Rae." Chuck chimed in, "We?" Ray-Rae muttered, "I knew it, I just knew it." Mack continued, either ignoring or not hearing either of them, "We are Hunters. This is what we do. We made a pact. If one of us had the infection, we would show no mercy! Remember?" Chuck tried to mediate, "Look Mack, the cure changes all that. We can fix this. All we need is…" Gunfire briefly drowned out all other sounds. Chuck yelled, "No, wait!" Mack fired at Ray-Rae who instantly transformed into her wolf.

Miraculously, only one of the many bullets actually hit her. Some of the shots had hit Quake, which infuriated him. Ray-Rae's wolf leapt, just in time to knock down Mack as an enraged Quake took a swipe at her. Without Ray-Rae's intervention, Quake would have taken Mack's head off. Quake had no time to refocus as Chuck finally joined in the shooting barrage Mack had initiated. He fired two pistols worth of darts into a charging Quake. Meanwhile, Mack and Ray-Rae struggled with one another on the ground. Mack lost her weapon during the ruckus and had to combat Ray-Rae with her bare hands. Ray-Rae remained a wolf. If it weren't for Mack's superior grappling skills Ray-Rae would have already mauled her.

With darts sticking out of his body, Quake changed directions and swiftly reached Chuck, knocking him on his back. Chuck's head and back screamed with pain. He'd dropped his pistols on impact so he instinctively reached up and grabbed Quakes furry neck to keep him at arm's length. Quake was on top of Chuck snarling, slobbering and breathing heavily. His eyes were beginning to show signs that the darts were taking effect. Quake's wolf was enraged and poised to kill. Ray-Rae's wolf was ready to fight as well. The pair was close to overcoming their prey when an explosion interrupted the mêlée.

DIANA & DR. VON SHELLEY

The cabin's bunker was dank and nominally lit. The two women sat on opposite sides of the room. Despite all the shelves and storage, they had each found a bare wall to lean on. There was no trust between them. Diana wanted the cure and to be left alone. She didn't trust that Dr. von Shelley would provide either, let alone both. Dr. von Shelley was in pain, feverish and her skull was on fire. Her blood felt so thick it seemed her heart could barely circulate it through her system. She needed to concentrate on improving the antidote, so they could escape this prison and get as far away from one another as possible. She didn't trust that Diana could hold out much longer. Her experience showed that stressful situations combined with a full moon made it almost impossible not to succumb to Lycanthropy. Diana was definitely facing this precarious scenario, since von Shelley knew they were in the last stages of a full moon.

Someone had to speak and since von Shelley felt she was a good facilitator in extreme situations, she broke the silence. "Look, we have nothing to lose here Mrs. Ragnorock. The only guarantee we have is that one or both of us will transform into a werewolf in the next few days. If that happens, we may very well tear each other apart, negating any chance either of us will escape or survive these circumstances." Diana sighed heavily before she responded. "How can I trust you or anything you say after everything you and your people have done to us?" Dr. von Shelley said, "I understand that, but in all honesty I cannot apologize for my job. At this moment, self-preservation is tantamount and there is no governing body to answer to down here. I cannot predict what will happen after we escape. I can only promise that I am willing to work together, at least until we escape. Common ground often unites the oddest of allies, what do you say?"

Dr. von Shelley struggled to rise, then walked slowly to the middle of the room and reached out her hand. Diana rose reluctantly and cautiously. She ambled to the middle of the room. As they clasped hands in a tentative handshake, a deep sigh of relief settled between them. A positive air of hope filled their underground sanctuary and the women began to relax. That feeling of goodwill was by an explosion followed by a cloud of dust permeating the darkness as the cabin collapsed above them.

AFTERMATH

The patrol car was abuzz with relentless radio traffic. Reports of gunfire and explosions dominated the airwaves. That was the least of their concerns. The back of the squad car was on fire from the blast. They hunched over in their seats, necks red, hair singed, baking from the heat of the blaze. Bray was desperately trying to maintain control of the wobbling car, driving with lights and heat distorted sirens all the way back to town. The open windows did nothing to help their plight. Josh had suggested that driving as fast as they could, might put out the fire, but the wind had only fed the flames, making them bigger and more intense. Bray thought in retrospect, "That was a friggin' stupid idea!" Arriving at the station, they tumbled out of the cruiser and realized they had an audience. The town was alive and littered with spectators.

Bray didn't like what he'd heard over the police band. The main roads and train bridges leading into La Mort Douce's had been blown to bits and the military was already on site to provide aid. Bray spoke his thoughts aloud, "Well that seems kinda early considering how remote this town is. Even New Orleans didn't get this kinda response after Katrina. Something's fishy." Bray looked at Jodi, "Kid, I don't know what sorta mess you've gotten into, but my advice to you is to make yourself scarce. You and your friends are gonna have to find a new place to hide out. La Mort Douce ain't friendly to your kind anymore." Josh interrupted; "No, I've seen what she is capable of. I'm arresting her!" Jodi stood, frozen in place, with the antidote case in one hand. She was tattered, bloody, burned-out and choking on the smoky stench of burned rubber, plastic and metal. Hanging her head, Jodi knew she had no energy to fight this new battle.

Josh was ready to arrest Jodi and stood in his cop stance with his gun drawn. Bray shouted, "Now listen here Deputy, we got more pressing matters then this one little filly here. Jesus... the squad car is still on fire. We gotta put that out and then we need to find out why the military is here in La Mort Douce. Where is she gonna go, right now, the citizens need us and that is more important than locking up some Were-Girl. Now let her go, we got work to do. Dag Nab It!"

Water sprayed all over them. What the La Mort Douce Fire Department lacked with tact, they made up for with perfect timing. The trio, completely soaked by their aggressive efforts, each welcomed the cold water and the interruption to their argument. It cleared the air and their minds. Bray said, without realizing he was being thematic. "Let cooler heads prevail Josh".

Bray stood in front of Josh, gently made him holster his weapon, looked him in the eyes and said, "Look around you Josh." Josh slowly surveyed his surroundings. There were people everywhere, cops and firefighters, civilians, old and young. Smoke billowed from the Institute, clouding most of the mountains and much of the view of Canada over the border. Fire, smoke and chaos permeated everything as Josh turned 360 degrees. This werewolf problem may have become a town problem, but La Mort Douce had a much larger threat now, the military. Bray said, "Josh, we need to get our town back. I liked when nobody knew we existed, so let's see what we can do to regain our anonymity." Jodi stealthily slipped away, thinking the same thing. "It would be wonderful to have anonymity again."

CHUCK

Chuck felt the thrum of the helicopter blades cutting through the air. The steady tempo pulsed in his chest. The vibrations he felt told him he was inside the bird. Eventually, he determined he was on his back in a stretcher looking up at a group of unfamiliar faces, except Major Bazzo. Despite all the noise, the Major was trying to speak to him with very little success. Someone put a headset on Chuck but he really didn't care to listen. In his opinion, it wasn't the right place or time. Chuck didn't need any reminders, especially not any fresh ones.

The Medevac chopper cut through the growing mountain fog. Chuck was too groggy to get a bead on the direction they were headed. Regardless, he was already planning his escape and expedient return to La Mort Douce. Chuck would not accept his team was lost. He was going back to locate them all and then he was going home to Toronto to retire.

There were many questions, about what transpired and the whereabouts of Dr. von Shelley. Not having the answers seemed to irritate Major Bazzo. Chuck responded as he felt necessary but eventually he grew tired of it all and mentally shut down. Instead, he watched the beautiful horizon disappear in to the fog and began reciting: "Ray-Ann Jackson aka "Ray-Rae", 31 238 176, Ballistics and Entry specialist, MIA. Lockhart Triplett aka "Low-Key," 20 602 562, Infantry Specialist, MIA. Adonis Kamahi, 16 265 381, Weapons expert, MIA. McKenzie Ochoa aka "Mack", 33 952 781, MAC, Hand-to-Hand specialist, MIA. Casanova Yamamoto, 32 498 366, Communications expert, DOA. Prabal Maitreya Sananda, 38 235 834, Long Range Marksman, DOA. Charles McElroy Robinson, 53 310 761, LRRP Commander, medically unfit for duty at present, Sir."

QUAKE

Quake came to with leaves and grass stuck to his face and body. He was dirty, bloody and once again healing from extensive injuries. Spent darts were falling off his body as he struggled to his feet. The darts clinked and cracked as they hit the ground, some broke under his feet cutting him. The fresh pain pushed him out of his lethargy. His head was on fire and he was loopy from the drug mixture the Hunters used. Smoking debris, small fires, charred and bloody body parts were everywhere. Quake could only think of Diana. He needed to make sure she was OK.

Quake stood up and looked around. Ray-Rae and Mack were long gone. He could smell that they had gone their separate ways. He thought to himself "Good luck, Ray-Rae." He wondered what had become of Chuck. Quake noticed Chuck's bloody trail lead to the Institute. Remembering the explosion, he assumed the place was nothing more than a mass of rubble and death. Quake surveyed his surroundings and spied the collapsed Cabin. Quake's heart sank.

Quake spent hours digging through the wreckage. Hope and emotions fueled his tattered and exhausted body until he finally found the bunker door. His heart raced and he felt tremendous hope wash over him. His pace was intense once he could see the door through the rubble. Quake grabbed the handle and swung open the heavy metal door.

Quake peered into the darkness, squinting his eyes. As he stared deep into the basement, his most beloved wife appeared before him. The woman of his dreams stood over the gutted and half-eaten carcass of Dr. von Shelley. Blood covered her tattered clothing, hands and face. Diana had the most pathetic look on her face and yet, from Quake's perspective, it was adorable as a little kid caught eating chocolates pilfered from the pantry. Sheepishly, she looked up at Quake, with sadness in her eyes and said; "I'm sorry, I just couldn't help myself" Quake looked down, torn between sadness and elation. Laughing, he shouted, "You know what? I sure do love you, woman!"

TERRY

The Andersen Pack

Terry sat in the lobby of the Institute and wondered, "How in the hell am I back here? This place was just destroyed?" Terry awoke from his nightmare drenched in sweat, his pajama pants stuck to his skin. The fire in his lungs felt like the first toke of a joint. He was unnerved and parched. He took slow, deep breaths in an effort to cool the inferno in his chest. The desire in him was overwhelming, he needed satisfaction and his body ached. He could feel the pull of the nearly full moon. He reached for the glass of water on his nightstand and gulped the liquid down. His brain throbbed from the rush of testosterone and adrenaline. The lava in his chest filtered through his heart. He felt spent, fatigued and jittery, all at once. An uncontrollable need raged from his lungs to his loins. His nerves were hypersensitive and he hungered for flesh. His skin was hot to the touch. The need mimicked that which an addict might feel after days of sobriety; only this was more primal, sexual even. He held on through this fervor to control it until his mind began to clear. Then he looked at Goldy lying picturesque in her sleep and Terry realized resistance was futile.

JODI

Several weeks passed and La Mort Douce was under "Martial Law" under the guise of helping them recover from an industrial accident. Most of the residents were uneasy under the watchful eye of the military. The pack had acclimated to it and eventually found a way around it. Besides, it was far better than imprisonment and torture. The pack hadn't experienced so much freedom for quite a long time. Jodi couldn't remember when she had last beheld the sky with such leisure. The noon sun had an amazing effect on her mood. The very same sun that Jodi enjoyed seemed to kiss Goldy's brown skin. The clouds were sparse, full and fluffy like cotton balls. Goldy was radiant and looked like her old self, very different from her mottled appearance in the woods when she had led a wolf pack into battle. The reunion with Goldy was pleasing to Jodi.

They spent much needed time getting their hair and nails done at the salon. They enjoyed plenty of girl talk, covering pretty much every topic, so long as it didn't have to do with anything that had happened over the last few years; particularly the events of recent weeks and months. They chatted, ad nauseam, about Jodi's relationship with Pierce and discussed Goldy and Terry's infant son, Sosthenes. Terry was over the moon with him and appeared to have a handle on the cub, even more so than Goldy. He was a doting father, watchful and strong. Terry allowed the boy just so much leeway before reining him in. Sosthenes was cute, brown, curly haired and wide-eyed. Terry gave all his spare attention to the baby so that Jodi and Goldy could have time together. Jodi knew Terry was privy to their conversations, but she didn't mind, they were family.

They had formed a new, underground pack. They assisted Weres, new and old, with their issues and problems, getting them in and out of town with relative ease. Occasionally, a La Mort Douce resident would seek help. The Andersen's revamped home was a refuge and place of solace. Goldy had finally gotten what she'd always wanted, a sense of stability in an otherwise unstable world. It wasn't perfect but it was an unexpected comfort and Goldy was happy.

Jodi and Goldy put their heads together to talk strategy. Jodi would be traveling as part of her planned Werewolf Underground Network. Secrecy was a necessity.

The Andersen Pack had no idea how many humans or vampires might be presently hunting in La Mort Douce. The government, having declared "Martial Law", had taken control of the roads and the railways in and out of La Mort Douce. Jodi would be responsible for directing those requiring assistance from the W.U.N. It would be a long time before the military vacated the town. Removing all evidence of the Institute's existence in La Mort Douce and cleaning up the mess was no small task for them. Goldy jokingly told Jodi that she was the Harriet Tubman of werewolves. That comment elicited a smirk from Jodi. There was really no comparison. Werewolves weren't slaves, just victims of a virus, but she got the gist of the humor and knew Goldy was simply trying to inspire her. Jodi owed much to this woman and she could never refuse her, so the pep talk wasn't really necessary. Goldy had secured the metal case containing the antidote vials that Jodi had retrieved from the Institute and already had a network of medical friends researching solutions to the "diminished cure" problem.

The local television news caught Jodi's attention as they continued to speculate about the source of explosions and fires that had occurred. The talking heads were wondering it would affect La Mort Douce in the long term and wondered how the Institute was involved. They frequently flashed the most recent death and missing person counts on screen. The only purpose served by the incessant reporting was to give fodder to the conspiracy theorists. The local gossipmongers simply relished in it. The sight of Sosthenes with Terry quelled any doubts Jodi had, giving her confidence and hope. They were a team, a pack and love provided Terry and Goldy's perseverance filled Jodi with a newfound hope.

GOLDY

Goldy looked over her shoulder at Terry staring at her. He must have been visually devouring her while she slept. Normally she woke up when Terry had these moments, but Goldy had been up late with Sosthenes. She turned and the sheets and blankets shifted to expose all of Terry's favorite parts. Terry told her she was gorgeous and sexy. She loved his voice and words, so it didn't take much for her desire for him to rise. Goldy could see the restless animal in Terry and she anticipated and cherished these moments. The beauty and passion of their lovemaking was wonderful, but every now and again, she liked it rough. She smiled, winked and spoke in a sultry voice. "Don't take it easy on me cowboy. The baby won't be up anytime soon." Terry was tall, dark, lean, muscular, solid and handsome. Goldy likened him to an African God and she loved every inch of him. Most of the time, he was romantic and sweet but during the time near a full moon, he was inspired. It was a great variation from his usual tenderness and took days to heal from, but it was worth it. She rolled over; kissed him and asked, "Rough night?" Goldy climbed on top of him, letting her gown fall off her shoulder, kissing him again.

Terry reached for her lace strap, telling himself to be gentle, but he ripped it anyway. The lace was no match for his passionate caress. Goldy was glad she hadn't worn panties to bed. They would have become a casualty to his passion as well. The tenderness of the moment disappeared as Goldy switched gears. She climbed off him and crawled across the bed on all fours. Grabbing the post with both hands, she flipped her hair, looked over her shoulder and smiled wickedly. Terry sat up and moved to her. Goldy wriggled her bottom against his groin. Terry nibbled her neck. Terry took her roughly and with purpose, satisfying both of them.

Breakfast nearly went unmade. The two of them lovingly glanced at one another from across the breakfast table, blushing, flirting and playing "footsies." The baby was in his high chair playing with his food, oblivious to his parent's romance. Sosthenes wasn't aware of what he was feeling but he did feel their love and the security and he relished in it. He was making sounds and playing with his utensils. Goldy and Terry were in there late 40s with a young child and still behaved as 20-year-olds. Breakfast was full of silent conversations, eye contact and giggles. Terry was calm and Goldy was sublimely satisfied.

Goldy and Terry entered the meditation room in their home. Kissing him, Goldy told Terry how much she loved him and then put Sosthenes in his playpen. Terry turned on some new age music as they prepared to meditate. This was the foundation for their success as a couple and as werewolves. It had helped bring Goldy back from her feral psychosis to human again. The meditation also provided an opportunity to practice what she preached, "The cure for what ails most werewolves" she claimed, was self-realization and self-discovery through physical discipline and spiritual meditation. The best way to control Lycanthropy was Goldy's Zen-lycan-therapy technique.

Goldy and Terry supported each other in this and their love for each other played no small part in their success. The moment she'd seen him and her child on that hill, her elation and happiness over-took all her mental and physical regression. All became right again and they journeyed together to recovery. Throughout this little sci-fi melodrama, she was forever grateful to have her life, her family and her sanity back.

Plus à venir

PLEASE...

[ ] READ

[ ] REVIEW

[ ] SELFIE

[ ] SHARE

THANK YOU

ACKNOWLEDGEMENTS

Thank you God, the positive force, the higher power, and the source of all creativity.

Thank you Michelle for the encouragement, support and patience.

Thank you Mari (M.e.) Hagan for the suggestions and Colleen for the intro.

Thank you Marie Antionette F4L, for the edit and props.

Thank you P. A. Cronin for the hard work and putting up with me.

Thank you Claudia, Teresa, Mai (book cover model), and Ashley for the book cover.

Thank you Adam Cushman, Justin DuVal, Amy Filbeck and Rocco Rivetti for the trailer.

Thank you Dackeyia Simmons Sterling for the guidance, thank you Nicole for the introduction

Thank you to all my Friends, Family, Fans, Relatives and beta Readers for reading my book, for the advice and encouragement.

Thank you Matty for believing in the brand.

ABOUT THE AUTHOR

LANCE OLIVER KEEBLE resides in Los Angeles, California. He has been an author most of his life. He has had a love for writing since the tender age of 10 and has appeared in various anthologies, books and periodicals under various pseudonyms.

His most current work is a firefighter superhero comic, appearing in several magazines, and the speculative science fiction, action, thriller, horror universe that is:

Globes Disease.